LOVERS' PARTING

Sheena had never loved a man before, and now that she did she knew she could never have him.

How could she admit to this man she loved that she had lied to him, deceived him, when she wasn't even sure why? How could she ask his forgiveness?

The only kind thing to do was to pretend she had never loved him at all. So, packing her belongings, and making her excuses, she left the Embassy—her heart broken in two . . .

THE
KISS OF PARIS

Barbara Cartland

PYRAMID BOOKS ▲ NEW YORK

THE KISS OF PARIS

A PYRAMID BOOK

Copyright © 1956 by Barbara Cartland

Pyramid edition published July 1972
Fifth printing, December 1976

Printed in the United States of America

Pyramid Books are published by Pyramid Publications (Harcourt Brace Jovanovich, Inc.). Its trademarks, consisting of the word "Pyramid" and the portrayal of a pyramid, are registered in the United States Patent Office.

PYRAMID PUBLICATIONS
(Harcourt Brace Jovanovich, Inc.)
757 Third Avenue, New York, N.Y. 10017

One

"*Por-teur! Por-teur!*"

The train came slowly into the *Gare du Nord* and from the window Sheena watched the blue-overalled porters with their wide leather belts as they hurried along the platform shouting and gesticulating to the passengers.

She was in Paris! She felt her heart leap at the thought. Yet her delight was followed by what was almost a sense of dismay. It was so noisy, so foreign, so big; and even the sense of adventure which had kept her alert and excited during the whole of the journey from England was now superseded by the feeling of her own insignificance.

Automatically she got to her feet and reached up to the rack above her head where the smaller portions of her luggage had been put by the porter at Calais. As she did so she caught a glimpse of the gold ring on the third finger of her left hand and felt herself shudder. For a moment she had forgotten it was there and now, with a sense of urgency and something almost akin to panic, she remembered that she must not forget it. She must remember it all the time—remember the ring and all that went with it!

"You'll be wanting a ring," Patrick O'Donovan had

said only two days ago when everything else had been thought of and her luggage was packed and labelled.

"A ring, Uncle Patrick?" she asked him enquiringly.

"Sure, me darling girl, it's usual for a married woman to wear one," he smiled.

"Of course. I had forgotten."

"I'll be buying you one at the jeweller's. 'Tis something I've never done before—not with all my experience of the fair sex. Begorra, but I'm all for learning."

He was laughing as if it were all a great joke. But Sheena's face was serious as she said in a low voice:

"I hadn't thought that I would have to wear a ring."

"Indeed they will be thinking it strange if you appear without one," Patrick O'Donovan answered lightly, and then something in the tense stillness of her figure communicated itself to him. " 'Tis not troubling you, Mavourneen?" he said in the soft, coaxing tone she knew so well.

"No . . . no . . . not really," Sheena answered, lying because she did not wish him to think her stupid or ready to make a fuss over such a small point.

"That's all right then," her uncle answered, with a note of relief in his voice. "I'll be away to choose you the symbol of happy wedlock. You had best give me something to show the size of your finger."

Sheena had taken a skein of silk from her workbasket and wrapped it round her finger to find the right size. Patrick O'Donovan had slipped it into the pocket in his waistcoat and gone off whistling.

Alone in the damp basement kitchen Sheena had stared down at her finger, and then, with an obvious effort, had gone back to the sink to start again on the endless pile of dirty dishes which always seemed to be awaiting her there.

"Por-teur! Por-teur!"

She signalled to a small, middle-aged man with a drooping moustache and his beret set jauntily on the side of his head. She handed him several packages through the window and then went along the corridor to where the other luggage was being sorted out by an attendant.

The woman in front of Sheena tipped the man and Sheena realised that she, too, would be expected to produce a *pourboire*. She fumbled in her bag. She had so very few francs left, but Uncle Patrick had been reassuring when she had pointed out how little money she had for the journey.

"They'll be meeting you in Paris," he said positively.

Now Sheena hoped that he was right, otherwise she had no idea how she could pay for a taxi. With a confidence she was far from feeling she told the porter that she expected there would be a private car to meet her.

"Venez avec moi, M'selle," he said, and only as he started to walk at a brisk pace down the platform did Sheena realise that he had called her *Mademoiselle*.

Did she look so unmarried, she asked herself, that even a porter could not credit her with the likelihood of a husband? She glanced at her luggage. The labels printed neatly in her own handwriting bore the legend "Mrs. Lawson."

"Why Lawson?" she had asked her uncle when he told her what name was to be hers.

"Why not?"

"It's such an ordinary name. You might have chosen something attractive."

"But Mavourneen, 'tis the one thing we wouldn't want; something which would draw attention to you, which would remain in a person's memory. Lawson is a commonplace name belonging to hundreds, perhaps thousands of English people; the sort of name you would never think about again. You understand?"

"Yes, I suppose so," Sheena answered. "But if I had the chance to choose . . ."

"The day will come, me darling, when you will change your name through your own inclination," Patrick O'Donovan smiled. "You will take a new one and a man with it, and Glory to God, what better chance have you got to find one than living in Paris?"

"Are you really suggesting, Uncle Patrick, that I should marry a Frenchman?" Sheena asked.

"I am hoping you will marry no one," Patrick O'Donovan said quickly. "Not while you have got me to look after—and I need a lot of looking after, me lovely girl."

"And yet you are sending me away from you," she answered reproachfully.

Patrick O'Donovan turned his face away. Sheena had noticed before that there were times when he had difficulty in meeting her eyes.

"It can't be helped," he said slowly. "Sure, it can't be helped."

He had sighed and then risen as if to leave the room, but Sheena had prevented him.

"Listen, Uncle Patrick, you know I do not want to go to Paris. You know I do not wish to take this job. I thought you had set your heart on it. If you want me to stay as much as I want to stay with you, then let us refuse."

"There are reasons why I can do no such thing."

"But what reasons?" she asked. "Who are these friends who ask such sacrifices of you? And are they friends? Aren't they more likely to be people in the position to give orders?"

Patrick O'Donovan walked across the kitchen to stand with his back to the fire. Even as he stood there and before he opened his mouth to speak, Sheena knew what was coming, knew by the expression on his face that he was putting on an act, that he was about to say words which came automatically to his lips.

"You must be trusting your poor old uncle," he began. "For haven't I always done what was the best for you? Ever since that day when you were no higher than my knee and your poor father and mother—God rest their souls—were drowned, I have taken you to my heart and looked after you as though you were a child of my own. Baby Sheena—a poor wee orphan with no one to care for you but meself. I fought for you, me darling, then, and I've fought for your interests always. And believe me, as the blessed Saints are me witness, I'm thinking of you now."

Sheena sighed. This was a repetition she knew only too well. This was the line Uncle Patrick always took when he wanted to get his own way and intended to have it.

"Very well," she said shortly. "Lawson it will be. And when do I go?"

"In a fortnight," he answered.

* * *

Never, it seemed to Sheena, had fourteen days sped past so quickly, and now she was here in Paris, starting upon an adventure which filled her not only with apprehension but also with an emotion which was strangely like fear.

It was all so unexpected, so unlike anything she had ever imagined. "I shall be a failure," she had thought over and over again these past two weeks. And yet now, walking behind the porter, she felt her spirits rising irresistibly. Whatever else happened, at least she had seen Paris!

There was something in the very smell of the station that was different from anything she had ever known before. There was something exhilarating in the difference in the people, in their voices rising on a high excitable note and in the sudden glimpse of the sunshine across the street where the cars were waiting.

It was then she remembered again how little money she had left. Would there be a car?

The porter had brought his truck to a standstill. Now they stood irresolute, Sheena looking about her, her blue eyes, fringed with their dark lashes, anxious as she glanced along the row of private cars.

Suddenly she became aware that a man was approaching her. He was tall and dark and as he swept off his hat she realised that his eyes were very grey against his suntanned skin.

"Mrs. Lawson?"

It was a question, and immediately Sheena began to shake her head.

"No. . . . I mean, yes. I am Mrs. Lawson."

"How do you do? I am Lucien Mansfield. Madame Pelayo asked me to meet you."

"How kind. . . . I was hoping someone would be here."

"The car is just over there," he said, pointing, and

the porter, without instructions, started off towards it with his truck.

"Had a good journey?"

"Yes, thank you."

The question was one of entire formality and Sheena, as she followed her luggage towards a big, expensive-looking limousine, thought that the man they had sent to meet her was stiff and a little frightening. There was something else about him, something which made her feel she must be on her guard, careful of everything she said. He must be English, for one thing, she thought, and that in itself was a surprise.

Her luggage was swiftly disposed of in the boot of the car, and before she could bring out her few remaining francs, the porter had been tipped and dismissed and she found herself sitting on the back seat of the car with a soft fur rug over her knees. A chauffeur wearing a cockaded cap shut the door, and then they were driving away into the sunshine, along the streets with tall, grey houses on either side, shops filled with colourful merchandise, and people sitting outside little bars at tables on the pavement.

For a moment Sheena forgot herself, her destination, her companion. She just looked, stared, and absorbed her first impressions of Paris. Then with a little start she realised that the man sitting beside her was watching her.

"This is your first visit abroad?" he said.

"Yes . . . yes, my first."

"You have always lived in England before?"

She was about to contradict him, to tell him that Ireland was her home, and then she remembered that Uncle Patrick had admonished her: "Say as little about Ireland as possible, Mavourneen. Remember that, thick-skinned though these English are, they must realise by now that we Southern Irish hate them."

"Yes, I have lived in England," Sheena replied stiffly.

"Do you speak French?"

Was this a catechism? she thought suddenly; and if so, what right had he to catechise her? She felt her chin lift a little. The pride of the O'Donovans was very easily aroused.

"I speak fluently," she answered coldly. "Although I cannot, of course, be sure that my accent is impeccable."

"I am glad about that," he said. "One misses so much that is worth seeing in Paris and in France if one cannot speak the language."

He smiled as he spoke and Sheena felt her resentment evaporate as quickly as it had been aroused.

"There is so much I want to see," she said confidently. "I have always dreamed about Paris. Paris in the spring —the chestnut trees, the Seine, the Louvre, all the wonderful things one reads about. And now I am here!"

"And anxious, of course, to see your charges."

She felt as though he deliberately poured cold water on her excitement.

"Yes, of course . . . my charges," she replied. "Will you tell me about them?"

"You will see them soon enough," he answered. "They are nice children, if a trifle spoiled."

The car turned, as he spoke, down an avenue where all the trees were in bud. It was beautiful and as Sheena caught her breath at the sight of it she hardly heard her companion's voice.

"You must have thought yourself very fortunate to get this job."

"Yes . . . yes, of course I did," she told him hurriedly.

"You have had a lot of experience?"

Again it was a question and again Sheena felt resentful that he should catechise her. With a little effort, because she found it difficult to challenge him, she turned to look into his eyes.

"Do you really want me to tell you the story of my life so soon on our acquaintance?"

There was an expression on his face which she did not understand.

"You must forgive me if I sound curious," he said. "But we have all been wondering what you would be like. The Pelayo children have had a large number of governesses."

"We?" Sheena enquired.

"The Embassy staff. Perhaps I should explain. I am one of them; my proper title is, I believe, Financial

11

and Confidential Adviser to His Excellency the Ambassador."

"It sounds very grand," she remarked quietly, "but why should the ambassador require an English adviser?"

"I am only half English," was the reply. "My mother was a Mariposan and I have lived in Mariposa for a great many years of my life; in fact I have estates out there."

"You will be shocked when I tell you that I had never heard of Mariposa until a few weeks ago," Sheena said.

"It is a very undeveloped country . . ." he began, but Sheena was no longer listening. She was thinking of that moment when Patrick O'Donovan had come down into the kitchen when she was washing up and said:

"I've news for you, Mavourneen."

"News, Uncle Patrick?" she asked, glancing at him over her shoulder.

"Yes, news. You are going to Paris."

"Paris!"

Sheena had very nearly dropped a plate and then, with a dexterity which almost twisted her arm, managed to save it.

"What on earth are we going there for?"

"Not we—you."

She had turned at that to look at him in surprise.

"Uncle Patrick, you have been drinking again.

"As I stand in the sight of Heaven itself, me darling, not a drop has passed me lips this day. No, 'tis news for you I have got. You are to go to Paris."

"And why and how should I be travelling to a foreign place?" Sheena enquired, still thinking he must be joking.

"You are going, me dear, as English governess to the two children of Don Veremundo Pelayo, the Ambassador of Mariposa."

"Are you mad?" Sheena had enquired.

"No, sane."

"But why should I be taking a job as a governess? You know as well as I do that I have no qualifications for teaching."

"Ah, but you have. The Ambassador himself has approved them and you have been spoken for by no less a personage than the Comtesse de Beaufleur."

"Uncle Patrick, if you are not drunk I am dreaming."

But she had not been dreaming and gradually the story had unfolded itself. His friends, those strange friends of whom she had never approved, of whom she knew little and the little she knew disliked, had planned this for her. It was these same friends who had brought them over from Ireland.

"Why should we go to England?" she had asked then. "You hate England, you have always said so."

"Sure, I loathe the guts of every Englishman," Patrick O'Donovan answered. "But we must visit the damned island, Mavourneen. What must be—must be."

That was the answer she always got, "What must be—must be," and now she must be off to Paris as governess to the children of some unknown Ambassador—and a nice mess she was likely to make of it.

Mariposa indeed! She had gone to the Free Library to read up about it. It was a small State, she learned, situated between Uruguay and Brazil. Its population consisted of Spaniards, Indians and the Mariposans themselves—a race deep-rooted in tradition and filled with a fierce pride in their long history of fighting each other and their neighbours.

"This is the *Place de L'Opera*."

The quiet deep voice beside Sheena jerked her back to the realities of the moment.

"And this is the *Rue de la Paix*. And now we are coming into the *Place Vendôme*."

"It is beautiful!" Sheena exclaimed.

She said the same thing a few minutes later as they passed the *Tuileries* Gardens and drove around the *Place de la Concorde*. Then the car was passing down a quiet street with high-walled gardens until it came to rest in front of an imposing mansion with a flight of steps leading up to the front door. Liveried servants came hurrying from the house to help Sheena from the car and bring in her luggage.

She walked into the hall. It was of marble with big impressive oil-paintings on the damask-covered walls. Feeling wide-eyed and impressed, she followed a footman up the stairs to the first floor.

"Is Her Excellency in the drawing-room?" her companion asked in French.

"*Oui, Monsieur.*"

A pair of double doors were flung open. Sheena had an impression of grey walls, glittering chandeliers of gilt and brocade-covered furniture, of huge bowls of exotic hot-house flowers; and, rising from a sofa, one of the loveliest women she had ever seen in her life.

Madame Pelayo was delicately made and small-boned, but at the same time comparatively tall. She had small classical features with a skin like alabaster which seemed in almost violent contrast to the raven's-wing darkness of her hair. There were diamonds flashing in her tiny ears and great ropes of elaborate pearls round her throat, and as she held out her hand to Sheena there was a fragrance of an exotic perfume that was both tantalising and seductive.

"Ah, Mrs. Lawson, you have arrived safely I see. The Colonel found you at the station. I was not afraid that he would miss you, he is so very reliable. Is that not true, *mon Colonel*?"

"Your Excellency flatters me."

"Could I possibly do that?"

Madame Pelayo looked up into the grey eyes looking down into hers, and for a moment it seemed to Sheena there was something vibrant and yet magnetic in the atmosphere. Almost simultaneously, they both turned again to her.

"Colonel Mansfield has told you about my children?" Madame Pelayo asked.

"I left you to do that," Lucien Mansfield interposed before Sheena could answer.

"I am glad. I want no tale-telling. I want Mrs. Lawson to judge for herself how charming, how very sweet they both are." Madame Pelayo paused for a moment and then looked at Sheena. "You are young," she said critically. "Far younger than I expected."

"I am afraid looks are deceptive, Madame. I am older than I appear," Sheena replied.

Even as she said the words she felt them stick in her throat. How she hated to lie and how hard it was to remember!

"They have got my birthday wrong," she had said to

14

Uncle Patrick when he handed her her passport made out in the name of Sheena Lawson. "Why, it's crazy," she went on before he could answer. "They have made me eight years older than I am."

"That is your age," he said.

"No, it isn't," she expostulated; and then, glancing up at his face, she understood. "But it is too ridiculous! I shan't be twenty-one until next month. No one is going to believe I am twenty-eight."

"Sure, but they will believe it all right," he answered. "No woman is going to make herself out older than she is—at least no woman they have ever heard of."

"Perhaps they are not as stupid as you expect them to be," Sheena expostulated.

"The Ambassadress wanted someone older still," he explained. "And incidentally, the last governess was sacked for looking too attractive."

"So I am to make myself ugly, am I?" Sheena asked ominously.

"You could never be ugly, me darling girl," Patrick O'Donovan replied. "But you needn't be shouting your attractions all over the place for all and sundry to hear and notice."

It was because she loved him so much that Sheena had done what he wanted of her. Habitually she wore her pale gold hair loose, falling to her shoulders. Now she had pinned it into a neat roll at the back of her head.

It was only when she was actually leaving for Paris that she had thought about her clothes. She never had any money to spend anyway, and it had not occurred to Patrick O'Donovan that she might want to buy anything new for the journey to Paris. Anyway, she knew only too well he had nothing to spare. She had the greatest difficulty in getting a few shillings out of him to pay for food, let alone anything else, and when there was anything in the house his so-called friends came and ate it.

She grudged them every mouthful they put into their lips; every bottle of beer and every glass of whiskey which was consumed upstairs in the front room during those long evenings when Uncle Patrick would leave her alone in the kitchen. He would stay with his friends,

15

talking, smoking and drinking, until she was too tired to wait for him any longer and would let out the fire and go to her own room.

What did he and those strange men, whom she seldom saw, talk about for such hours on end? she used to wonder, and then push the question away from her mind.

"I really meant to have a very much older governess this time," Madame Pelayo was saying. "But the Comtesse de Beaufleur spoke so very warmly of you and we all know that she is a difficult person to please."

"Yes, of course," Sheena murmured.

She realised with a sudden sense of dismay that she did not know if she was supposed to have met the Comtesse or not. Fortunately Madame Pelayo turned to Colonel Mansfield.

"I am going to take Mrs. Lawson up to the Nursery," she said. "Will you wait and have a cup of tea with me when I return?"

"I am honoured, but, as you know, my desk is piled high with work."

"And you prefer to return to it rather than to waste time with tea and—me."

"To refute such an accusation may I say I shall be delighted to stay for tea?"

There was a little twist on his lips which made Sheena question whether he was being sarcastic or not. But Madame Pelayo smiled at him delightedly, her lovely face seeming to light up.

"Will you order it then?" she said. "And the chocolate biscuits that you like better than anything else. See, I remember everything—even your *penchant* for biscuits."

"You are too kind."

Again Sheena felt there was a touch of sarcasm behind his bow. A foreign bow, she thought, and she wondered now how she could have thought that he was entirely English. There was, in fact, something very foreign about him.

"Come upstairs, Mrs. Lawson," the Ambassadress said. She led the way as she spoke, her full-skirted dress of black faille rustling as she walked as if it rested on innumerable silk petticoats.

16

It was then, as she turned towards the door, that Sheena had a glimpse of herself in one of the long mirrors which decorated the grey walls. She saw reflected the lissom elegance of Madame Pelayo—the flash of her jewels, the lovely lines of her dress—and following her a small, undistinguished figure in a shabby, badly cut suit of brown tweed.

The felt hat which Sheena wore pulled down over her fair hair had seen better days. Granted, her white silk blouse was clean; but her heavy shoes with their low heels seemed to make an unconscionable noise as she followed the spindle-heeled, toeless sandals of her hostess across the polished lobby outside the drawing-room and up the wide staircase, with its beautifully chased balustrade.

"I hope you will be comfortable here, Mrs. Lawson," Madame Pelayo said as they climbed the stairs. "I am very anxious that the children should feel settled and we should have no more changes in the house. I wish them to learn English—in fact it is essential that they should speak English fluently."

"Can they speak a little already?" Sheena asked.

"Oh yes, indeed, they know quite a lot. We have had two English governesses, but they both had to leave for reasons that I need not enumerate to you now. Sufficient to say that I promised myself that never again would I have a young, unmarried woman in the place. It is too much responsibility, too much trouble for everyone—including me."

"I understand," Sheena murmured.

She was beginning to understand now why Uncle Patrick had insisted that she should be a widow.

"The children, of course, already speak French as well as Spanish. My husband talks to them in Spanish, which is his own language, and I in French, which is my native tongue."

"They must be very talented," Sheena suggested.

"On the contrary. You will find they know very little—except how to get their own way," Madame Pelayo said, with a flash of humour which seemed to make her even more lovely. "And here they are, my little ones!"

She opened the door of a room as she spoke and

17

there were cries of, "Mamma! Mamma!" from two children who were playing with bricks on the floor. They sprang to their feet and ran towards their mother, looking, Sheena thought, exactly like two expensive dolls that she had once seen in a shop window.

Madame Pelayo bent to kiss her children and then introduced them to Sheena.

"This is Madeleine," she said. "Although I am afraid we always call her Madi. She will be seven next week and is already very excited about what she is going to have for a birthday present."

"A pony-cart, Mamma! You promised me a pony-cart," Madi cried.

There was no pleading in her voice, rather it was a statement of fact. She already promised to be a beauty like her mother. She had dark hair curled on either side of her face, and tied on top of her head with a huge bow of satin ribbon. Her dress, of pink organdie, fell from an embroidered yoke to stand stiffly above her bare, dimpled knees. She was slim and elegant, moving like quicksilver, and having an engaging manner of setting her head on one side when she asked a question.

The boy was sturdier and much darker. It was easy to see the Spaniard in him, and already there was an in-bred pride to be seen in the way he carried his head, despite the fact that he was plump and had difficulty in following the quick movements of his sister.

"Pedro is only just five," Madame Pelayo explained. "My husband adores him and spoils him inordinately. But I am very strict, *n'est pas*?"

The children laughed at that as if at some great joke, and Pedro, throwing his arms around his mother's knees, held her close to him.

"Now, children, I have got to go downstairs," Madame Pelayo said. "Show Mrs. Lawson where everything is. Show her, too, how nice and polite and good you can be. All English children are very good because they are brought up so very, very strictly."

"I am sick of hearing about English children," Madi said petulantly.

"Now, Madi, that is naughty," her mother replied. "Mrs. Lawson will not get a good impression of you if you talk like that."

Madi looked at Sheena as if inwardly she said, "Who cares?" But she did not reply and Sheena smiled in what she hoped was an ingratiating manner.

"I certainly won't tell you how good English children are," she said. "To begin with I don't think they are better or worse than any other sort of children. And when I was small, my Nanny was always telling me about some children she had been with before she came to me and how good and well behaved they were, with the result that I hated them."

"Did you really?" Madi asked interestedly.

"Yes, really," Sheena answered.

She saw the interest quicken in the child's eyes and felt she had scored at least one point. But when Madame Pelayo closed the door behind her and she was alone, she felt her heart sink. She really knew so very little about children. She had been brought up an only child and she had had very little to do with other children.

She had gone to school spasmodically. Once for a few terms in Dublin; another time to a small school right down in the south of Ireland; and once for only a few months in Cork. For the rest she had picked up things here and there, taking lessons when she could find them from widely diverse types of teacher and finding that the sum total meant that she was extremely badly educated.

Only one thing had been fortunate. Her mother's old maid, who had stuck to them through thick and thin until she died of a heart attack when Sheena was eighteen, had been French. Sheena had talked with the maid in her native language from her earliest days—in fact it became so like second nature to her that she often found herself thinking in French. Old Marie had been in many ways the only mother she had ever known. Patrick always spoke of himself as being both father and mother to her, but Sheena hadn't been very old before she realised that she had to look after him rather than the other way about.

Poor Patrick! With his prejudices and his enthusiasms, his violent hatred of England and his almost idolatrous love of Ireland. Dear Patrick! With his warm heart, his sweetness and his understanding.

Sheena felt a sudden surge of homesickness come over her. Why had she consented to this wild, mad scheme? What was she doing here? As out of place as a cuckoo in a nest, if it came to that, in this exotic, over-decorated nursery with two children who looked more capable of instructing her than she them.

She looked round at the elaborate toys—at the dolls' house with electric light, exquisite furniture, and real silver *accoutrements* which must have cost a fortune; at the rocking-horse as big as a real pony; at the electric train which ran through tunnels and stopped at minia-ture stations; at the teddy bear which was as big as Pedro himself; and at the dozens of dolls decked out with tiny ear muffs and dresses trimmed with real lace. Any of these toys, Sheena thought, had cost more than she and Uncle Patrick had to spend in a month on their food!

And now she let herself be led from the Nursery into the rooms which opened out of it. The single bedroom for herself with a fitted dressing-table; clothes cupboards that lit up when you opened the doors; thick, soft carpets into which one's feet seemed to sink; and a long, narrow French window which opened on to a balcony which overlooked the gardens at the back of the house. It was all so lovely, so luxurious, that Sheena felt she had nothing to say as the children dragged her away to show her their own room and the blue-tiled bathroom which they both shared.

Then, when they felt she had seen everything, and had gone back to her bedroom, they stood looking at her.

"Are you going to make a time-table?" Madi en-quired.

"Do you usually have one?" Sheena asked quickly.

"All the governesses we have had made one," Madi replied. "But we never kept to it. It would say 'History' or 'Scripture' on the time-table, but Mamma would come and say 'Come for a drive in the car,' or Uncle Henri would arrive and then Miss Robinson would giggle and forget all about history and the time-table."

"Well, perhaps we had better not have a time-table to start with," Sheena said—thankfully because she was not certain how to draw one up. "We will just try and

20

get your lessons in when nobody else seems to want us to do anything."

"Have you met Uncle Henri yet?" Madi asked.

"No, who is he?" Sheena enquired.

Madi looked at Pedro and gave him a little nudge. The little boy had not been listening, but now he looked enquiringly at his sister.

"She doesn't know who Uncle Henri is," Madi explained.

Pedro with almost a sly look in his eyes smiled at Sheena. "Uncle Henri liked Miss Robinson," he said at length. "Do you think he will like you?"

"Hush, Pedro." Madi obviously understood enough to realise the impropriety of such a remark.

Sheena, a little embarrassed, turned towards the dressing-table and pulled off her hat.

"You run into the Nursery, Madi," she said, "and see if tea is ready. I expect you have tea at this time."

"We have milk," Madi answered. "Pedro doesn't like milk, but Mamma says he has got to drink it to grow big and strong."

"Will you go and see if your milk is ready?" Sheena asked.

The children ran from the room and she sat down at the dressing-table. Her hair was uncomfortable, pinned up so tidily with such unaccustomed severity, and she pulled out the pins and taking a comb from her bag combed it free. It seemed to spring out joyfully into its natural waves and curls. For a moment Sheena sat staring at her reflection, seeing not a small, heart-shaped face with what Uncle Patrick called its "blue eyes put in with a smutty finger," but instead the dark, flashing beauty of Madame Pelayo.

How she would love to be as pretty as that, she thought. Then she heard a sudden tumult from the Nursery and without thinking, and still carrying the comb in her hand, she ran into the adjoining room. The children appeared to be shrieking at something by the fireplace. Thinking they must have hurt themselves Sheena ran towards them, and only as she reached them did she look down in astonishment to see that Pedro was sitting on the chest of a young man who was lying on the hearth-rug.

21

Pedro was being bounced up and down, shrieking at the top of his voice, while Madi was dancing round them both, uttering shrill cries which did not sound unlike an Indian war chant. Comb in hand, Sheena stood and stared, and found herself looking into a pair of sparkling eyes above a wide laughing mouth. Then suddenly Pedro was sitting on the floor and the young man was on his feet.

"How do you do? I am Henri de Cormeille, and you, I understand, are Mrs. Lawson." He took her hand in his and raised it to his lips.

For a moment she was astonished and then she remembered that it was conventional for a married woman in France to have her hand kissed.

"How do you do?" Sheena said. "I . . . I thought something was wrong. The children were making such a noise!"

"That, I may as well inform you, is their usual reception of their uncle."

"Then . . . then that is all right," Sheena said, and realised she was blushing. It was not only because she was conscious of feeling rather foolish, standing there with her comb in her hand, but because of the expression in the young man's eyes. Eyes which seemed to take in every detail of her golden hair falling about her shoulders; eyes which made her uncomfortably aware that she could not meet them and keep her composure.

"I am astonished!" the young man said suddenly.

"Astonished?" Sheena queried.

"Yes. My sister informed me that she was getting a very staid, very proper English governess. 'She will be old,' she said. 'An old married woman.' Is there some mistake or have you changed identities with the person who was originally engaged?"

Sheena thought that she must put an end to this conversation. She became aware that the children were watching them—standing surprisingly silent, looking from one face to the other. No wonder Miss Robinson had giggled when Uncle Henri came to the Nursery! She could understand that now.

"I'm afraid you are seeing me at a disadvantage," she said stiffly. "I was just doing my hair when I heard the children scream. But I assure you that I am in fact very staid and very strict."

"*Mon Dieu*, I'm terrified!" There was no mistaking the twinkle in his eyes or the laughter which seemed to keep his mouth perpetually smiling. "But if I am good, please, Mrs. Lawson, may I stay to tea?"

"Oh, yes, Uncle Henri, stay to tea, stay to tea," the children cried.

"You see, they are pleading on my behalf."

"You must do as you think best," Sheena said. "I am not certain, having only just arrived, whether I have the authority either to invite or refuse you."

She turned away as she spoke, walked across the room in what she hoped was a dignified manner, and disappeared into her own bedroom. Only when she was alone did she allow herself to chuckle a little.

There was no doubt that Uncle Henri was going to be a handful. No wonder the other governesses had got into trouble over him!

"I must be very sensible," Sheena told herself, and then realised, even as she said it, that she didn't feel sensible at all. From the moment when she had got out of the train a sense of excitement had been rising in her.

This was a world she had never known before—not only Paris with its trees and its buildings, its traffic and its strange people, but also the beauty and luxury at the Embassy. The pictures, the curtains, the carpets—everything was so different from the life she had lived with Patrick O'Donovan, with its pinching and scraping, the worry of wondering where the next meal was coming from, and—yes, why not admit it?—never having anyone except Uncle Patrick to talk to for months on end.

And now, in the space of an hour, she had met three people who intrigued and interested her. Colonel Mansfield—serious, rather frightening, and yet in his own way definitely intriguing. Madame Pelayo—beautiful, exotic: the sort of person Sheena had imagined existed only between the pages of an expensive magazine. And now, Henri de Cormeille—gay, debonair; someone of whom she must be careful, someone she knew, instinctively in her own heart, she would have to fight against every inch of the way.

23

She went to the window and looked out into the garden. The sun had set and already pale blue twilight was creeping over the sky. There was something magical in the very shadows beneath the flowering bushes below and in the soft dusky translucence of the sky above.

Could this really be happening to her? Suddenly Sheena knew it was all the prelude to adventure—an adventure so exciting, so thrilling that already she was almost breathless with the thrill of it. Through the closed door she heard the children laughing and hurriedly she returned to her dressing-table.

Quickly, lest she should weaken in her resolve to look staid and respectable, she pinned back her hair, striving to brush smooth the springing waves on either side of her temples. And then, without even another glance at herself in the mirror, she walked across the room and opened the door which led into the Nursery.

Two

"May I come in?"

The Nursery door opened and Sheena looked up from the small white sock she was darning to see Colonel Mansfield standing in the doorway.

"Of course," she answered, but at the same time she felt a little apprehensive. She did not know why, but Lucien Mansfield always made her feel afraid. There was something in the way he looked at her, in the almost penetrating quality of his grey eyes, and perhaps, too, it was because his personality was so strong, so obtrusive, that it was impossible to ignore him.

Even when other people were there—the beautiful Madame Pelayo, her brother, and even the Ambassador himself—Sheena found it impossible not to be conscious all the time that Colonel Mansfield was in the room.

She had not seen much of him for the first two days after her arrival; and that, perhaps, was fortunate because she felt in an utter state of chaos. There was so much to learn, so much to absorb, so much that was utterly new to her that she was terrified all the time of making a mistake, of revealing how woefully ignorant she was—not only of being a governess, but of the type of life in which she found herself.

Now, as Colonel Mansfield crossed the room, she forced herself to a composure she was far from feeling, but she was at least a little more self-assured than she had been on the first day of her arrival.

Lucien Mansfield, however, appeared utterly at his ease as he walked to the hearth-rug and stood with his back to the fire looking round the elaborate, luxurious Nursery.

"The children are resting," he said. It was a statement rather than a question.

"Yes. I make them lie down for an hour after luncheon."

"I heard you had started such an innovation. I thought it a good one."

Sheena glanced at him quickly. She had an idea there was very little that went on in the Embassy that Colonel Mansfield did not know. She made no comment, continuing to darn Madi's little sock.

"I hope you have found everything to your liking, Mrs. Lawson," Colonel Mansfield said after a moment. "I was expecting to have a series of requests and complaints, but so far have had neither."

"I am sorry if that has disappointed you," Sheena answered with a smile, "but I find everything so perfect here that I really have nothing to complain about."

"You are certainly different from your predecessors," Lucien Mansfield commented drily. "And now I have one or two things to ask you. To start with, may I have your passport? There are certain formalities that have to be completed."

"Yes, of course," Sheena said.

She rose, walked quickly across the room and into her bedroom. Her passport was lying on her dressing-table because she had half expected that she would be asked for it. As she picked it up, she had a quick glance at her reflection in the mirror. She was looking pale, she thought, but with her hair sleeked back tidily she looked at least demure and unsensational—the sort of quiet girl anyone would be pleased to have as a governess.

She went back into the Nursery. Colonel Mansfield was standing where she had left him and she fancied there was a frown between his eyes. And then, as she held out her passport, he smiled. It made him look young, almost boyish, and for the first time she realised how good-looking he was. There was, she thought, something purposeful about the squareness of his jaw, and perhaps something hard and obstinate in the line of his lips. And yet, when he smiled, he had an almost irresistible charm and instinctively she found herself smiling back.

"Thank you," he said. "And now there are just a few questions I have to ask you."

He drew a paper from his pocket and sat down at the Nursery table. He opened the passport and scrutinised it. There was a long silence and despite every resolution to remain calm Sheena felt her fingers tremble a little.

"You must have had a very happy and uneventful life," Lucien Mansfield remarked, breaking what seemed to Sheena an almost ominous silence.

"Why . . . why do you say that?" she asked, surprised.

"Because you look so very young," he replied. "It is almost impossible to believe that you should be as old as your passport reveals. But, of course, a passport cannot lie."

"No, of course not," Sheena said quickly. And then because some comment seemed to be expected of her she added: "All my family look young." She was thinking of Uncle Patrick who looked far less than his age.

"Yes, your family; I was just going to ask you about them," Lucien Mansfield told her, and instantly Sheena saw the dangers that lay ahead. "I see your maiden name was Ashburton."

For a moment Sheena did not answer him. It seemed so funny to hear the name, which Uncle Patrick had forbidden her to use, spoken in a matter-of-fact tone and in a matter-of-fact way.

"I gave you my name, Mavourneen," he had said, "when you first came to me, and it was your mother's name too. I would not be asking you to use the name of a black-livered devil who was after stealing my only sister from me. An Englishman he was, and the only good thing he ever did in his life was to father a child as sweet as you, me darling girl."

"Why was he so bad, Uncle Patrick? Why did you hate him?"

"He was English, child, and surely that's a reason for hating every one of them—God rot their souls!"

27

"My mother must have loved him!" Sheena could hear herself saying the words. She must have been nine at the time, just being old enough to reason, to think things out for herself, to try and remember what her father and mother had been like.

Vaguely she could remember their voices, feel their arms, hear the sound of their laughter. But she had only been five when they had died at sea, racing a small boat, which everyone had told them was unseaworthy, across the bay in a gale in which no sensible fisher-folk would have ventured out. That had been typical of them, she learned—not only from Uncle Patrick, but from the other people who had known them. Young, reckless and daring, they had defied fate all their lives because they had liked to live dangerously. . . .

"Yes, my maiden name was Ashburton," Sheena said now, and savoured the word as it came to her lips. A nice name, almost a beautiful name, and yet Uncle Patrick had never let her even breathe it in his presence.

"I used to know some Ashburtons very well," Colonel Mansfield answered. "The head of the family is, of course, Lord Avon. I wonder what relation you are to him?"

"None that I know of," Sheena replied. "I'm afraid I have very few relations. I'm an orphan; my father and mother were both drowned when I was very small."

"That must have been very sad for you," Lucien Mansfield commiserated, and there was a sympathy in his voice which Sheena felt made him almost human. "I was going to ask you," he went on, "who is your next of kin?"

There was a moment's pause.

"I . . . I have an uncle," Sheena said slowly. "But there is no need to bother you with his name."

"I'm afraid I must have one, just in case you fall down the stairs or get run over in the street," Colonel Mansfield insisted, with a twist to his lips.

"Then I had best give you my uncle's name and address," Sheena said. "Of course, I have seen very little of him these past years."

She felt herself blush even as she told the lie, but Uncle Patrick's advice had been explicit.

"Don't be after mentioning my name in Paris," he had admonished her. "Remember I'm Irish—true Irish—and, Glory be to God, that's likely to be suspect before you start."

"Suspect of what?" Sheena asked. "Oh, Uncle Patrick, do explain. Why should everything be so secretive? Tell me what is happening and why we have to go through all this when I would much rather be here with you—and in your heart of hearts you know you don't want me to go."

She made the appeal passionately and even as she spoke she knew it was useless. Patrick O'Donovan could never give a straight answer to a straight question.

"Now, me darling," he coaxed, "you know I'll be missing you every moment of the day and night. Yet what must be must be. But guard your wee tongue, Mavourneen, and play your cards cleverly."

"I haven't got any cards," Sheena said helplessly.

And she felt now that she wanted to say the same thing to this serious-faced young man who was asking her questions it was almost impossible to answer. If only she could tell him the truth. If only she could say: "I'm not a governess really—I never have been one. I was brought here by a trick, by a false reference, and now that I've seen Paris you had better send me back."

And yet, even as such a fanciful notion came to her mind, she knew she did not want to go back—not yet at any rate. She had seen Paris, but how little of it! Already the magic of it was creeping into her heart, into her mind. There was so much more she wanted to see, so much more she wanted to do.

Speaking quickly, almost too rapidly for her companion to take it down, she said:

"My uncle's name is Patrick O'Donovan, and his address is 339 Fulham Road, London."

"That was the address at which we wrote to you," Colonel Mansfield commented.

"Yes, but he is not there. A letter would be forwarded," Sheena improvised quickly, realising she had made a mistake.

"At the moment, for instance, is your uncle in England or Ireland?"

"I have not the slightest idea," Sheena answered. "I

have not seen him for several years." She could feel the colour rising hotly in her cheeks and she bent her head as if to look closer at the hole she was darning.

Colonel Mansfield wrote for some moments and then he asked:

"Your husband—when was he killed?"

"Two years ago—or was it three?" Sheena replied. She was trying desperately hard to remember what Uncle Patrick had told her.

"I'm sorry to bother you with all these questions," Colonel Mansfield went on. "But I assure you they are necessary. Do you mind telling me how he was killed?"

"In . . . in a . . . motor accident."

"And what did he do?"

Sheena felt as if she must scream as one question followed after another. Why hadn't she thought of this? Why hadn't Uncle Patrick warned her these details would be required? What did her husband do? What could she say he did? Madly the question seemed to echo in her mind and then she realised that here again there were pitfalls. Had he been in a good position there might have been a pension for her. If he had money of his own, she should have some now.

"He was not in a job when he was killed," she said at last in a low voice. "He . . . was looking for something to do."

"I understand. Any children?"

"No! No . . . of course not."

The positiveness of her tone made Colonel Mansfield glance at her in surprise. She bent her head still further, realising as she did so that her hands were trembling. To her great relief he closed her passport and put both it and the paper on which he had been writing into his pocket.

"I think that is everything, Mrs. Lawson. Will you think it impertinent if I say I'm sorry for you having to earn your own living?"

The fact that the interrogation was obviously finished gave Sheena a sense of relief, so that she could speak almost naturally as she replied:

"But why? It is what most girls do, isn't it?"

"Most girls perhaps," Lucien Mansfield answered. "But it is hard on a married woman. You must have

30

thought when you married that you would have a home and, perhaps, children of your own, not spend your time looking after other people's."

"Yes . . . yes, of course."

"Ours is the gain," Lucien Mansfield smiled. "Madame Pelayo told me last night how delighted she is that the children have taken to you and that you seem to be settling down."

"They are sweet children," Sheena answered. "And not a bit spoilt as you led me to expect."

"I wanted you to anticipate the worst and not be disappointed by our best," he said. "Isn't that always the wisest way of tackling things?"

Sheena considered this idea seriously.

"No, I do not really think so," she said at length. "I hate anticipating the worst. I always believe that everything is going to be wonderful until it turns out differently."

"You must have an awful lot of disappointments."

"Not many. Paris, for instance, is just as wonderful as I expected it to be."

"But you haven't seen anything of Paris yet," Colonel Mansfield answered. "Perhaps one day . . ." He checked himself suddenly and she wondered what he had been going to say. Then he rose to his feet and stood looking down at her.

"I wondered when I first saw you," he said at length, "why you looked so un-English. Now I know. It is because your eyes are completely and absolutely Irish."

"Blue eyes put in with a smutty finger," Sheena laughed. "That is what my Uncle Patrick always says."

The words were out before she could stop them. "Why, why do I have to lie?" she thought despairingly. "One always gets caught out sooner or later."

"Your uncle's description is very apt," Lucien Mansfield remarked. His voice was somehow dry; there was a questioning note in it which made Sheena realise that he had noticed her lapse in quoting her uncle so easily when she had said that she saw so little of him.

"Do you know Ireland well?" was his next question.

"I was there as a child, before my parents were drowned," Sheena answered. That was true enough at any rate.

31

"And who brought you up after they died?"

Sheena took a deep breath and then held up her hand as if to call for silence.

"Listen!" she said. "Did I hear the children?"

There was no sound at all from the adjoining room, but she got quickly to her feet.

"I think I hear Madi calling me," she mumbled, and without waiting to see if there was any response or reply from Colonel Mansfield she ran from the room.

The children were lying on their beds. Madi was looking at a picture-book and Pedro was half asleep, his eyes tight shut, a golliwog clasped tightly in his arms.

"Is it time to get up?" Madi asked.

"Not yet," Sheena answered.

She moved across the room as if she were fetching something from the chest-of-drawers. She lowered the blind a little further to shut out the afternoon sun and fiddled around with their clothes for a moment or two before returning to the Nursery. To her relief the room was empty. Colonel Mansfield had gone.

Sheena sat down in her chair by the fireplace and put her hands up to her burning cheeks. How difficult it was, how complicated! Why, oh why had she ever let herself embark on such a mad adventure?

Then she told herself that she had no alternative. When Patrick O'Donovan made his mind up about anything it was practically impossible to circumvent him, and he had been determined, with an iron determination that nothing could gainsay, that she should come to Paris.

What hold had these friends over him? What did they do to ensure that he carried out their commands? Sheena had no idea; she only knew that short of defying her uncle and breaking with him for ever she could do nothing but come here, because he had asked it of her— because he had, in fact, insisted.

She had a sudden longing for the easy, uneventful life they had lived in Ireland. Patrick, who had always been a rolling stone, had moved into her parents' house when they were drowned and had lived there with her and old Marie.

He had gone away for periodical visits. He had given no explanation of his movements and they had no idea where he was until they would sometimes receive a highly coloured picture postcard with a few words of greeting on it. When Sheena grew old enough to ask questions, he had always told her that he was off to the races.

"Sure, me darling, and have you ever met an Irishman who could resist a good piece of horseflesh?" he would ask. And she had believed him implicitly until she grew older.

When Sheena was fourteen they started their travels, and she had memories of dark, cheerless houses in big towns. The back streets of Dublin, Belfast and Cork all became familiar. She went with Uncle Patrick to race meetings, boxing contests, football games, and to dozens of places where great numbers of people were gathered together. In a few years she had thousands of acquaintances and no friends. They never stayed long enough to make friends or returned soon enough to keep alive the first spark of friendship.

But there were periods of real happiness, periods of rest, holidays for Uncle Patrick, when they went back to the little house on the cliffs below which the great waves came rolling in from the Atlantic.

How she loved it! And how, always when she was away, she would ache for the feel of sea-spray on her face and the sight of green grass undulating away over the distant hills.

It was true what Patrick had said himself. He had been father and mother, uncles and aunts—in fact all the family she had ever known. He had brought her up and had loved her as if, indeed, she were his—and she could never be sufficiently grateful to him for that. What would have happened to her if he had not been there? Sometimes she had frightened herself with the thought that, if he had not come to her rescue, she might have been brought up in an orphanage.

"There was no one else, Mavourneen," Uncle Patrick had told her often enough. "Your father's family know of his death of course. I wrote and told them what had happened, but never a reply did I get. They disliked your mother. They had not wanted her in the family—them with their stuck-up noses and their grand ideas of what was good enough for an Ashburton. They would have none of the O'Donovans—though we are descended from the Irish kings themselves. Kings, we were, me darling, when the upstart English were walking about with naught but woad on their bodies. But why should we trouble ourselves? 'Tis Irish you are; Irish from the crown of your blessed head to the soles of your darling feet. Irish and an O'Donovan, and don't you ever forget it."

She never had forgotten it, Sheena thought. At the same time she could not force herself to hate the English as Uncle Patrick hated them. She could never forget that her father had been English. Bad he might have been and neglected by his family, but still she was a part of him—an Ashburton, however much Uncle Patrick might deny it.

It was as if Colonel Mansfield's questions now made her curious for the first time. Had she any relations left? Who was Lord Avon who he had said was the head of the family? With almost a sense of dismay Sheena realised how ignorant she was about her father. All she knew about him was that he had been English and that Uncle Patrick had said that he was bad.

How could she have lived so long without asking questions? she wondered, and then remembered that it would have taken the rack and the thumbscrew to make Patrick O'Donovan tell her anything he wanted to keep to himself.

Even to speak of her father put him into a rage, and she had learned, when she was quite tiny, to avoid questions and suggestions which upset him. "When I next see him I will insist on knowing the truth," Sheena thought to herself and wondered with a smile if she would really have the courage.

The clock on the mantelpiece chimed the hour and she rose to her feet. She had not even finished darning Madi's sock, and she realised that the children's rest hour had passed unprofitably with questions from Colonel Mansfield and flights of her own fancy which had left her only restless and disturbed.

She was just putting the sock away in her work-basket when she heard the door open and turned to see the Vicomte de Cormeille enter the room.

"Bon jour, Madame, I have come to take the children

34

for a drive," he smiled. "I have got a new car and I promised them weeks ago that they should come out in it."

"I will go and get them ready," Sheena said, turning towards the night nursery.

With a quick movement the young *Vicomte* stood in front of her.

"There is no hurry."

"But it is time for them to get up," Sheena protested.

"They can wait," he said. "They will be excited enough when they hear where we are taking them."

Sheena raised her eyebrows.

"We?" she asked. "I didn't think you would want me to come."

"Do you think I would take them otherwise?" he asked.

There was something in the expression on his face and the look in his eyes which made her own drop before his.

"I think it would be much better if they went for a walk," Sheena tried to say firmly.

Henri de Cormeille laughed at her, and now his hands went out towards her, taking both hers in his before she could prevent it.

"Oh, Sheena, Sheena!" he cried. "Do you know that today was the first time I heard your name? What a sweet name for a sweet person! Sheena! I have never known a girl called that before."

"My name is Mrs. Lawson, *Monsieur*," Sheena tried to say firmly. But it was difficult to be firm when one of the most attractive young men you have ever seen in your life is holding your hands in his and swinging them gently.

The *Vicomte* was not very tall but his body was perfectly proportioned and he had, Sheena thought suddenly, the lithe grace of a young fawn. He made her think of Pan, and in her mind's eye she almost saw him blowing on his reed pipes with little horns sprouting in his wavy hair.

"We will go in the *Bois*," he said gaily. "I want to show you the *Bois*—the trees beginning to bud, the lovers walking beneath them, their arms entwined, their eyes seeing only themselves and their love. We will

35

drive beside the Seine. I want to see the expression on your face when you see the silver river in the sunshine, the barges moving down it, the grey buildings on the other bank reflected, shimmering as the ripples widen out and the birds come down to the water's edge to drink."

"I . . . I will go and get ready," Sheena told him, trying to take her hands away from his. But he would not let her go.

"You are so young, you are younger than Madi even, in many ways. I have been watching you these last two days. You are like the sleeping princess in the fairy story, before the kiss woke her up. What was your husband like?"

His question took her by surprise, and then swiftly, before he could stop her, she wrenched herself free.

"I'm going to call the children," she told him over her shoulder as she hurried from the room. "If we do not get out quickly, the afternoon will be over."

She ran into the night nursery.

"Get up, children," she cried. "Uncle Henri is here and is going to take you for a drive in his new car."

There were cries of delight from Madi and rather less excitable ones from Pedro, who was still sleepy. Sheena pulled on their long, white woollen leggings, which fitted snugly and were held over their shoes by a piece of elastic under the instep. Then she buttoned them into their bright red coats, put a white beret on Pedro's head and tied a little red bonnet trimmed with white ermine over Madi's dark curls.

"Now go and talk to Uncle Henri while I get my hat and coat," she commanded.

They rushed away with whoops of joy while Sheena went into her own room and took from the cupboard the old jaegar coat she had worn for over five years, and pulled on the plain brown felt hat in which she had arrived in Paris and which was the only one she possessed. She felt a sudden rebellion against her appearance, against the dull brown of her tweed suit, the colourless beige of her coat and the severity of her hair pinned back under the felt hat.

She had seen Madame Pelayo leave the house that morning in a coat of wine-coloured velvet trimmed with a huge collar and cuffs of rich sable, and for the first time in her life Sheena had longed for beautiful clothes and to look elegant and *soignée,* like some of the other women who came to the Embassy.

She only had glimpses of them when she took the children down to the drawing-room after tea or when Madame Pelayo and her friends came up to the Nursery for a few moments, but they opened up vistas of a new world—a world where women were beautiful, fêted and admired.

Yet even dowdy and drab as she was there was something in Henri de Cormeille's eyes which told Sheena she was attractive, and she had a wild desire, at this moment, to look as she might look for him if she had the chance or the money.

Severely she repressed such a thought, and picking up her handbag and gloves walked demurely into the Nursery. The children were dragging their uncle towards the door, chattering nineteen to the dozen in French, but when he looked at Sheena he spoke in English:

"You are ready for this expedition?"

"Yes, I'm ready."

"The *Bois* can be very romantic in the spring. You are prepared for that?" There was a look in his eyes which she should have thought impertinent, but somehow she could not help laughing with sheer high spirits as she answered:

"I'm prepared for anything."

"Et voilà, we can go then."

The children ran ahead of them, shouting and laughing, until they reached the top of the stairs, where Pedro waited for Sheena to hold his hand. Instead, she picked him up in her arms and carried him down the wide staircase. She felt suddenly in need of protection. She wanted something to hold on to, something to remind her that here was her duty.

Her face was half hidden by the heavy child. It was not until she had actually reached the foot of the stairs and was crossing the hall that she looked up to find Lucien Mansfield standing outside the door which led to the Ambassador's study.

"You are going driving?"

Sheena hoped that his remark was addressed to the

37

Vicomte; then she saw he was looking at her. Somehow she felt uncomfortably guilty.

"Yes," she answered. "We are going in Monsieur de Cormeille's car. He wished to take Madi and Pedro for a drive."

"How nice for them." There was no mistaking the sarcasm in Lucien Mansfield's voice, and almost with a feeling of dismay Sheena glanced from him towards the *Vicomte.*

"Any objections?"

There was no doubt that Henri de Cormeille meant it as a challenge.

"Many! But doubtless you would not understand them."

"In which case shall we consider them unsaid?"

"You may prefer to do so."

There was antagonism between the two men which seemed to vibrate around them. For a moment they faced each other—Lucien Mansfield's face severe and expressionless, yet his grey eyes were very steady and almost steely as he looked into the *Vicomte*'s handsome face. Then, with a little laugh, Henri de Cormeille turned away.

"I don't interfere with your pleasures," he said. "Keep your hands off mine!"

Sheena was not quite certain how it happened, but somehow, before there was time for any more or even for her to hear what Lucien Mansfield replied, the *Vicomte* had hustled them down the steps and they were in his big car. There was room for all of them on the front seat. Madi sat between Sheena and her uncle and Pedro sat on Sheena's knee. One of the footmen put a light rug over their knees, slammed the door and they were off. The big car purred like a contented cat as the *Vicomte* drove it dexterously down the quiet streets and into the *Champs Elysées.*

"Faster! Faster! Uncle Henri," Madi was soon crying as they passed the *Arc de Triomphe* and started down the long avenues which led towards the *Bois.* Paris was bathed in pale golden sunshine, but there was a nip in the air and Sheena bent to fasten the top button of Madi's coat and pull her own a little closer round her.

"You are not cold?" the *Vicomte* asked solicitously.

"No, it is lovely," Sheena answered.

"A lovely day for lovely people," he said, and somehow managed to make it a compliment just for Sheena so that she dare not look at him but turned to watch the road slipping away as they went faster and faster. Even the children were hushed into silence until they had reached the *Bois,* and beneath some Chestnut trees just coming into bud the *Vicomte* brought the great car to a standstill.

"Can we run amongst the trees?" Madi asked. "Oh, please, Uncle Henri."

"You must ask Mrs. Lawson," he replied.

"Yes, of course," Sheena answered. She turned to the door, but swiftly the *Vicomte* had jumped from the driving-seat and hurried round to open it for her. He took Pedro from her arms and set him on the ground.

"Go for a run, old man," he instructed him, and then, bending past Sheena, he lifted Madi in the air and deposited her beside her brother. "Go and explore, *ma petite.*"

"I must go with them," Sheena said quickly, but as she tried to rise he barred the way.

"There is no hurry. Let them look after themselves. They have got to learn to be independent sooner or later."

"But I must look after them," Sheena expostulated.

"They will come to no harm," he replied. "We will keep them in sight. I want to talk to you."

"What about?" she asked.

"There are a lot of things. I want to ask you what you are thinking about, what is your opinion of us all? There are so many things we can talk about."

He was watching her as he spoke, his eyes quizzically on her lips, noting the way the colour came and went in her cheeks, seeing the little flicker of her dark eyelashes and, because she felt shy, the way her eyes refused to meet his.

"Of course if you do not want to talk about those things," he continued, "we can always talk of love."

"Of love!" Sheena's eyes were wide for a moment.

"But, of course. Isn't it the one subject which engages all our hearts? The one subject which is inevitable when a man and a woman are together?"

"I think that must be a French way of looking at things," Sheena said, trying to speak sensibly, but aware of the tremor in her voice.

The *Vicomte* was not listening; instead he leant on the door of the car so that his face was very near to hers as he said quietly:

"You would be very lovely, you know, if you made the most of yourself."

"I don't know what you mean," Sheena answered.

"I think you do," he said. "You are woman enough for that. Do you know what you looked like that first evening when you came into the Nursery and found me lying on the hearth-rug playing with the children? Your hair was falling about your face—soft, golden hair, Sheena, the colour of the sunshine in the early morning. I had expected the new governess to be someone middle-aged—and instead, I looked up to see a girl, indeed someone who was little more than a child and beautiful as an angel itself."

Sheena gave a little laugh.

"You were seeing me upside down," she said. "When you were the right way up, you must have seen that you were mistaken."

"I am not mistaken," the *Vicomte* answered. "I can still see that you are just a little girl masquerading—pretending to be grown-up and sophisticated, and yet as innocent of life and of love as a babe unborn."

With an effort Sheena fought against the magnetism in his voice. She felt herself slipping away into some exciting dream. It was almost like being hypnotised, she thought. And then, as she moved her hands, the sun glinted on the gold wedding-ring which Uncle Patrick had bought her.

"You forget, *Monsieur,* that I am a widow," she said severely. "I know a great deal more of life than you think. And now I must go to the children."

She pushed resolutely at the door of the car as she spoke and to her surprise he made no effort to prevent her descending from the car.

"Now you are running away," he said softly. "But one day you will stop running and then I shall catch up with you."

"I think you're talking nonsense, *Monsieur,*" Sheena

answered. She was out of the car, her feet were on the ground, but although she had made the effort to evade him, now she did not want to go. The children were both in sight, searching beneath the trees for primroses. She could see them quite clearly and they were coming to no harm. It seemed so pointless to run after them, to run away, as the *Vicomte* had said she was doing. She hesitated, and sensing her hesitation he laughed gently.

"You are very severe with me, *Mrs. Lawson*," he said, accenting her name. He made it impossible for her not to smile as she answered:

"That is better, *Monsieur*. You must not call me by my Christian name. I feel sure that Her Excellency would not like it."

"Of course my sister would not like it," the *Vicomte* agreed. "That is why I shall be very careful. I will call you Sheena when we are alone together and in my thoughts when I think of you—which is always, all the time—and in my heart, where I will cherish you."

"You should not say such things to me."

"Why not?"

It was a question which she felt she must answer.

"Because . . . oh, because it is wrong," she stammered. "I am only the governess and you know that both the Ambassador and Madame would be seriously annoyed if they heard you. And also . . . well . . . also because the things you say are not true."

"Can you be certain of that?" the *Vicomte* enquired. "Oh, Sheena, how sweet you are! Have you ever flirted with a man before? I doubt it; and if you have, it was with one of those heavy-handed, lugubrious Englishmen, who know nothing about love and less about women."

"But I do not wish to flirt, *Monsieur*," Sheena protested. "It is true that I have never flirted before. That is all the more reason why you must not say such things to me. I do not understand the game you play and . . . and I do not want you to make a fool of me."

"My sweet! Do you really think that I would make a fool of you?" the *Vicomte* asked. "You must have a very poor opinion of me."

"I think, *Monsieur*, that you have very little to do with your time, and at the moment must be very short of friends. There are many beautiful, smart women in

41

Paris who would like to hear you say the things you say to me. They would not be frightened or ignorant, as I am."

"Have you ever thought how exciting it is to find somebody who is so ignorant?" the *Vicomte* asked softly. He took her hand suddenly and raised it to his lips. "Let me teach you a lot of things that you have never known before."

Quickly Sheena took her hand away.

"No, *Monsieur*. This is wrong—I know that. You must leave me alone or else I must . . ." She paused suddenly. What would she do? She didn't know what the answer was.

Seeing her hesitation he laughed.

"Yes?" he inquired. "What would you do?"

"Oh, please, please," Sheena pleaded. "You are making me feel so stupid and so embarrassed. I do not know what to say to you."

"Why not say the truth—that you find me a little interesting, a little charming, and a little different from anyone you have ever met before?"

"That is true enough," Sheena said. "But if Madame Pelayo finds out that you are behaving like this I shall lose my job. I shall be dismissed, as I gather Miss Robinson was."

For a moment he looked slightly embarrassed. And then he laughed.

"So, someone has been telling tales," he said. "Was it the inestimable, self-righteous Colonel who informed you about Miss Robinson?"

"Colonel Mansfield! No, of course not," Sheena answered. "He would not speak to me about such things. It was the children, as a matter of fact, who made me guess what had happened—and also something that your sister said."

"Miss Robinson was a very stupid girl," the *Vicomte* said. There was something in the tone of his voice which told Sheena the truth.

"You mean," she asked, "that she fell in love with you?"

He shrugged his shoulders and spread out his hands.

"It was not my fault—I beg you to believe it was not my fault."

"No?" For the first time since her acquaintance with the *Vicomte* Sheena felt sure of herself. "I'm afraid I do not believe you. But one thing is very certain. I will not fall in love with you. I will not be stupid, as Miss Robinson was."

"Can you be sure of that?" the *Vicomte* asked, and there was an expression on his face and in his eyes which brought back all her feeling of insecurity.

Almost feverishly she turned away from him.

"It is time we went back," she said sharply. "I will collect the children and you must take us home, otherwise we shall be late for tea."

As she ran towards Madi and Pedro busy collecting the primroses, she heard him laugh—and it was the laugh of a man amused, satisfied and yet expectant. And as it echoed in her ears Sheena felt afraid—not only of him, but of herself!

Three

Sheena was awakened in the morning by Jeanne, the head house-maid, bringing her a cup of tea. This was an honour, because usually one of the under-maids was deputed to perform the unimportant task of calling the governess.

Jeanne, who was middle-aged, bossy and married to one of the men-servants, pulled back the curtains, opened the shutters with a kind of flourish, then set down the tea-tray at Sheena's bedside.

"Thank you! How kind of you, Jeanne!" Sheena exclaimed, and looking at the delicate china arranged on the spotless lace-edged tray-cloth she added: "It is a surprise to find that people drink tea in the early morning in France. I expected there would only be coffee."

"And so there is, *M'selle*, in any correct French household," Jeanne said with something approaching a sniff. "But although Madame is French, she allows His Excellency's foreign ideas to supersede our national customs. In South America I understand they drink a kind of local tea—and a very inferior one at that."

Sheena smiled at the disdain in Jeanne's voice; then, pouring her tea into the cup, she said:

"Well, this looks delicious at any rate!"

"I'm glad you think so, *M'selle*," Jeanne replied. "Personally I prefer coffee. What good is tea to anyone

44

I should like to know? Just coloured water when all is said and done."

Sheena laughed. Jeanne's manner of talking, positive and almost passionate in its intensity, was somehow amusing in a stout elderly woman with the beginnings of a moustache on her upper lip.

"I am afraid I'm English enough to like coloured water," Sheena chuckled. "And what I like even better is having it brought to me while I'm still in bed. At home I usually get up and make tea for other people."

Jeanne, however, did not appear interested in Sheena's reminiscences. "And now, *M'selle*," she said, in almost an impatient manner: "Perhaps you will be kind enough to tell me your plans for today."

"My plans?" Sheena asked in surprise. "But I don't think I've made any."

"Don't you realise it's your day out?" Jeanne enquired.

"No, I had no idea," Sheena answered. "In fact no-one has told me that I even have one."

"Of course you have one, *M'selle*. All the governesses were most insistent on that. Madame will no doubt tell you you can choose any day of the week you want, but as I take the children when you are out, I prefer Wednesday. Any other day would be very inconvenient."

"Then of course I will choose Wednesday," Sheena smiled. "You must tell me what happens, Jeanne. At what hour does my day start?"

"Whenever you please—although M'selle Robinson did get the children up and dress them. I usually took over from her about eleven o'clock."

"Then that will suit me, too," Sheena said. "Do I . . . have to go out for luncheon?"

"No, no, not if you do not wish it. A tray will be brought to your room if you stay in; and if you intend to be out, perhaps you will tell me so that I can inform the chef. It is for you to choose entirely what you wish to do, *vous comprenez?*"

"Yes, I understand," Sheena answered. "And thank you for telling me about it. I think . . . I should like luncheon up here, if it is not too inconvenient—and as early as possible, so that afterwards I can go out and look at the shops."

"I will inform them downstairs," Jeanne said. "And I will come to the Nursery, *M'selle,* at eleven o'clock to take the little ones for a walk."

"Thank you, Jeanne."

The elderly maid turned towards the door and then as she reached it she turned back.

"Pardon, M'selle!" she exclaimed. "But I had forgotten there are two letters for you. I put them in the pocket of my apron in case they fell off the tray as I was carrying it upstairs." She turned back towards the bed and handed Sheena two envelopes.

The one on top was from Uncle Patrick and Sheena tore it open impatiently. It was the first word she had had from him since she left London, and now she felt a sudden surge of homesickness—not for that tall, dirty house with its back-breaking stairs, its dark, airless basement, and evil-smelling sink, but for Patrick O'Donovan himself, for his warm brogue which seemed to transform every word he spoke; for his twinkling eyes and broad smile which made one feel the world was a happier place just because he was in it.

For a moment, as Sheena held his letter in her hands, the writing seemed to dance before her eyes. She missed him! Missed him more than she could have believed it possible. Ever since her parents died he had always been there with her. Sometimes they had been apart for a few weeks, but never for longer, and now that feeling of isolation and loneliness which she had felt when she said good-bye to him at Victoria Station swept over her afresh.

"Good-bye, me darling girl; it will not be for long," Uncle Patrick said as she clung to him.

"I don't want to go! Oh, Uncle Patrick, I don't want to leave you."

She had spoken urgently with something near to anguish in her voice. For a moment he had held her close against his broad chest, and then he had almost pushed her up the steps into the carriage.

"It won't be for long, Mavourneen; it won't be for long."

It was only as the train moved slowly out of the station and she had waved from the carriage window until he was out of sight, that she realised, with a sense of dismay, that he had not said how long. There were so many questions that she had wanted to ask him —which, in fact, she had asked him, but in his own inimitable way he had avoided answering them.

Now Sheena wiped her eyes with the back of her hand, clearing her vision so that she could see Uncle Patrick's erratic yet somewhat individual handwriting on the cheap, unheaded writing paper. The letter began characteristically:

How are you, me lovely girl? I got your letter this morning to say you had arrived safely, and the Saints be praised that the crossing was not worse. I am interested in all you tell me about the Embassy and the people who are living there. Here the weather has been wet and cold and I caught a chill at the races, which is making me awful low. My luck was out and if you can spare a little of your salary this week it will be much appreciated. You can't send it to me through the post, of course, but you could ask for it to be brought over in the Diplomatic Bag. If you can send anything, address it to Mr. John Lawson and I will be calling at the Embassy in London on the off chance.

Take care of yourself, me darling, and the Lord bless you.

Your loving Uncle Patrick

Sheena read the letter through twice, and then, with a little burst of emotion, held it against her cheek. It smelt of tobacco—the strong, pungent tobacco which Uncle Patrick always smoked in his pipe. And as she shut her eyes, she could almost see him sitting and writing to her with that little pucker between his brows that meant he was concentrating.

But he was not well. She gave a little sigh at the thought. He would never take care of himself, for all that he was getting on in years. However cold the weather, he would never wear an overcoat—although, when she came to think of it, it might be because he did not possess one. A race-course can be bitterly cold place in early spring and if Uncle Patrick had caught a bad chill, it meant that he would be depressed and morose for perhaps a week.

If only she were there to look after him. She gave a little sigh of exasperation and thought how helpless she was to do anything for him. Then she remembered that he was in need of money. There at least she could help him, provided she received her salary—though how much it was to be and when she was to be paid it she had not the slightest idea.

What was meant by the Diplomatic Bag? Vaguely she seemed to have heard that the Embassies of different countries were immune from censorship and other local laws and restrictions. She worried over it for a moment and then shrugged her shoulders. She could find out. She wondered whom she would ask and then remembered that the Ambassador's private secretary was a rather nice-looking girl who came in daily. She would ask her.

Quickly, because she was impatient and felt there was so much to do, Sheena jumped out of bed; and as she did so, an envelope fluttered from the bed-clothes on to the floor. It was the other letter which Jeanne had brought her and which, in the emotion for reading Uncle Patrick's letter, she had entirely forgotten.

She looked at it curiously as she picked it up. Her name and address were typed, so it gave her no clue to who might be the sender, and it bore a French stamp. Indifferently Sheena slit open the envelope with her finger and then drew out a small piece of thin paper on which were typed a very few words:

At the first opportunity go to the bookshop in the Rue St. François off the Rue de Rivoli. Take your passport with you and ask for a parcel. Speak of this to no-one.

She read the message through once and then again. What did it mean? she wondered. What extraordinary instructions and what could be in the parcel? She was expecting nothing; and why should she speak of it to no-one? It all seemed so extraordinary.

It must be something to do with Uncle Patrick, she thought at last. Perhaps he had found a Diplomatic Bag of his own and was sending her something which could not come in the normal way through the post. Whatever

48

it was, she had the chance to collect it this afternoon. She had already planned to walk down the *Rue de Rivoli* and look in all the glittering jewellery shops that she had noticed when she passed that way with the children in a taxi. A parcel! Now what could Uncle Patrick be sending her?

And then she thought not of the second letter but of what Patrick O'Donovan himself had written to her. If only he wasn't so far away, she thought, she could telephone him and find out how he was. But what was the point of wishing? He was in London and she was in Paris, and Continental telephone calls were far beyond the reach of her purse.

She woke the children, dressed them and they all had breakfast in the Nursery. Afterwards they did a few easy lessons together, and punctually on the stroke of eleven o'clock Jeanne came into the room.

"Madame wishes to speak to you," she said. "I told her it was your day off, but she would like to have a word with you before you leave the house."

"But, of course," Sheena said. "Shall I go to her now?"

"Yes, she has been called," Jeanne said, "and had her breakfast. But I shouldn't annoy her. She is never at her best first thing in the morning."

She spoke with the familiarity of an old servant who considers she has a right to criticise. Sheena made no comment but went down one flight of stairs and along the passage to where Madame Pelayo's suite was arranged at the back of the house, overlooking the peace and quiet of the big garden. She knocked at the door and heard an answer: "Come in!"

Sheena had never been in Madame Pelayo's bedroom before. For a moment she could only stare in astonishment and admiration. The huge bed, of carved silver in the semblance of a sea-shell, was raised on a platform at the far end of the room. Behind it, draped from a corolla of flying cupids, hung great clouds of apple pink chiffon caught at the side of the bed with huge bows of silver ribbon.

Pink taffeta of the softness of a moss-rose curtained the windows, and the carpet was also pink—a deeper shade—which covered the whole floor and seemed a fitting background to the exquisite furniture of inlaid Spanish walnut. There were great bowls of flowers, the same as Madame Pelayo surrounded herself with in her living-rooms, and there was an exotic fragrance of expensive perfume which seemed to pervade everything.

Madame Pelayo was sitting up in bed, her dark hair framed with lace pillows, and on the bedspread, of pink satin edged with white mink, were spread the morning's papers and a great pile of invitations and letters.

As Sheena entered, Madame Pelayo put down the letter she was reading and drew from her eyes the horn-rimmed spectacles which she was forced to wear when she was reading. She was very vain about her spectacles and would never wear them in public. Without them, and with her hair loose on her shoulders, the Ambassadress looked little more than a girl. But her voice as she spoke to Sheena was sharp and authoritative.

"Good morning, Mrs. Lawson. I wanted to speak to you."

"Good morning, *Madame*."

Sheena advanced until she stood at the side of Madame Pelayo's bed. There was a chair near, but the Ambassadress did not ask her to sit down.

"I understand, Mrs. Lawson," she said, "that you went driving with my brother yesterday."

"Yes, *Madame*. He said he had promised the children to take them out in his new car. We went to the *Bois*."

"I was told that you were out for nearly two hours."

"It must have been about that, *Madame*."

"Now listen, Mrs. Lawson! This is not to occur again. My brother is a very impulsive, over-generous young man. He is fond of the children and even fonder of giving pleasure to people like yourself who perhaps have not the chance of many treats or amusements in their lives. Though such sentiments do him credit, they are not to be encouraged. Do I make myself clear?"

There was something in Madame Pelayo's tone and in the look in her eyes which made Sheena flush angrily.

"I did not seek such an invitation or such entertainment," she said quietly. "And I did not think it was part

50

of my duty to refuse to allow the children to go with their uncle."

"Mrs. Lawson! You are a married woman and as such should be capable not only of taking care of yourself but of managing a situation such as this. I think I am making myself quite clear. My brother's impulses—and they will doubtless occur again—are not to be encouraged. Need I say any more?"

"No, *Madame*. I understand."

"I may as well say now, and quite frankly," the Ambassadress went on, "that I was disappointed when I saw you. I had made it very clear that I wanted a much older governess for the children; someone who would prove in no way likely to be distracted by—how shall I put it?—the temptations of Paris. You not only look young, but you appear to be very inexperienced."

Sheena felt her pride rise. If Madame Pelayo meant to be insulting she was certainly succeeding!

"Looks can be deceptive, *Madame*," Sheena said quietly. "You will not have to complain again."

She turned as if to go and Madame Pelayo looked at her in sudden surprise as if she had not expected her to answer back.

At that moment the door opened and the Ambassador came in. He was at least thirty years older than his wife. A short, not particularly attractive man, it was, as Sheena had already discovered, impossible not to realise that he had an exceptionally intelligent mind and strong personality.

"Good morning, Yvonne!" he said to his wife. "I slipped away from a Committee Meeting because I felt certain you would be awake by now. Good morning, Mrs. Lawson!"

"Good morning, Your Excellency!" Sheena answered. And then, as she would have slipped from the room, the Ambassador put up his hand as if to stop her.

"One moment, Mrs. Lawson, before you go," he said. And turning to his wife he continued: "Listen, Yvonne! I have an idea. I was thinking last night that we see far too little of the children. Don't you think, now they are older and Mrs. Lawson is, I am sure, improving both their manners and their behaviour, that when we are alone here, just *en famille,* they might come down to

51

luncheon? When there are guests, of course, it is a different matter. But Lucien and Henri are both, I believe, devoted to my little ones, and they, even as we are, would be delighted for this opportunity of having more of their company. What do you think, my dear?"

"Just as you like, Carlos," Madame Pelayo said, with a little gesture of indifference. "We are not often alone and, of course, when there is company the children must stay in the Nursery."

"Then it is settled," the Ambassador said. "In future you bring them down to luncheon, Mrs. Lawson."

"But not today," Madame Pelayo said. "It is Mrs. Lawson's day off."

"Then tomorrow," the Ambassador conceded. "We shall look forward to see you, Mrs. Lawson."

"Thank you, Your Excellency!"

Sheena went from the room and shut the door behind her. Only when she was outside did she realise that she was trembling—not with fear, but with anger. How dared anyone speak to her as Madame Pelayo had done? Inferring that she was encouraging the young *Vicomte*. And yet she asked herself honestly, had she not been glad to go for that drive? To listen to him, even while she protested at what he said? To feel the strange excitement at the compliments he paid her and the admiration in his eyes?

Oh dear, how difficult it was! But in future she would be very firm. She would refuse to listen to him; she would refuse the invitations he would offer her and the children. She must be firm. She must behave as was expected of her.

"Young and inexperienced." She thought of the Ambassadress's words and shivered because they were so accurate and so true. If the people here knew that she was only twenty and had had nothing to do with young children until this moment . . .

As if to escape from her own thoughts she ran downstairs to the small room behind the library, where she knew the Ambassador's private secretary worked. She was typing as Sheena entered, her fingers flying over the keys, and only when she came to the end of the line did she pause and look up with a smile.

"Good morning, Mrs. Lawson!"

"Good morning, *Mademoiselle*. I want your help."

"But, of course, what can I do for you?"

"I wanted to ask you about my salary."

"Strangely enough I was going to speak to you about that this morning," a deep voice said behind Sheena.

She started and turned round. Colonel Mansfield was standing in the doorway which led to another room.

"I'm feeling very remiss, Mrs. Lawson," he went on, as Sheena appeared to have nothing to say. "Will you come into my office a moment and we will try and get things straightened out."

For some reason that she could not explain even to herself, Sheena wanted to refuse. But there was nothing she could say that would not sound either rude or ridiculous; and besides, the Ambassador's secretary seemed to think the conversation had nothing further to do with her and was already rattling away on the keys of her typewriter again.

Feeling rather like a small boy entering the headmaster's study, Sheena followed Colonel Mansfield into a room she had never seen before. It was austere and almost bare in contrast to the ornate luxury of the rest of the Embassy. The walls were panelled and there were one or two very beautiful and obviously valuable pictures. A big desk stood in the centre of the room and seemed to focus the beholder's attention upon it. There was only one comfortable arm-chair by the fire-place. The rest, like the one Colonel Mansfield pointed to on the opposite side of his desk, were stiff and upright.

"Won't you sit down, Mrs. Lawson?" he asked.

Sheena obeyed him.

"I must apologise," he said, "for not speaking to you before about your salary. I made a mental note when you arrived to suggest that we should pay you weekly even though the terms of your employment entail a month's notice on either side. I thought perhaps you might be glad of the money on a weekly basis and at any rate not find yourself short of cash as you were in a strange country. Unfortunately the whole thing slipped my memory. Will you forgive me?"

He smiled as he spoke and Sheena, suddenly at her ease, smiled back.

"Yes, of course."

"It was only this morning that I heard that this was your day-out," Lucien Mansfield went on. "And even then, when I should have come to find you, I became involved with several telephone calls which kept me at my desk. And now, if you will forgive me, we will get down to business. I suggest that as you have been here already over a week, I give you two weeks' wages right away. Is that agreeable to you?"

"Thank you," Sheena said.

Colonel Mansfield opened a desk and drew out a wad of notes. He counted off a number of them and laid them in front of Sheena.

"There are fourteen thousand francs," he said. "And I am afraid I must ask you for a formal receipt."

"Fourteen thousand francs!" Sheena said in astonishment.

"Yes! Seven thousand a week—that was the agreement, you remember."

"Yes . . . yes, of course," Sheena said.

"It sounds much more in francs," Colonel Mansfield smiled. "It is only a little over seven pounds a week, you must remember."

"Yes! I . . . had forgotten," Sheena answered.

She had never expected so much, and now, with a sudden thought of what this would mean to Uncle Patrick, she said impulsively:

"Please, can I send some of it back to England? In . . . in the Diplomatic Bag, if it can't go through the post."

"What do you know about the Diplomatic Bag?" Lucien Mansfield smiled. And then he said: "But if you want to bank it, I can think of a much better way than that. I will just instruct the Embassy in London to pay so much money into the bank each week."

"No, but I don't want to bank it," Sheena said. "I want to give it to someone . . . a . . . a relation of mine."

Even as she spoke she realised she had made a mistake. She had already told Lucien Mansfield that she had no relations. And then, floundering a little because lies came so hard to her tongue that had always told the truth, she added:

"Well . . . it's not . . . exactly a relation of mine but
54

. . . of my husband. He is . . . not well and is in need of money. I thought . . . if I could send him some . . ."

"But, of course," Lucien Mansfield said. "It is your money and you must do as you think best with it. Could you tell me who it is for and how much you want to send? And the Embassy in London will do all that is necessary."

"Could they just leave it there in an envelope for . . . for this person, who will call?" Sheena asked.

"I expect so. But isn't it rather a laborious way of doing things? They will send it to him direct at whatever address he lives."

"No! I think it would be best if he could call," Sheena persisted.

Why? Oh why? she asked herself despairingly, did Uncle Patrick always make things difficult? She knew by the look on Colonel Mansfield's face that he thought it extraordinary. There was nothing she could do or say.

"And the gentleman's name?" Lucien Mansfield enquired.

"Mr. John Lawson."

"It is your husband's brother?" he asked.

"No, no! Only a distant cousin."

"And how much do you want to send him?"

"All of it," Sheena said eagerly. And then, seeing Colonel Mansfield's look of astonishment and realising suddenly that she had only a few odd francs left in her purse, changed her mind. "Perhaps I had better keep one thousand francs, but please send the rest."

"Are you quite sure you are wise?" Colonel Mansfield asked. "You will find a lot of things in Paris which you will want to buy for yourself."

"Oh no! That's quite all right," Sheena answered. "I don't want to buy anything. I have got everything I need."

"Indeed! Then you are very different from most women when they find themselves in Paris for the first time."

She thought that his eyes rested for a moment on her plain white blouse and badly fitting shoulders of her tweed coat, and quite suddenly she felt she hated him not only because he frightened her, but because he also made her feel so gauche and inexperienced.

"It is my money," she said angrily. "And I know exactly what I want to do with it."

He raised his eyebrows as if her outburst surprised him, and then he said quietly:

"But, of course! As you say, it is your money—even though the amount of it is much more than you expected!" He waited a moment and as she did not reply he added: "Didn't you read the letter I sent you setting out the terms of your engagement and the salary that the Ambassador was prepared to pay?"

This was another trap, Sheena thought wildly, and she must be careful lest she fall into it.

"I am often very forgetful of such things," she replied, rising to her feet.

She did not look at him as she spoke and yet she was uncomfortably aware that his eyes were on her face. Holding the thousand-franc note in her hand, she moved towards the door. Although he did not appear in any way to hurry, he was there before her.

"I hope you enjoy your first day of freedom," he said. "Take care of yourself, and don't get lost."

He was smiling, but she did not smile in return.

"I hope I am too sensible for that," she answered.

She did not look back as she hurried up the stairs, although she had the uneasy feeling that he was still watching her. In her own bedroom she thrust the thousand-franc note into her handbag, pulled on her hat and coat and then, on an impulse, entered the Nursery.

Jeanne had just finished dressing the children preparatory to taking them out for a walk.

"I have changed my mind," Sheena told her. "Would you be kind enough to say that I will be out for luncheon today?"

"Yes, of course," Jeanne replied. "And if you are eating alone, there is no need to be extravagant. You will find lots of small cafés where you can get a good meal and a bottle of wine for three hundred francs."

"I shan't be extravagant," Sheena promised.

She wasn't going to explain to Jeanne that she didn't intend to have any luncheon at all. She had eaten a good breakfast and it wouldn't hurt her to wait until suppertime. Her interview with Colonel Mansfield had made her feel that she wanted to be free of the Embassy. She began to feel that all this intrigue was suffocating her. It was so difficult not to say the wrong thing, not to become involved in her own lies—or rather those of Uncle Patrick.

As she went out into the sunshine she felt a sudden sense of escape, which in itself was exhilarating as the air which seemed to carry with it the fragrance of mimosa. The sunshine was in her eyes as she walked along the quiet street until she came to the hustle and bustle of the *Place de la Concorde*. The fountains were iridescent with tiny rainbows playing among the marble figures; and then, hardly realising where she was going, Sheena had crossed the *Tuileries* Gardens and was standing on the banks of the Seine.

It was as lovely as Henri de Cormeille had described it to her, and yet they had never reached it yesterday because she had insisted, when they left the *Bois*, that they should go straight home.

Now the river did not seem grey but blue, reflecting the sky above it. The ripples of the passing barges were silver and the reflections of the houses and buildings opposite shimmered and broke and reconstructed themselves again on the moving water.

How long she leaned over the parapet—watching and looking and feeling as if she herself became part of the scene—Sheena did not know. It was only after a little time that she realised she was singing a song beneath her breath. It was an Irish song and yet somehow it seemed to be perfectly attuned with the Seine and the loveliness of its surroundings.

After a long time she started to walk and found herself staring at the great grey wonder that is *Notre-Dame*. And after that there were bridges and houses and churches, whose spires pointed up towards the sky, and strange little bookshops against the parapet of the river itself, and old gentlemen who sat fishing for hours on end with apparently never a bite.

Never, Sheena thought, had she known anything more exciting or more thrilling than Paris in the spring— this wonderful, fascinating, entrancing city that she had discovered for the first time.

It must have been early in the afternoon before she realised that she had no idea where she was and that she had not yet even looked in one shop window. Slowly she retraced her steps, following the river back the way she had come. Her progress was slow indeed—there was so much to see, so much to watch. Once or twice she had an impulse to go and sit outside a little café and order perhaps a *brioche* or a cup of coffee. And then a sense of shyness prevented her. She would be alone and the people she could see sitting on the pavements were usually a man and a woman together or else it was only a man who sat by himself.

And so she walked on, stopping here and there, watching this and that, even sitting for a while on a bench which overlooked the water and feeling herself almost hypnotised by the colour and movement of it. At last determinedly she set off to find the *Rue St. François*. She must find out what this parcel was that Uncle Patrick had sent her.

After being obliged to ask the way of a policeman she at length found the *Rue St. François*—a narrow street with tall houses and a few unimportant shops.

The bookshop was tucked away between two houses which had their shutters closed and an air of emptiness about them. The shop itself was small and there was only one customer when Sheena entered, but she had to wait until he left before she could reach the counter, behind which an elderly man with grey hair and pince-nez managed to shuffle to and fro.

Sheena still had to wait while he put the money he had received from the last customer away in a drawer, and then he glanced up and peered at her near-sightedly.

"Oui, Mademoiselle?"

"There is a parcel for me to collect from here," Sheena said. "I am Mrs. Lawson and I was told to show you my passport."

She brought it from her bag as she spoke and handed it to the elderly man. He took it into his hands, opened it slowly, reading first the name and then turning it round so that he could inspect her photograph. He looked at it for several seconds, then looked at Sheena and back again at the photograph. Without a word he handed the passport back to her and went from the shop into what was obviously a room at the back. He shut the door behind him and Sheena waited.

It seemed to her that he was taking a long time to find the parcel, and after a moment she leisurely turned over some of the magazines which lay on the counter. They were crudely illustrated and after reading the caption to one drawing Sheena felt herself blush and closed the magazine quickly.

Still the man did not return and she began to wonder if he had forgotten her very existence. Another customer came into the shop—a woman with a shawl over her head and a string bag filled with shopping. She also had a yard-long loaf of French bread under her arm, besides several other packages, and after a moment she sighed and sat down on her bundles.

Sheena began to wonder if she should go and knock on the door through which the elderly man had disappeared; but even as she hesitated, the door opened and he came out. He carried nothing in his hands and her first thought was that either he had mislaid the parcel or it had not arrived. Then he spoke to her.

"You're to speak on the telephone."

Sheena stared at him, thinking she could not have heard aright or had misunderstood what he said, but impatiently he pointed to the room from which he had come.

"In there, in there," he said. "Hurry!"

Too surprised to argue, Sheena moved behind the counter and through the door which led into an inner room. It was small, rather dark and was piled with books and packing cases, torn paper and parcels that were partially unpacked. In one corner, attached to the wall, was one of the old-fashioned telephones, and Sheena saw that the receiver was lying on a small, rather dirty table beneath it. She went towards it and as she did so the door was shut behind her. She picked up the receiver.

"Hello!"

"Is that Sheena O'Donovan?"

It was a deep man's voice that asked the question in English although she thought he had a slight foreign accent.

"Yes. Who are you?"

59

"Never mind. You got the letter which was sent to you this morning? It had not been opened before you received it?"

"Opened! Why should it have been?"

"That is not what I asked you. Had it been opened?"

"No, of course not. . . . I don't think so. Who are you and who am I speaking to?"

"Listen, Sheena! There is no time for questions to which you will get no answers, and no need to trouble your head about anything but what is of importance."

"Surely I can ask you who I am speaking to—and how do you know my name?"

"Shall I explain that I am a friend of your uncle's?"

"A friend of Uncle Patrick! Oh, have you news of him? I had a letter this morning to say that he was not well. Have you seen him recently?"

"Questions! Questions! Instead of talking, Sheena, listen. I am a friend of your uncle's who got you your present post and arranged for you to be sent to Paris. Now do you understand?"

"Yes . . . yes, I suppose I understand."

"Then tell me, how are you getting on at the Embassy?"

"All right, I think."

"Do they trust you?"

"I suppose so."

"They are not suspicious in any way?"

"Suspicious of what?" Sheena asked.

"Come, come," said the voice. "You are not so stupid as that. Suspicious of who you are and why you are there."

"I wish I knew that myself," Sheena said. "If you are responsible for sending me to Paris, perhaps you will tell me why . . ."

"I have told you, I am not prepared to answer questions," came the interruption. "Now, attend to me carefully. There may be talk amongst the people at the Embassy of contracts. A contract with regard to something which lies in Mariposa. You are to learn all you can of this—understand? Be careful how you ask questions, but make what enquiries are permissible, and when you have found out anything, however trivial, however unimportant it seems to you, come here and ask, as you have done today, for a parcel."

"What does all this mean?" Sheena asked. "What are you asking me to do?"

"I am asking you to do what you are told," was the reply.

"It is fantastic, ridiculous. How can I find out about a contract?"

"You must do your best. You are friendly with Colonel Mansfield. He could tell you if he wished to do so."

"I can't talk to him about things like that."

"I think you will find you can if you try."

"Why should I?" Sheena asked.

"I am prepared to answer that question. You are fond of your uncle?"

"But, of course!"

"If things should go wrong with him, you would be sorry?"

"Naturally I should be very upset," Sheena cried. "What are you inferring? What are you trying to say?"

"I am trying to tell you it is of vital importance to your uncle—to his health, his well-being, his finances —that you should do as you are told."

"But surely you will not expect . . ."

"I have given you your orders. That will be all."

"But listen . . . I must . . ."

There was a click at the end of the line. Whoever had been talking had replaced the receiver.

Sheena stood for a moment staring at the open mouth of the telephone, and then very slowly she sat down on a packing case. What did this strange conversation mean —not so much to her as to Uncle Patrick? Even as she asked this question of herself, she felt that she knew the answer, and in a terror such as she had never known before she heard her own voice whisper:

"No! No! No!"

Four

For a few moments Sheena sat with her hands to her face, distraught by her thoughts. And then, with an effort, she pulled herself together and got to her feet. She felt as though she would go mad if she stayed another second in the untidy, packet-strewn room, which smelt of dust and mice and the strange, pungent odour of newsprint.

Her feeling of despair gave way to one of anger and something that was almost akin to hatred as she walked through the shop with her head held high and without even a glance at the old man, peering at her short-sightedly through his pince-nez. She thought he mumbled something at her, but she did not wait to hear what it was.

The sunshine and fresh air gave her a sense of freedom as if she were escaping from something utterly horrible, and she almost ran down the street—wanting to get away not only from the bookshop but from her own thoughts. She turned left on leaving the shop and soon found herself in another and wider street, then turned again until she was hopelessly lost and, at the same time, almost oblivious of her surroundings.

She was seeing Uncle Patrick in her mind and hearing all the time in her ears that deep voice on the telephone which seemed, with every word it spoke, to exude poison.

It was some time before she realised how fast she was walking until, with what was a sense of surprise, she found she was very hot. Her breath, too, was coming very quickly and irregularly as if she had been running across country; and almost like waking from a dream, she wondered where she was.

There was a small café just ahead of her with half a dozen tables set out on the pavement, none of which was occupied. And because she felt her legs could carry her no further, Sheena walked to one of the empty tables and sat down. Almost instantly the elderly, rather dirty waiter appeared and asked her what she required. She ordered coffee and he brought it in a few moments.

It was not very good coffee, but it was hot and black and Sheena drank it as she might have done a glass of medicine, feeling that it would pull her together and perhaps enable her to think more clearly.

Who, she asked herself, over and over again, were these people with whom Uncle Patrick had got involved? What power had they, not only over him but over her? She thought of that high, ugly house in Fulham Road where they had stayed in England, and of the people who had come there.

Patrick O'Donovan had always made a mystery as to who were the owners. He had been lent accommodation in the basement and the ground floor by his friends, he told Sheena.

"They must be rich to own a house in London," she remarked before she had seen it. When they arrived, she had been sure that Uncle Patrick's friends were not so rich as they sounded. The house, damp and dirty, was in a lamentable state of repair. The furniture was only cheap, battered pieces which looked as if they had been picked up at odd times in bargain basements. But it was a roof over their heads and she knew only too well that neither she nor her uncle could afford to quarrel with any habitation that was offered them, however poor it might be.

What she had not understood were the people who came and went to and from the other parts of the house. There were two flats at the top, she learnt, although she never saw them. But they were occupied spasmodically by their owners or their tenants, both of whom were men.

On the first floor were sitting-rooms which were used continually by men who came late in the evening or else arrived at odd times with typewriters at which they worked feverishly for hours on end.

"Is it a club?" Sheena asked once.

"No, just a meeting place for various friends," Uncle Patrick answered.

"They don't sound very friendly," Sheena commented, and to her surprise he had turned quite angry.

"I have told you before that you are to stay downstairs and not listen to what goes on up above. For the love of God, must I be repeating it to you again? It is your own business I am asking you to mind, and surely that is not hard in return for a bed to sleep in and a fire to cook at?"

"Don't be angry with me, Uncle Patrick," Sheena pleaded—upset because she had not expected him to fly into a rage over such a small thing. And his anger had evaporated at the look of pleading on her face.

"Sure and I'm a crotchety old fool to be swearing at you," he apologised. "But ask me no questions, me darling girl, as I'm not able to answer them."

She had tried to obey him after that and to remain oblivious to the sound of feet tramping up the stairs. And she would efface herself quickly if she came out of her bedroom, which was on the ground floor, to see shabby, rather sinister-looking men letting themselves in at the front door or coming down the stairs with the collars of their overcoats turned up and hats pulled low over their eyes.

It was impossible not to wonder what was said and what was done upstairs. There was certainly no joviality about their parties, because, however many men there were up there, their voices were never raised and there was never so much as a hint of laughter.

Sheena supposed that she was not very curious by nature. After the first few days she ceased to wonder or even to think very much about the other occupants of the house unless she actually ran into one of them downstairs or in the dark, airless passage-way which was called the hall. There were occasionally women visitors, but they were few and far between. It seemed to Sheena that these were usually middle-aged or extremely unattractive, with their hair cropped close to their heads and as often as not wearing trousers.

They were strange friends for Uncle Patrick, who had always, in Ireland, liked people as gay and as inconsequential as himself and always swore that he loved pretty women as much as a well-bred horse.

Why, Sheena asked herself now, hadn't she taken the trouble to find out more? To discover the objectives and perhaps the danger of these people, and if possible to get Patrick O'Donovan out of their clutches. She did not ask herself how she could have done this, she only felt that it was what she should have done.

Uncle Patrick always talked of looking after her, but she had, in fact, looked after him—seen to his clothes, cooked his food, saved his money and even, once or twice in times of crisis, advised him so sensibly that he had taken her advice and thanked her for it.

Why, knowing how weak, how improvident he was, had she let those months in London drift by without making any effort to have a show-down? Was it, she asked herself now, because she had been afraid of what she might discover if she had been too inquisitive?

Now she did know—at least, had a very good idea of what was going on. What was she going to do? Should she go back to London and face Uncle Patrick with the truth? Or might any unexpected or unwise action on her part do him real harm?

With a little constriction in her heart she remembered the ominous threat in the voice over the telephone. Could such things really be happening? she asked herself wildly. Had it been true or had she imagined the whole thing?

She pulled a piece of paper out of her pocket and stared at the typewritten message which had taken her to the bookshop in search of a non-existent parcel. The paper was cheap; the typewriting was undistinguished. There was no clue, nothing to tell her, or anyone else for that matter, anything about the sender.

If she went to the Police with such a story, who would believe her? And if she went to the Ambassador, what would happen then? She knew, even as she asked herself the question, that was the one thing she dared not do—not without knowing how deeply involved her uncle was in this or what lay behind it all.

"I must try and see him," she thought. "I must write to him and suggest that either I go to England to him or he comes here to me." She could save enough money for either contingency, she thought, in two or three weeks. But what might happen in that time? What might be required of her? There was always that to be considered.

Her coffee was finished and Sheena pushed the cup to one side and then put her arms on the little round table and looked almost despairingly out into the sunshine and at the traffic passing up and down in front of her. One part of her brain was still busy with her own problems, the other part was watching the people moving past, the cars, the 'buses and the cyclists—as if they were a film unrolled before her eyes, something with which she had no personal contact.

In the same detached manner she noticed a big, grey car with its chromium plating shining in the sunshine, waiting a little way down the street outside a flower shop. The chauffeur was dressed in grey, too; his livery ornamented with what appeared to be a profusion of silver buttons. There was a small, white poodle in the car, jumping about, its nose first pressed to this window and then to another. Its funny, perky little face made Sheena smile in spite of her troubles.

It was as she was watching the dog that she saw its owner come from the flower shop carrying a huge bunch of Parma violets in her hand. Almost in spite of herself Sheena found herself watching the girl—for she appeared little more—with interest. She was beautifully dressed in a pearl-grey dress which seemed to match the car, and had a wrap of platina mink draped over her shoulders. She wore a little hat of red feathers and her bag and shoes were the same colour.

Sheena could only see her profile, but she had a quick glimpse of a sudden flashing smile as she spoke to the chauffeur seated at the wheel of the car. He turned to get out, but something she said stopped him and he slammed his own door shut just as she opened

66

the back door of the car for herself and climbed in beside the excited poodle.

As she did so, Sheena saw something fall unnoticed into the gutter. She got to her feet, but the car had already begun to move. She ran forward. The flower shop was only two doors away from the café, but already the car was edging into the flow of traffic. Sheena waved to the girl sitting in the back, feeling that she must attract her attention. To her surprise she received a smile and a wave of a grey-gloved hand before, gathering speed, the car had carried its occupant down the street and out of sight.

Reaching the edge of the pavement Sheena bent forward. Now she could see what had been dropped—a notecase of pale blue leather stamped with a gold monogram. She picked it up. It was quite bulky and must have fallen, Sheena thought, from the girl's open bag. She brushed some dust from it, opened it and saw that inside it was packed with notes. She was staring at them when a voice beside her said in French:

"*Mam'selle* has found something?"

Sheena started, then realised it was the waiter who stood there.

"Yes," she answered. "The lady who got into that car dropped this."

"If *Mam'selle* will give it to me, I will return it to her."

"You know who she is?" Sheena asked.

The waiter's eyes flickered before he answered, and she knew that he was lying.

"*Mais oui!* An old and valued patron."

Sheena looked at the small, rather squalid little café, at the waiter's dirty apron and badly shaved chin, and then remembered the opulence of the grey car and its grey-liveried chauffeur.

"I will return it myself," she said firmly. "The people in the shop will know her name."

The waiter started to expostulate, but Sheena said sharply:

"If not, of course, the notecase must be taken to the Police."

"The Police are not always trustworthy, *Mam'selle*."

There was something insidious in the quiet, almost

whispered reply, and Sheena, hating the greed in his eyes and the sudden craftiness about his mouth, replied:

"How much do I owe you for the coffee?"

He asked double what she felt he would have asked her had she not held what appeared to him a small fortune in her hand. She paid without argument, giving him a small tip and turning resolutely towards the flower shop. As she went, she heard his voice saying:

"Bon chance, Mam'selle!"

She knew he was suspecting her of keeping the money for herself. Because his suspicions made her also suspicious of other people, she slipped the notecase into the pocket of her coat before she went into the shop.

"Would you mind telling me the name of the lady with the red hat who has just bought a bunch of violets from you?" she asked a woman behind the counter.

"I am afraid I don't know, *Madame,*" was the reply.

"Hasn't she been here before?" Sheena enquired.

"I don't know," the woman answered. She was middle-aged with a pale face and looked ill. "I don't often help in the shop," she explained. "But this afternoon my husband had to go to the dentist and so I told him I would look after the place while he was gone."

"How long will he be?" Sheena asked, thinking that perhaps she could wait and describe the customer when the proprietor appeared.

"I don't know," the woman said vaguely. "About another hour or so I should think."

Sheena felt that she could not bear to wait that long.

"Thank you very much," she said. "I may come back later." And she went from the shop without saying any more.

The waiter was watching for her, but resolutely she turned the other way, walking up the street. There were so many people about that she did not like to stop and examine the notecase until she was able to turn down a less frequented road. Here she examined what she had found without the fear of being overlooked.

There was a great wad of notes, as she had seen on first sight, and Sheena did not even bother to pull them out but searched the other pockets hoping for a visiting card. What she found instead was a letter folded small

68

and tucked down into the silk lining. She pulled it out and saw it was an envelope of very thin, grey paper. The postmark was an old one, but the letter was addressed to:

Mlle. Fifi Fontés,
192, Avenue Marcel,
Paris.

That must be the address of the owner, Sheena thought; and now, for the moment at any rate, her troubles were over.

She did not know why, but she instinctively shrank from having to take the notecase to a Police Station; and to have to explain how she had found it and what she had been doing when she had seen it fall into the gutter. She did not want to explain her movements during the afternoon. Naturally it was absurd, but at the moment the thought of any enquiries that might become personal frightened her.

She put the notecase into her pocket and went back to the busy street. It took her some minutes to find a policeman and, when she had found him, to ask the way to the *Avenue Marcel.* He told her, with a wealth of detail and gesticulation, while the traffic that he was supposed to be directing appeared to be tying itself into knots. And finally, after thanking him, Sheena set off in the right direction, although whether she was likely to be able to follow the rest of his instruction remained to be seen.

She had gathered from his directions that the *Avenue Marcel* was some distance away, and although he had advised her to take an autobus she decided to walk. Her first objective was the *Champs Elysées,* and after walking for perhaps ten minutes she found herself in the *Rue de la Paix* and remembered it from that moment when Colonel Mansfield had pointed it out to her on the way from the station.

Looking in the shops as she went, Sheena walked on until she came into the beautiful, symmetrical square of the *Place Vendôme.* It was then that she suddenly recognised a big car drawing up outside a hotel, and a moment later saw the *Vicomte* as he stepped out beside a beautiful woman dressed in the very latest fashion. She said something to him and as he turned to make a laughing reply, his eyes fell on Sheena as she came slowly along the pavement. It seemed to her there was only a momentary hesitation on his part, then he turned to his companion and said:

"Will you excuse me for a moment?"

He walked towards Sheena, lifting his hat as he held out his hand in greeting.

"Good afternoon, Mrs. Lawson! Have you lost Madi and Pedro or are they just hiding round the corner?"

"Good afternoon, *Monsieur!* It is my day off, as it happens."

"I wish I had known."

There was no mistaking the implication in his words, and slowly, with a sense of guilt, Sheena remembered what Madame Pelayo had said to her that very morning.

"I must not keep you, *Monsieur*," she said quickly.

But the *Vicomte,* despite the fact that his elegantly dressed lady friend was waiting for him, appeared to be in no hurry.

"Will you have tea with me in an hour's time?" he asked. "I will meet you at Rumpelmayer."

"No, thank you, *Monsieur*," Sheena said.

"Why not? You don't have to be home until late. Miss Robinson often dined out."

It was not very difficult for Sheena to guess who had given Miss Robinson dinner, and with a severity which was quite unlike her usual manner she said:

"Thank you for the invitation, *Monsieur,* but I cannot accept it."

"Why not?" he asked. "Let us have tea together— just you and I. I have got a lot to say to you."

"It is quite impossible," Sheena replied. "Surely you realise that?"

He looked at her for a moment and then he smiled understandingly.

"My sister has been talking to you," he said. "I suspected that she would. Now listen! Pay no attention. I will explain everything to you when we meet. Come to Rumpelmayer at five o'clock. No-one will know."

"No, *Monsieur*. I cannot do that."

"Please! Do not be silly. It is quite all right; I promise you."

Sheena shook her head.

"No, *Monsieur!* Your friend is waiting."

Henri de Cormeille glanced impatiently over his shoulder. There was no doubt that his companion was looking restive and tapping her foot in a suggestive manner.

"I shall go to Rumpelmayer at five o'clock," he said hastily. "Don't let me down."

He was gone before Sheena could say any more— hurrying back to the woman who had been with him in the car and slipping his arm in hers as in a low voice he obviously began to apologise. Sheena moved on quickly. She could not hear what the *Vicomte* said, but the woman's words, spoken in French in a voice high and annoyed, came to her ears quite clearly.

"*Tiens,* Henri, who is your so smart little friend?"

There was no doubting the sarcasm in the words and Sheena felt her cheeks burn as she hurried on, forcing herself not to look back. She was well aware now, after only such a short time in Paris, how she appeared in contrast to Madame Pelayo and the beautifully dressed women who came to the Embassy.

Over and over again she had thought it fortunate that she did not come much in contact with them. Now, with a sudden sinking of her heart, she remembered that she was to appear at luncheon day after day. There would often be three men there to see the contrast between her and the elegant, exquisitely dressed Ambassadress.

She knew that the Ambassador would look on her kindly, and she did not like to think what expression she would see in Henri de Cormeille's eyes. And what would Colonel Mansfield think? she wondered. Was she beneath his contempt or would he understand how ignorant she was about clothes—as about so many other things?

Then she remembered his questions and the shrewd, penetrating look in his eyes, and she felt herself shiver as if it were difficult to hide any secret from him. Somehow, the gold seemed to have gone from the sunshine as she walked on, finding her way into the *Champs-*

Elysées and moving on towards the *Arc de Triomphe*.

Finally she arrived at the *Avenue Marcel* and discovered that No. 192 contained four apartments. Mademoiselle Fontés was on the first floor, she noted, and the *concierge* directed her up a beautifully ornate staircase to where she found another door and beside it a bell. She rang, and after a few moments a maid appeared, elegantly dressed in the same shade of pale grey that the chauffeur had worn, but with a cap and apron of frilled organza.

"Is Mademoiselle Fontés at home?" Sheena asked.

"What name shall I say?" the maid enquired with a supercilious glance at Sheena, so that once again she was uncomfortably conscious of her own shabby appearance.

"Will you tell Mademoiselle Fontés that I have brought back something she has lost?"

The maid seemed surprised, hesitated and then finally asked Sheena into the apartment. She closed the door and left her in the hall while she disappeared, apparently in search of her mistress. Sheena had, however, hardly time to glance round before a door was flung open and a young woman wearing a little red hat, which she recognised, came hurrying impetuously towards her.

"You have found my notecase?" a voice asked excitedly in French.

There was no doubting that the face beneath the red hat was as pretty as Sheena had expected it to be. Fair hair was a frame for long, dark, curling eyelashes, big liquid eyes, and a very red mouth.

In answer Sheena drew the notecase from her pocket.

"Oh, how wonderful! I had only this minute discovered it was not in my bag. I have just telephoned for the car to come back so that I could go and look for it, I thought I must have dropped it in the flower shop."

"No, in the gutter outside," Sheena explained. "I waved to you, but you did not stop."

"You waved to me . . . of course!" Mademoiselle Fontés exclaimed. "And I waved back. But I did not understand that you wished me to stop."

"But didn't you think it rather strange that I should be waving?" Sheena enquired.

"No, of course not!" Mademoiselle Fontés replied. "People often wave to me."

There was no mistaking the surprise on Sheena's face, and after a moment the French girl said:

"Perhaps you don't realise who I am."

"I am afraid I don't," Sheena answered. "I am English and I have only just come to Paris."

"English!" the French girl cried. "I thought you couldn't be French. I was wondering what you could be. You speak so fluently and most English people are . . . well, so tongue-tied."

Sheena smiled.

"I had a French nurse."

"And that explains why you speak so beautifully," Mademoiselle Fontés said. "But now I must introduce myself. I am Fifi Fontés of the *Casino de Paris.*"

For a moment this did not convey any more to Sheena than she knew before. Then vaguely she remembered that the Ambassadress had said one night that they were off to the *Casino de Paris.*

"You are an actress?" she asked.

"Mais oui," Mademoiselle Fontés smiled. "The star of the *Casino de Paris.* Now you understand why, when you waved, I thought you were someone who had seen me act and perhaps had been kind enough to admire me." Her eyes twinkled and she added:

"I am a great success!"

"I'm sure you are," Sheena replied. "I was watching you because I thought how lovely you looked, and then I saw your notecase fall just as you shut the car door."

"I was in a hurry, so I told Pierre not to get out and to drive as quickly as he could to my next appointment," Mademoiselle Fontés said. "It is my worst sin—I am always late and so I am always in a rush. It is a bad fault. One day, perhaps, I shall cure it." She gave a little mock sigh which said more surely than words that she would not make any great effort to alter herself. And then she added: "But I must not talk about myself. We must talk about you—and thank you so very much for your kindness in returning what I had lost. There was a lot of money in my case, but that wasn't in the least important. What mattered was that it contained my most precious possession and all my luck."

"Your luck?" Sheena asked.

"Yes, my luck," Mademoiselle Fontés repeated. She held the notecase for a moment against her breast and then she said, looking down at it: "What can I give you to show how grateful I am?"

"Nothing! Nothing, of course!" Sheena said quickly. "I am only glad I was able to bring it back. And now I can go."

She knew that the French girl had thought of rewarding her in money, and it was not only pride but a vast embarrassment which carried her quickly to the door. But even as she reached it Mademoiselle Fontés was there before her.

"No, no!" she said, putting her hand out to stop Sheena reaching the handle. "You must not go like that. I cannot let you! You have been so kind, so very kind. Please stay while I tell you how much this means to me." She hesitated a moment and added: "I know you would like a cup of tea. All English people drink tea at four o'clock, and it is later than that already."

"No, really," Sheena replied. "There is no need for you to bother about me. I am only so glad to have been of service."

"You are going to have a cup of tea," Mademoiselle Fontés said firmly. "Why, you haven't even told me your name."

She took Sheena by the hand and drew her, half reluctantly, half curiously, into the sitting-room, calling out to the parlour-maid, over her shoulder, to bring tea and *pâtisseries* for them both.

The sitting-room was not very large, but furnished with gay, satin-covered chairs and big cushions of coral-coloured silk. The walls were grey and silver and the furniture, while nondescript, was in good taste. Seated in a basket by the electric fire was the white poodle, who jumped up as Mademoiselle Fontés entered and ran excitedly towards her, barking shrilly and dancing around her as if he thought she was ready to play some new game in which he must take part.

"I saw your dog in the car," Sheena said. "I thought he was so sweet."

"Bo-bo is the light of my life," Fifi laughed. "Although he is very noisy and often very naughty. Now

74

please sit down and make yourself comfortable while we wait for tea. Won't you tell me your name?"

"My name is Sheena Lawson," Sheena replied. "And I am governess to the children of Don Veremundo de Pelayo, the Ambassador of Mariposa."

"Now, where have I heard of him?" Mademoiselle Fontés asked. "I know—the Vicomte de Cormeille. His sister is married to the Ambassador."

"Yes, that is right."

"He is very naughty, that one," Mademoiselle Fontés said, looking at Sheena under her eyelashes. "Have you discovered that?"

For a moment Sheena hesitated and then, because she liked the little French actress, she said:

"Do tell me what you know about him. I have been in Paris such a very short time that I find it difficult to know what are my own impressions."

Mademoiselle Fontés gave a little chuckle.

"I think you have already found that Henri is a big flirt," she said. "Always, always he wants to flirt—first one and then another. He is gay and irresponsible—like a little boy. But even little boys can sometimes be tiresome—or dangerous to one's peace of mind."

"He is a great friend of yours?" Sheena asked.

Mademoiselle Fontés shook her head.

"No, no," she replied. "You need not be afraid of stealing him from me. When I first came to Paris, I met Henri and he made, how you say in English, 'a big pass' at me. But I was not interested in him and now we are very friendly. After my first nights he always comes round and brings me flowers, but usually he is looking for new faces. He likes very young and very inexperienced girls."

So that was Henri's secret, Sheena thought.

"And how do you like Paris, *Mademoiselle?*" the French girl went on.

Sheena drew in a little breath.

"I think I ought to explain that I am married and a widow."

"A widow! It is not possible," Mademoiselle Fontés cried. "You look so young. I cannot believe that you are more than nineteen or twenty."

"I am older than that," Sheena said. But somehow

she could not bring herself to lie any further. She liked this French girl so much that it was difficult to say as much as she had. And yet she dared not let the conversation continue under false pretences, seeing that Mademoiselle Fontés knew the *Vicomte*.

At that moment the parlour-maid came in with the tea on a tray. She set it down between their chairs, and Sheena saw, with amusement, that there was no milk provided with the tea, but only slices of lemon laid neatly on a small saucer. Fifi Fontés poured out.

"Do help yourself to a *pâtisserie*," she said. "I wish I had known you were coming and we could have had more delicious ones. When I am alone, I try to have nothing between luncheon and the very light meal I eat before a performance. I have to think of my figure, you see."

"But you are very thin," Sheena said.

"Not as thin as you," Fifi Fontés answered. "Perhaps I am taller—but no, it is because I am wearing much higher heels."

She stared at Sheena as she spoke and then said suddenly:

"Do you know, it is funny, but we are rather alike!"

"That is very flattering to me," Sheena answered. "I only wish it were true."

"But it is," Fifi Fontés insisted. "Will you stand up a moment? Come to the mirror."

Sheena did as she was asked, and then the French girl said:

"Do take off your hat."

Sheena pulled it off. Her hair had escaped a little from the tight pins in which she had arranged it and was curling round her face in little wispy curls. Her cheeks were still pink from the exercise and although her lashes were naturally dark they did not compare unfavourably with the heavily mascara-ed ones of the little actress.

"You see?" Fifi Fontés asked triumphantly. "We are alike. My hair isn't quite natural, like yours. It was fair when I was a child, but it began to get darker until I touched it up. And my eyes aren't as blue and, of course, you don't make up very much. But you do see what I mean?"

76

Sheena could see it although she felt to herself that the contrast was rather a harsh one where she was concerned. The pearls round the actress's throat, the diamonds flashing in her little ears, the beautiful lines of her grey dress enhanced the prettiness of her heart-shaped face.

"My complexion is better," Sheena thought. Her clear, pink and white skin was absolutely natural whereas in the actress's case it was easy to see the sallowness beneath the rouge and powder.

"I have an idea," Fifi Fontés said suddenly, "and, please, you must agree to it."

"Agree to what?" Sheena asked.

"That I should give you a dress as a present," was the answer.

"But I don't want a present . . ." Sheena began.

"You can't leave me under an obligation to you. It isn't fair. You can't begin to know what you have done for me. First of all let me explain. There was over a hundred thousand francs in my notecase. Do you know how much that is in English money?"

"A little over one hundred pounds," Sheena said.

"Exactly!" Fifi Fontés nodded. "I was going to pay for a fur I bought yesterday at a shop where I haven't got an account, and then I hadn't got time to go there because I was late—as usual. That was why, when I realised I had lost my notecase, I was so worried. I knew if anyone unscrupulous picked it up I should never see it again."

Sheena thought of the glint in the eyes of the waiter. If he had got it before her, there was no doubt that the notecase would never have been returned to its rightful owner.

"And now the second thing—and much the most important," Fifi Fontés went on. "That letter which you found, and which told you my name and address, is the one thing I value above everything else. You see, five years ago, when I first came to Paris, I loved somebody very much. I had only just gone on the stage—much against my parents' wishes. My real name is Marie Armand and my father is a notary who lives at Amiens. They are very quiet and very respectable people and

77

they didn't wish me to act but to stay at home and later to make the usual arranged marriage.

"But I came to Paris to go on the stage and I fell in love at the same time. He was a very wonderful person, but he was not at all the type of husband my father would have chosen for me. He had no money, no ambitions and the only thing he liked to do was to fly. He had a job with an aircraft factory. It was a dangerous job, but he loved it. We used to plan that in the future he would take something safer, but I think we both knew in our hearts that there was no future for him.

"This is the last letter he wrote me—before he was killed testing a plane, which just fell to bits in the sky. Nobody knows why or what went wrong, they only knew that there was nothing left of the aeroplane or of Antoine."

"I am sorry," Sheena said softly.

"At one time I couldn't talk about it," Fifi Fontés went on. "But now I realise it was the one beautiful, perfect thing in my life that can never be spoilt and never taken from me. And Antoine brought me luck in my job as well as giving me the greatest happiness I have ever known. It was through him that I got into the chorus at the *Casino de Paris*. It was because I was so happy and so keen to succeed, for his sake, that I danced and sang better than I have ever done in my life —before or since.

"I got my chance. The night that Antoine's letter came I went on to the stage with it lying between my breasts. I swore then that it would be my talisman all my life. I didn't realise it would be the last letter I would ever have from him or that two days later he would be killed."

"Oh, I am so glad I found it for you," Sheena cried.

"If I had lost it, I feel everything would have gone wrong with me ever afterwards," Fifi told her. "That sounds stupid I know, but I can't help being superstitious. If I go on to the stage to play a difficult part, I feel Antoine's letters against my skin and I know it will be all right—that somehow, somewhere, he is watching me, wanting me to succeed, wanting me to do well."

There was a sudden pause as Fifi Fontés took a little handkerchief from the belt of her dress and wiped her eyes.

"I don't often talk about him," she said. "There is nobody now in my life who knew him and so he just remains a secret hidden away in my heart, but somehow still a very big part of my life."

She smiled through her tears.

"And now do you understand what you have done for me?"

"I am so glad that I was able to do it."

"But you understand, too, that I have got to give you something? I wouldn't feel right if I took so much from you and didn't give anything back. Let me give you a dress—your first from Paris."

"Only if it is one for which you have no further use," Sheena said.

Fifi Fontés looked surprised.

"But I meant a new dress. One from Dior or Balmain."

"No, no! Of course I wouldn't take that," Sheena protested. "But you said yourself that we are about the same size. If you have an old dress—something you were going to throw away—then I would love to have it. I shall never have any money to buy one for myself."

Fifi Fontés suddenly clapped her hands together.

"Oh, but this is fun!" she said. "You don't know what fun this is going to be."

She jumped to her feet and ran to the door.

"Anastasia!" she called. "Quick, quick! Come here."

There was the sound of footsteps coming down the passage and then in the doorway appeared a black woman, smiling so that her teeth were very white against her dark skin.

"This is my maid, Anastasia," Fifi Fontés said to Sheena. "She was brought up in the Convent. She sews more beautifully than the angels themselves—isn't that true, Anastasia?"

"Oh, no, *Mademoiselle!* You are being kind. But I like to sew. I love pretty clothes and I like to see my lady looking prettier than anyone else."

"Now we have got to make someone look as pretty as me," Fifi told her.

She burst into a flow of French so quick, so spirited that Sheena had difficulty in following what she said. But somehow she got the drift of it and got to her feet.

"Only one dress. Just one!"

"I am taking charge of this," Fifi replied delightedly. "Come along into my bedroom. Quick, Anastasia; find all the things I told you about."

She took Sheena by the hand as she spoke and almost ran her across the room to where a door opened into her bedroom. It was a pretty room, but Sheena had no time to look at the decorations. Cupboards were opened and Fifi began to pull out dresses, suits, evening gowns, blouses and hats.

"I have been wondering for months what to do with these things," she said. "I couldn't bring myself to throw them away and there was no-one to whom I could give them. Most people are much too fat to get into my things."

"Please, only one dress . . ." Sheena tried to repeat, only to have her words swept on one side.

"I want you to try on this and this," Fifi Fontés cried, holding out one lovely gown after another.

Swept along irresistibly by a tide which seemed to overpower her, Sheena did as she was told. First of all both Fifi and Anastasia uttered cries of dismay and horror at the shapelessness of her underclothes. She found herself being hustled into elegant little bits of chiffon; into nylons—which were so fine that she was half afraid to touch them—and then one of Fifi's dresses was slipped over her head and, with cries of delight, they discovered it fitted her perfectly.

"If anything it is a tiny bit big," Fifi said critically. "You will have to eat more. Oh, how lucky you are! I only wish someone could say that to me. And now the belt. Oh, and there is a hat that goes with it."

She looked at Sheena then with a comical little expression of dismay.

"But your hair!" she exclaimed. "That is terrible! So English and not a bit suitable to a Paris hat."

In answer Sheena pulled out the pins and let her hair go loose.

"That's better," Fifi said approvingly. "But it wants cutting and shaping."

Darting across the room like a small humming-bird, she picked up the telephone. She dialled a number and a moment later said:

"Hello! This is Mademoiselle Fontés speaking. Is Emil there? Good! Then ask him to come round at once. At once, do you understand? Yes, yes! Of course I am keeping my appointment tomorrow. I just want him to come here now."

She put down the receiver. Sheena turned with a bemused glance towards her.

"Who is Emil?" she asked.

The hairdresser arrived almost before Fifi's explanations and Sheena's expostulations were ended. He swept into the room and took charge, as only a French *coiffeur* can do, of a woman who does not look her best. Before Sheena really realised what was happening great lumps of her hair were being snipped on to the floor, and he was parting it in a new manner—sweeping it back from her forehead to fall in heavy, natural curls on either side of her face. It was only when he had finished and she could see herself in the mirror that she saw how different she looked.

"Lovely! Oh, Emil, you are a genius!" Fifi cried.

"Mademoiselle est revissante!" the hairdresser remarked.

"I can't believe it is me," Sheena said slowly, "I had no idea my hair could look like this."

"It wants washing and setting, of course," Fifi said. "If you could come with me tomorrow . . ."

Tomorrow! Her words seemed to awaken in Sheena a sense of responsibility.

"No, of course I can't," she replied. "I shall be working tomorrow. And now I must get back. Oh, thank you for everything. I have had such a wonderful time."

She reached out towards her own clothes, but Fifi picked them up before her and swept them into Anastasia's arms.

"You are not going to have those. I know exactly what you will do—you will wear them and put my things away in the drawers."

"But I can't wear this dress every day," Sheena said in horror.

It was, in fact, very unsuitable—being of black satin,

81

cut by a master hand and ornamented with tiny touches of velvet which gave it a smartness almost beyond description.

"No, that is for best," Fifi answered. "And here is the coat that goes over it and the hat that goes with it." She hesitated a moment and then cried: "The suit that I wear *pour les sports,* Anastasia. That will be perfect for Mademoiselle when she takes the children for walks. And there is the coat—a lovely blue wool which is just the colour of her eyes!"

"But I can't take all these things from you," Sheena expostulated for the hundredth time.

"You are going to have them all," Fifi replied. "There are dresses for everything you will do. I promise you I wouldn't have worn any of them again. Isn't it fortunate you can wear my shoes as well? Really, we might have been twins!"

"But how can I thank you?" Sheena asked.

"I am still in your debt," Fifi answered, suddenly serious. "If you only knew what it meant to be able to say 'thank you' in such a very small way for something which, if I had lost it, was quite irreplaceable."

She bent forward suddenly and gave Sheena's hand a little squeeze.

"This is a perfect arrangement," she said. "You have given me something and now I have been able to give you something in return. And do you know what it is? What I have been able to give you?"

"Yes . . . of course," Sheena began, only to be interrupted.

"Look at yourself in the mirror," Fifi cried. "Look how different you are—so smart, so pretty, so—how shall I put it? . . . irresistible! Then you will understand that I have given you not clothes—but a new personality."

"Yes! I think I do understand," Sheena said slowly, staring out bewildered at the strangely attractive reflection in which she could hardly recognise her former self.

"And there is a name for what I have given you," Fifi went on, in her soft, excited voice. "It is called, *ma chérie*—'The Kiss of Paris.' "

Five

It was after six o'clock when Sheena arrived back at the Embassy in a taxi with three large suitcases and a hat-box. She was thankful to see there was no-one about as they stopped at the broad steps which led up to the front door.

She had thought that there was every likelihood that Madame Pelayo would have gone to a cocktail party. She usually went to one in the evening, escorted either by the Ambassador or by Lucien Mansfield. It seemed to be part of the latter's job to act as escort when the Ambassador was otherwise engaged.

Sheena had no desire to be seen until she had time to collect herself and realise what Fifi had done to her. Both Fifi and Anastasia had absolutely refused to allow her to keep her old tweed suit, her underclothes or even her shoes.

"We are going to throw them away," Fifi said. "Or else I am certain you will feel shy at appearing in your new things! They will just hang in the cupboard and no-one will ever see you in them."

It was so obviously what Sheena would have done that she had to laugh, and after that she became help-less in Fifi's and Anastasia's generous hands. Anastasia especially seemed to be glad to get rid of the clothes which were encumbering the cupboards and which she protested over and over again that her mistress never wore.

"You never liked this one, *Mademoiselle*," she would suggest, holding up a dress which seemed to Sheena to be so lovely that she could not imagine how anyone would wish to part with it.

"No, no! I hate it!" Fifi would answer, and Anastasia would set it with the growing pile of other things which Sheena was to take away with her. When she protested, they wouldn't listen, and after a while she sat helpless, her eyes wide, feeling as Cinderella must have felt when by a wave of the wand she became transformed from a ragged slattern into a fairy-tale princess.

Gowns, suits, hats, shoes, gloves, bags, were all piled one on top of the other, until finally Fifi sank exhausted into a chair and exclaimed:

"That is wonderful! Now we have had a good spring-clean and what we all deserve is a cocktail."

Again Sheena tried to refuse, protesting that she had drunk a cocktail only once or twice before and didn't like the taste of them.

"You will like the ones that Anastasia makes," Fifi told her. "They are mostly passion fruit, which is delicious."

Once again Fifi was right. Sheena did like it and she felt it gave her courage to dress herself in her new clothes. She put on the black dress which had been the first gown of Fifi's she had tried on, because Anastasia protested that the coat which went with it was too heavy to pack. Fifi set a little hat, trimmed with velvet leaves, on her head and gave her a handbag of black lizard-skin, which she assured Sheena was worn out but which looked, as far as the latter could see, quite perfect.

"And now you will dazzle everyone!" Fifi said finally. But as Sheena neared the Embassy, she hoped there would be no-one to dazzle.

She could not help feeling shy and also a little awkward in her new high-heeled shoes. She paid the taxi, with what she hoped was an air of assurance, and told the footman to take the suitcases up to her room. Fifi had lent them to her and she had promised to return them as soon as she could manage it.

The footman entered the house by a side door and

Sheena hurried up the steps and into the hall. She thought there was no-one about and was just preparing to run towards the broad staircase when Lucien Mansfield came out of the Ambassador's room and stopped as he saw her coming across the marble floor. For a moment he hesitated and then he spoke.

"Good evening!" he said—and she knew by the tone of his voice and the expression on his face that he did not recognize her.

Overwhelmingly self-conscious, the mere action of being able to speak seemed to have deserted Sheena. She could only stand in the centre of the hall and look uncertainly at Lucien Mansfield as he moved slowly and with an air of politeness towards her. And then suddenly he recognised her.

"Good Lord!" he exclaimed. "It's Mrs. Lawson."

"Yes . . . yes," Sheena managed to stammer, angry with herself for her own nervousness and yet suddenly helpless and at a loss just because he was looking at her.

"What have you done to yourself?" he asked. "You look . . ." He paused and then, as Sheena still seemed unable to speak, he finished his sentence . . . "Beautiful!"

"I . . . I ha . . . I mean . . . thank you," Sheena faltered.

And then he smiled—that irresistible, charming smile which, for some unaccountable reason, always set her at her ease.

"What's happened to you?" he asked. "You have been transformed into somebody very different. Is it magic or is there some very rational explanation for it?"

"It's magic," Sheena smiled back. "In fact it is what someone has just told me is called 'The Kiss of Paris.' "

"So that's what it is," he said quietly.

And as she smiled up at him, her blue eyes looking into his grey ones, a voice from the stairs interrupted them.

"Who is talking about kisses?" Madame Pelayo asked, as she came sweeping down towards them in a cape of Russian sables covering a cocktail dress embroidered with glittering sequins. She had reached the bottom of the stairs before she realised who was talking with Lucien Mansfield, and then, when she saw who stood

85

there, the smile on her face froze and the expression in her eyes hardened.

"Can it possibly be Mrs. Lawson?" she enquired. There was an asperity in her tone which Sheena had never heard there before.

"Yes, *Madame*."

Sheena's nervousness had returned to her and her fingers trembled as she clutched her handbag.

"You have certainly spent your first day out shopping to advantage," Madame Pelayo said. And as her eyes inspected Sheena more closely, she exclaimed: "But that was in Dior's last collection! How can you possibly . . ." She stopped because Lucien Mansfield put out his hand to touch her arm.

"I am sure Mrs. Lawson has a very good explanation," he said, "and will want to tell you about it later. At the moment we must go."

There was something insistent about his voice; something authoritative, too, to which Madame Pelayo surrendered even though the glance she cast at Sheena was far from pleasant. She turned away with a little flounce of her skirts, and as she and Colonel Mansfield disappeared through the front door, Sheena heard her say, "But it is my business, Lucien," and guessed that Colonel Mansfield had been telling her that it was not her business to enquire where the governesses got their clothes.

Thankful to be free and to have to make no further explanations at this particular moment, Sheena ran upstairs and arrived panting on the second floor to find the Nursery in darkness and that the children had been put to bed.

They were not asleep however, and when she opened the door they both sat up and called out to her excitedly.

"I am so glad you are back, Lawie," Madi said— using the nickname which they had both instinctively adopted as they had grown to like and trust her.

"Did you have a nice day?" Sheena asked, coming into the room.

"No, horrid!" Madi pouted. "Jeanne took us for a very dull walk; and when we went down to see Mamma this evening, she was too busy talking to Uncle Lucien to play with us."

Sheena knew that Colonel Mansfield enjoyed the courtesy title of Uncle and she could not help wondering now what he and Madame Pelayo had to talk about which had kept them so preoccupied when the children were there.

"Uncle Henri came later," Pedro chimed in. "But he was cross—very cross."

"Cross with you?" Sheena asked.

"Oh, no, not with us," Madi answered. "He came in just as Jeanne arrived to take us upstairs, and Mamma asked him what he had been doing, and when he said 'Nothing,' she teased him and said, 'Was one of your little girls unkind to you, then?' Wasn't that a silly thing to say, Lawie? Because Uncle Henri hasn't got any little girls, has he?"

"No, of course he hasn't," Sheena agreed. "Your mother must have been playing make-believe."

"That's what I thought," Madi said. "But Uncle Henri said, 'Oh, damn!' and went out of the room and slammed the door. That was naughty, Lawie, wasn't it?"

"Very naughty," Sheena agreed. "And now you must go to sleep."

"It's very early," Madi protested. "Jeanne always puts us to bed early because she is bored with us. Isn't that true, Pedro?"

"Quite true," the little boy lisped solemnly.

And then the feminine instinct in Madi recognised the difference in Sheena.

"You don't look like our Lawie," she said critically. "I thought you were Mamma when you first came in."

"It is because I have got a new coat," Sheena replied.

"It's nice, isn't it?" Madi asked, putting out her hand to touch the soft cloth and stroke the velvet cuffs.

"Very nice," Sheena answered.

"Did you buy it all yourself?"

Sheena shook her head.

"No, it was given me by someone who was very kind."

"A present?" Madi enquired.

"Yes, a present," Sheena agreed.

The child snuggled back against her pillows.

"I love having presents. Don't you, Lawie?"

"Yes, but I don't get many as a rule," Sheena answered.

"Uncle Henri used to bring presents for Miss Robinson," Madi said. "Chocolates and flowers; and she used to giggle like anything when he gave them to her."

"Now go to sleep," Sheena commanded hastily. "If I tell you a story, will you promise not to talk any more?"

"Yes! Yes! We promise," Madi cried.

And Pedro, as usual following his sister's lead, cried: 'I pwomiss, I pwomiss!"

Sheena sat down on the children's bed and told them the old, old story of the three bears. And when they had shouted with laughter at the fate of poor Goldilocks, she kissed them both good night, reminded them of their promise, and went out of the room, leaving the door a little bit ajar so that she should hear them if they called out.

She went to her own bedroom and saw that the three suitcases and the hat-box had been set down in a tidy row at the end of the bed. For a moment she stood looking at them, savouring the delight of what lay ahead of her. For the first time the big, empty cupboards in her room were going to be filled. For the first time she would need the deep drawers in her dressing-table and the cupboard which had been built for shoes and the one for hats.

How wonderful it was for the first time in her life to have clothes—real clothes, not just ugly things which covered her body. She drew a deep breath of sheer delight and looked at herself in the mirror. She had no idea that the cutting of one's hair could alter a person so completely. Her face seemed a different shape; her eyes bigger than they had ever seemed before. Perhaps it was because they were shining, she thought.

"I don't believe even Uncle Patrick would recognise me," she told herself; and then, at the very thought of his name, she remembered what else had happened to her that afternoon.

In the excitement of being with Fifi she had forgotten the horrid, sordid little bookshop in the *Rue St. François;* that voice, deep, disembodied and yet somehow terrifying, speaking in her ear; the feeling, almost of terror, which had shaken her when finally she had understood what was said.

And now, what was she to do? she asked herself. With an effort she refused to allow herself to think of it any more. She forced it into the background of her mind, and taking off her coat turned resolutely to the suitcases.

They proved a distraction, as she had known they would.

She had hardly had time in Fifi's bedroom to examine what was being given her—in fact she felt, as she drew out most of the clothes, that she had never seen them before.

There were suits and dresses which were so lovely and so exactly what she had always longed for that she wanted to cry at the sight of them. There were dozens of other things too, equally lovely, but which she felt she would never have the chance of wearing. Cocktail dresses, dinner gowns and a great ball dress of soft, blue tulle with a cascade of pink roses down the front, which seemed to Sheena more like a poem than a dress.

"I shall never wear it," she sighed, "but how lovely it is to have it—to know that it is there, to be able to look at it when I am feeling miserable!"

She hung the gown up in the cupboard, put the shoes and hats and handbags away, and then, because she could not resist it, changed into an evening dress. It was a very simple dinner frock of pale green chiffon, embroidered round the neck and waist with tiny brilliants. It made her seem very thin, and almost ethereal; and when she had brushed her new, short curls until they danced around her head, she went into the Nursery to find that her supper was waiting. One of the footmen had brought it up on a tray and left it there on the table.

As Sheena walked across the big, empty room she pretended, to herself, that she was going to a restaurant with some charming young man who had asked her out for the evening. He pulled back the chair so that she could seat herself comfortably at a small table with shaded lights, and then, as the waiter brought the long menu, he asked her what she would have.

As Sheena played her game of pretence, she sat down at the Nursery table, and now, peering under the covered dish which was set on the tray, she ordered cold chicken and ham—because that was what was waiting for her there.

There her game of pretence ended. She could not think what she would say to a young man if one did take her out, nor what, in fact, the restaurant would be like. She had lunched and dined out at some of the cheaper places in Dublin and Belfast. And when they had been in London Uncle Patrick had taken her on two occasions to a small restaurant off the King's Road, where she had been entranced by watching the other diners and had found the food delicious—even though Patrick O'Donovan declared that he wouldn't offer such rubbish to the pigs back home in Ireland.

He was only finding fault because they were in England, Sheena thought, and enjoyed to the full the excitement of being able to order something she hadn't cooked, and of hearing the noise and chatter of other people around her.

"Dressed like this I can go anywhere in Paris," she thought. And then she remembered that no-one was likely to ask her, except perhaps the *Vicomte,* and if he did she would be unable to accept his invitation. She found herself wondering what it would be like to have dinner alone with Lucien Mansfield.

She was frightened of him and yet, in some strange way, he fascinated her. There was so much character behind the reserve in his face She longed, sometimes, to be able to talk to him; to ask his opinion; to listen to what he had to say on any subject, however unimportant. And yet the moment she was in his presence she became tongue-tied.

"How stupid he must think me," she thought resentfully, and wondered if, now that she had beautiful clothes, she would alter and perhaps become poised and self-assured like Madame Pelayo and the other ladies who came to the Embassy.

Her supper was over and the footman took away the tray. Sheena walked restlessly to the window and looked out into the darkness of the night. How she wished she could go out if only for five minutes!

"Haven't you had enough adventures for one day?" she asked herself, and felt that she was ungrateful and

90

greedy to want more. It was Paris that was making her restless, she thought. Paris, which gave so much and yet made one hungry for more!

She felt as if there was a strange stirring in her heart that had never been there before. Her whole being reached out towards something outside herself—beyond her narrow experience, and yet somehow impossible to put into words. It was tangible and yet so intangible!

"I will get something to do," Sheena said sensibly. She took up her work-basket. There was a pile of things to be done for the children—buttons to be sewn on; woollen jackets to be mended; the lace to be repaired on Madi's small but elegant underclothes. But somehow her fingers would not obey her will, and after a time she sat staring into the fire, her thoughts running away from her like wild horses which could not be caught or controlled.

She was startled when she heard the door of the Nursery open and awoke from her reverie with a sudden jump. Henri de Cormeille was looking round the door, and when he saw that she was alone he came quickly into the room and shut the door behind him. Slowly Sheena got to her feet.

"You oughtn't to come here, *Monsieur*," she said.

"Nonsense!" he answered. "I want to see you, and my sister and the redoubtable Colonel are both out to dinner. I came back early specially because I wanted to talk to you."

He had crossed the room to stand at her side as he spoke, and now he gave a little exclamation of astonishment.

"What have you done to yourself, Sheena? You have cut your hair, and that dress is entrancing—it makes you look like a water sprite. Why have you never worn it before?"

"*Monsieur*, please be sensible," Sheena pleaded. "You know you will get me into trouble if Madame Pelayo finds you here."

"I have told you that she is out," the *Vicomte* said with a grin. "Haven't you got a proverb in England which says, 'While the cat is away, the mice will play'?"

"Well, I'm not going to play with you," Sheena replied positively. "I'm going to bed."

"Not until you tell me why you never came to tea with me today."

"I told you that I couldn't come," Sheena answered.

"You said 'no' because you were afraid of my sister. But you would have liked to come—admit it!"

"No . . . ye . . . I don't know."

"But I do," the *Vicomte* said confidentially. "You would have liked to have tea with me alone at Rumpelmayer's. We could have sat in the corner and I would have fed you with cream cakes and ice-cream while I watched the colour coming and going in your face, and those long eyelashes of yours trying to veil the blue of your eyes. Have you any idea how attractive you are, little Sheena?"

"No . . . no . . . no!" Sheena cried, half scolding, half laughing. "What am I to do when you won't listen when I say you are not to talk like that—when you won't go away?"

"Now you are beginning to talk sense," the *Vicomte* smiled. "Come, sit down and tell me what you have done to yourself. I thought you were pretty the first time I saw you, with your gold hair hanging over your shoulders. But now that it is short it makes you look even lovelier. Where did you get that dress?"

"Why are you so curious?" Sheena asked.

"You drive me mad!" the *Vicomte* said, reaching out to take her hand in his. "I can't make up my mind if you are being very clever or if you are really as simple and inexperienced as you appear. There is not one woman in a hundred who would have kept me waiting at Rumpelmayer's today, cooling my heels and making me mad with rage because you didn't come. There is not one woman in a hundred who would manage to remain as elusive as you have contrived to be this last week."

He waited for a moment and then, as she did not speak, he said very softly:

"Don't run away any longer."

She tried to take her hand from his, but he held on to it.

"I . . . don't know . . . what you are trying . . . to say," she stammered. "As I have already . . . told you, I want to go to . . . to . . . bed."

"That's a lie," he answered. "And you know it. You

92

are lovely, Sheena, and you fascinate me. I find myself thinking about you at all hours of the day—waiting for the sight of your little pointed face, for the flicker of your eyelashes when you know that I am watching you and it makes you feel shy. Shy because of the things that I am thinking."

"Please let me go?" Sheena asked.

In answer he raised her hand to his lips, and because his mouth was warm and insistent she felt herself tremble a little.

"Shall I tell you what I am thinking, Sheena, when I look at you?—or have you already guessed? How much do you know about life? As I have asked you before, are you as inexperienced as you look? Or are you so clever as to be able to conceal all that that husband of yours must have taught you?"

Sheena stiffened suddenly.

"So you don't like to speak of him," the *Vicomte* said. "Did you love him very much, I wonder?"

"You have no right to ask me so many questions," Sheena cried.

"I am not asking you questions," Henri de Cormeille answered. "I am thinking aloud. I am thinking that you are very lovely and yet you know so very little about love. And who should blame you, for you have only been married to an Englishman—and Englishmen think of love as just another sport, inferior in every way to cricket and football. Let me teach you about love, Sheena. Let me teach you all the things that love can mean when two people want each other."

Almost in spite of herself Sheena found herself hypnotised by the *Vicomte's* voice, by the touch of his lips.

Now he turned her hand over in his and kissed first the palm and then each finger—his mouth lingering on the smooth softness of her skin, then finding the blue veins on her wrist. His kisses grew more passionate and more insistent until, with a sudden movement that surprised him and a strength he had not expected from her, Sheena drew herself free.

She set a chair between herself and the *Vicomte,* and stood holding on to the back.

"Please go," she said. "Your sister may return at any

moment and she will be very angry if she finds you here."

"Is that the only reason you are asking me to go? My dear, aren't you being a little ridiculous? We are both grown-up people, both well aware that life is short and that happiness is hard to find. We are not children to believe that something better will always happen to-morrow. You have been married and widowed, Sheena. You know that love is a precious thing that comes and goes; that can be given and lost. Why do you deny what I can see in your eyes, what I can feel in the trembling of your fingers? You want me as I want you. Are you too frightened to acknowledge it?"

"Please go away."

White-faced, Sheena could think of nothing else to say. She felt as if he drew her by his words, by the magnetism which reached out from him towards her. And yet at the same time, even while she acknowledged his attraction, she wanted to run away from him. It was not only because he thought she knew more than she did. It was something deeper, something more fundamental —and yet she could not deny there was a strange excitement in his words and the look in his eyes, in the hungry desire behind his kisses.

"Please, go away," she said again.

"And if I won't?"

She looked up to see an obstinacy in his face and a light of triumph in his eyes which she had not expected.

"Don't you understand?" she asked. "I have got a job to do here. I have been accepted for the position of governess. It is important that I should stay—not only for selfish reasons but because I am helping someone by doing so. If your sister finds us—or even finds out that you are making love to me—I shall be dismissed without a reference, without, perhaps, enough money to get me back to England."

"And if that happened, do you think I should let you starve?" Henri de Cormeille asked. "I would look after you, Sheena. How could you doubt me? Listen, I have a little flat of which my sister knows nothing. I live here, but when I wish to entertain my own very special friends I take them to my apartment. Will you come there with me one evening? We will dine somewhere first. No-one will know; no-one will see us. And then we can go back to my apartment and I can make love to you without you being afraid, without you having to think about anything but me."

"Is that the sort of suggestion you make to every young girl you meet?" Sheena asked. And now there was a hardness and something like scorn in her voice which had not been there before.

The *Vicomte* smiled disarmingly.

"Do you really believe that I should make such a suggestion to a *jeune fille?*" he enquired. "But, of course not. How could you suspect me of being so reprehensible? But to a married woman one may say anything. The little gold band on your left hand gives me permission to speak as my heart dictates. Come with me one evening—just you and I alone. We should be so happy."

"I don't think you mean to insult me," Sheena said slowly. "And so I shall not say that I am insulted by such a suggestion. But the answer is no—never!"

"Perhaps I have asked you too quickly," he replied, quite unabashed by her reply. "I have always been told that English women are cold, difficult to get, and that one must woo them for longer and more ardently than any other nationality. Is it because the cold sea encircles your island that there is so little warmth in your blood? Or is it because you have never learned how thrilling love can be and therefore you are both ignorant and afraid of it?"

"Perhaps by love we mean something very different," Sheena said.

"What is love, but the need of a man for a woman and a woman for a man?" Henri de Cormeille enquired.

"There is more to it than that," Sheena answered. "I am sure of it. You are making it sound as if it is entirely a physical thing."

"And isn't it?" Henri de Cormeille enquired. "Give me your hand."

Without thinking she obeyed him, and was quite unprepared for the movement by which he drew her swiftly round the chair into his arms. For a moment he held her close against him, laughing down into her face, and then his lips were on hers.

It was the first time in her life that Sheena had ever been kissed. Never before had she felt herself held captive by a man's mouth, known the softness and yet the strength of lips which seemed to possess her so completely that for the moment her brain ceased to function. She wanted to fight against him, wanted to push him from her—and yet she could not move. She felt as if she could not breathe, as if she sank beneath deep waters which were closing over her head and she could not even gasp for breath.

And then suddenly her mouth was free and his kisses were on her face, her neck, her eyes, her hair.

"You are entrancing!" he cried. "I want you! I want to love you! Say you want me too."

Still she could not move. She could only stand captive in his arms, feeling the world whirl around her, knowing that once again her mouth was soft and pliant beneath his.

It was then that the interruption came. It was the sound of a car door being slammed and voices rising to their ears through the open window. A second later there came the soft thud of the front door being closed.

Henri gave Sheena one last kiss which seemed to take all her breath from her; then he moved swiftly across the Nursery floor. He opened the door and was gone like a shadow from the room.

The door closed behind him and Sheena sank, limp and trembling, into the armchair. She put her hands up to her cheeks and realised that they were burning. She touched her mouth and felt that it could never be the same again but must carry the imprint of his kisses all her life.

She did not know in that moment what she felt—or, indeed, what she thought. She only knew that she was quivering because she had passed through a tremendous experience such as she had never known before in all her life. The time seemed to have passed so quickly since the *Vicomte* had come into the Nursery, but when she looked at the clock she saw, to her surprise, that he had been there for over half an hour.

What was she to do about him? Somehow she could not think of tomorrow, but could only remember what had happened today—this moment. She had been kissed for the first time in her life. Was she in love with the young *Vicomte?* Was she, indeed, attracted to him as he was attracted to her? She did not know the answer to any of her own questions. She only knew that she felt giddy and distraught by all that had occurred.

If only she could think clearly. But somehow it was impossible while the passion of his kisses still burned against her lips and neck, while she could still feel the strength of his arms around her shoulders.

"I must go to bed." Sheena whispered. She went into her own room and, as she switched on the light, she hesitated. There was a key in the door. She turned it and heard the lock click home. Was she locking against Henri de Cormeille—or against the love which might be knocking at her own heart? She was not quite certain.

Six

Sheena awoke very early and got up before the children were awake so that she might be able to write her letter to Uncle Patrick in peace. She had felt she could not attempt it yesterday when her brain was so bemused with all that had happened that it was almost impossible to think straight or to set her thoughts in order.

Now, as the pale sun came flooding over the roof tops, she opened her window wide and felt the spring air invigorate her as though it was a glass of wine. There was, she decided, something special in the air of Paris; something she had never known before; something which made her feel young and gay and impetuous so that even the dark cloud of worry over her uncle or the difficulties of keeping up her own masquerade seemed not to matter so much as they might have done.

It was enough that she was here and that Paris was altering and changing her in some magical way of its own.

It was with an effort that she tore herself from the window to sit down at the neat little writing-able which stood in one corner of her bedroom. She picked up a pen and laid one of the sheets of thin paper, engraved with the arms of Mariposa, in front of her. She stared at it. How was she to begin? What was she to say to bring home forcibly to Uncle Patrick that she must know the truth?

98

She knew only too well his easy manner, the habit he had of shelving anything unpleasant, of turning his back on something which he did not understand, or disliked. He was a past master at evasion, and because of this characteristic he was one of the happiest people she had ever known. Nothing really worried him, because he wouldn't allow it to. If he had money, he spent it; if he hadn't, he went without. There was always someone who would stand him a drink for the sake of his smile and the irresistible appeal of his brogue.

Uncle Patrick was never without friends Sheena thought. It was only that she, trailing behind him like a small, unimportant shadow, had not been able to throw herself wholeheartedly into that strange, feckless, precarious life where the only security she had ever known was the four walls of a small house on the cliffs.

Resolutely she put the thoughts of Ireland out of her mind and forced herself to write the first words of her letter:

Darling Uncle Patrick—and then she stopped, seeing him come striding into the room, as he had done when she was a child, to lift her high in his arms above his head so that she had a distorted view of his face laughing up at her. She could remember him sitting by her bedside when she was recovering from being badly concussed through a fall from her pony. How kind he had been, telling her stories by the hour or making her amusing toys out of pieces of newspaper and old cotton reels! It seemed to her then that the sun rose and set on Uncle Patrick—and how much she still loved him!

She couldn't hurt him—that was one thing she could never do. And yet she had to know the truth. With a sudden urgency in case her resolve should weaken, she made her pen fly over the paper, setting down in detail what had happened yesterday when she had gone to the little bookshop. Telling him of the threats which the deep voice had made to her over the telephone, and begging him either to come out to Paris or to let her come to him.

I will send you my salary as soon as I receive it [she wrote]. *And if it is imperative, I will ask for one week in advance. What I sent you yesterday should bring you*

99

here, and somehow we will find enough for you to get back. Please, please, Uncle Patrick, if you love me at all, come over and explain. I am frightened by all this mystery and I want to see you more than I have ever wanted anything in the whole of my life.

There were tears in Sheena's eyes as she finished writing. It was, indeed, true that she was frightened—not for herself but for Uncle Patrick. Suppose, she thought, he had done something wrong and given these people a hold over him. There were so many things he might have done. No-one knew better than she how careless he was about money, or how ardently patriotic to the point of being fanatical. Either might have involved him in a situation which, if disclosed, would bring him up against the law.

"The law is an ass!" How often had she heard him quote that. And when she was a child he used to tell her half seriously: "They'll tell you at school that a policeman is a man's best friend. The best part of a policeman that you'll ever see is his back when he's walking away from you."

She had laughed at him then, thinking he was teasing, but now she was not so sure. Supposing there had been a deeper meaning in such casual words!

She put her letter into an envelope, addressed it and then slipped it into her handbag. She was not so stupid as to leave a letter to Patrick O'Donovan, whom she had told Lucien Mansfield she had not seen for two years, lying about the Embassy.

"I am beginning to suspect that there are spies everywhere," she thought to herself with a little shiver. And yet, remembering how badly she had lied to Lucien Mansfield, she felt there would be some justification in his suspecting her. She felt her cheeks burn again as she remembered her slip when he told her that her eyes were Irish, and she felt ashamed when she recalled how she had run away from him when he had asked her questions about her married life.

But even the memory of such things, or the expression on Madame Pelayo's face when she had seen her last night in her new clothes from Fifi Fontés, could not dim Sheena's joy as the sun crept further into her room and she went to her wardrobe to take out the suit she was going to wear that day.

She could hardly believe that it was herself whom she saw in the mirror when finally she was dressed. Nothing could have been more simple than the coat and skirt of pearl-grey suiting which Fifi had given her to wear under the overcoat of blue tweed. There was a little blouse of the same colour, shoes which matched almost exactly, and a tiny hat that was nothing more or less than a twist of ribbon. Very plain, without ornamentation, the whole ensemble should have made anyone who wore it look unobtrusive and demure. And yet, as Sheena discovered, it revealed things about herself that she had never known before.

She had never known, for instance, that her breasts curved sweetly down to a tiny waist; that her hips were so slim or that her legs, revealed by the shortness of the skirt, were so well made. As she looked at herself, she realised that her eyes were vividly blue, her skin clear and her curls, touched by the sunshine, were like tiny gold tongues against the clear lines of her face. It was with a sense of guilt that she turned away from the mirror.

"I'm getting vain," she said out loud. And yet she knew that she was only making up for nearly twenty-one years of self-effacing humbleness.

She had never thought of herself as being of any consequence. Yet now a few new clothes had given her the knowledge not only that she was pretty but that she was a person.

"I suppose," she thought, "it was because I was so busy looking after Uncle Patrick that I had no time to think of myself."

And yet was it the clothes that had awakened her to a knowledge of her own charms or was it the look in Henri de Cormeille's eyes and the touch of his lips on hers? With almost a sense of dismay Sheena realised that this was the thought from which she had been trying to escape all the morning, and instinctively the tips of her fingers went up to touch her mouth. Then, almost running, she went into the children's rooms to draw back the curtains.

"I have been awake for hours and hours, Lawie," Madi said reproachfully.

"So have I," Sheena replied gaily.

"But you could get up," Madi pouted. "We have had to lie here thinking the day would never start."

"Let us start it now," Sheena said cheerfully. "Get up quickly and we will think of all the wonderful things we can do because the sun is shining."

"No lessons?" Pedro asked hopefully.

"Very short ones," Sheena promised. "Perhaps we could do them as we walk along."

"That would be fun," both the children cried.

Sheena had invented a game for them in which she pointed out an object in the street and they had to tell her what it was called in English. Usually, she discovered that she learned more than they did, because if their English was sometimes at fault, at French, Spanish and Mariposan they were extremely proficient.

"We are teaching Lawie to speak Spanish," Madi announced at luncheon that day.

Sheena wished, as the eyes of the other people at the table were all turned upon her, that the child would keep silent. She was well aware, as they came down to luncheon, that Madame Pelayo's lips had tightened as she saw the new grey suit, while Henri de Cormeille was looking at her in a way which she felt must reveal to everyone present what his feelings were as far as she was concerned. Only Lucien Mansfield looked as usual —calm, serious and with somehow a feeling of strength about him.

"Eat up your lunch, Madi," she said hastily. "And don't talk so much."

"I hope the children are definitely concentrating on their English, Mrs. Lawson," Madame Pelayo said disagreeably. "I asked Pedro to read me two or three of the simplest words yesterday morning and he had no idea what they were."

"You chose wery difficult ones, Mamma," Pedro said suddenly.

"I knew them, didn't I?" Madi asked.

"So you ought to, a great big girl of your age," Madame Pelayo replied.

"What we ought to do is always to talk English to them," Henri de Cormeille interposed.

"I think it would be far better, Henri, if you left the children's education to Mrs. Lawson," Madame Pelayo said, with meaning.

Quite unperturbed the *Vicomte* gave his sister a little bow.

"Touché, ma chérie."

She smiled at that, put pettishly, looking, even when she was annoyed, so beautiful that Sheena found it difficult not to watch her instead of attending to the children.

She could quite see that these family luncheons were going to be an ordeal. And yet, when the Ambassador arrived, full of apologies for being late, the atmosphere changed. Madame Pelayo might be thirty years younger than her husband and she might, at times, find him difficult or somewhat staid in his manner, but at the same time she both respected and admired him, and being a Frenchwoman, she did not hide her feelings but flattered him with her attentions and made it very clear, whenever he came into her presence, that she was pleased to see him.

"How late you are, *mon cher,*" she said now. "I have been worrying as to what could have kept you."

"Business, business—what is diplomacy but business?" the Ambassador answered.

"The chef is making you a fresh omelette," Madame Pelayo smiled. "Henri, please get Carlos a glass of sherry—you know, that special bottle which we said no-one was to drink but him."

The *Vicomte* rose to his feet and fetched a decanter from the sideboard.

"You will like this, Carlos," he said to his brother-in-law. "And it would put new life into a corpse!"

"That's almost what I feel myself to be," the Ambassador replied. He lifted his glass to his wife, then, as he took a sip, he turned to Lucien Mansfield. "I thought I should never be rid of them," he said. "They talked and talked, determined to make me sign there and then."

"You didn't do so, I hope, sir."

103

"No! I told them I must have time to consider it in all its details."

"Have they left the contract with you?"

"Yes! It is on my desk. We will talk about it this evening. I have got to see the Spanish Ambassador immediately after luncheon."

"There is no hurry," Lucien Mansfield said. "Except as far as they are concerned."

"They certainly convinced me of that," laughed the Ambassador.

Listening, Sheena felt her heart begin beating. This, then, was the contract of which the voice on the telephone had spoken. This was what she had to discover. And almost immediately she decided that she would have nothing to do with it. Not until she had seen Uncle Patrick would she go near that bookshop. Not unless it was, for him, a matter of life and death would she demean herself to go down and speak again to that voice which had threatened and bullied her.

"If you don't want Lucien this afternoon," Madame Pelayo was saying to her husband, "can I take him to the Reception at the Argentine Embassy? You know how much I dislike going alone to these official functions."

"Yes, my dear, of course," the Ambassador said. "I told you that I wouldn't be able to go with you."

"Yes, I know!" Madame Pelayo pouted. "But you know how much I want you to come with me."

"*Ma chère,* I would do anything for you except offend the Spanish Ambassador. Already he accuses me of not treating him with sufficient respect; and if I do not go to the Council that he has called this afternoon, I fear that I should be in his black books for ever."

"*Mon pauvre,* of course you must go—so long as I can have Lucien."

"Lucien must deputise for me."

"I will do my best, sir."

"And does nobody want me to do anything with them this afternoon?" Henri de Cormeille asked with exaggerated plaintiveness.

"We want you, Uncle Henri," Madi cried.

"Then you can't have him," Madame Pelayo said

sharply. "Surely, Henri, you have got something better to do with your time."

"I don't think I have," the *Vicomte* answered lazily. There was a challenge in his eyes as he looked at his sister.

"I forbid it," Madame Pelayo said, in a low voice.

She looked none too pleasantly at Sheena as the children, having finished their luncheon, were shepherded from the room. And after Sheena had put them to lie down in their beds, she came from the night nursery to find Madame Pelayo waiting for her.

The Ambassadress was looking even more beautiful than usual in a dress of sapphire blue velvet with a long wrap of platina mink round her shoulders. But for the first time since she had come to the Embassy Sheena, in the grey suit and with her hair arranged by a master hand, did not feel gauche as she advanced to meet her.

"I was not able to see you this morning because I slept late," Madame Pelayo said. "And I have only a few seconds now. But I feel that you owe me an explanation of this amazing transformation in your appearance."

"I am perfectly ready to give it, *Madame*," Sheena replied. "It must appear a little strange to you."

"A little strange!" Madame Pelayo retorted, her voice rising on a high note. "It is, in fact, extremely peculiar. You come here dressed in a adequate, if unobtrusive, manner; and suddenly, within twenty-four hours, you appear in the very latest models from the great fashion houses. That suit is by Dior, if I am not mistaken, and his prices are hardly possible on your salary."

"Yes, I know . . ." Sheena began, only to be interrupted by Madame Pelayo, who continued:

"I was assured by the Comtesse de Beaufleur that your credentials were of the highest respectability. I have had trouble before with young governesses who lost their heads in Paris. If it is a man who has been giving you these presents . . ."

"But of course it isn't!" Sheena interrupted angrily. "I think, *Madame,* if you will be kind enough to listen to me, it would be best if I told you exactly what has happened."

She was angry that the Ambassadress should think,

even for a moment, that her clothes should have been given her for any immoral reason. She could understand that the difference in her appearance must cause comment, but the pride of the O'Donovans brought the colour to her face and there was a flash in her eyes as she told Madame Pelayo exactly what had happened and what reward Fifi Fontés had given her for the return of her notecase.

"So that's what happened!" Madame Pelayo said, when the story was finished. "Well, I understand, Mrs. Lawson, and I can't of course, exactly blame you for taking such a gift. At the same time, I must ask you to remember that the clothes worn by the star of the *Casino de Paris* are not likely to be suitable for someone in your position."

"I will only wear the very simplest of them, *Madame,* while I am on duty." Sheena said.

She did not speak humbly because she was angry. A week ago she might have been crushed and humiliated by the Ambassadress's anger, but now there seemed to be a new spirit in her, something which made her want to fight for herself—and perhaps for her new appearance.

"That suit is simple enough," Madame Pelayo said reluctantly. And then, with a sudden flash of petulance, she added: "Oh, it isn't only your clothes, Mrs. Lawson. I thought I was getting someone middle-aged and staid. The *Comtesse* was so insistent that you were exactly the right person I was looking for."

"Would you like me to resign my position?" Sheena asked in a low voice.

Even as she said the words she knew she didn't want to go. How could she bear to leave Paris now, so soon? To go back to that airless basement in London? Perhaps to start on her wanderings again with Uncle Patrick? To give up this adventure just at the very moment it was starting?

"No! I don't want that, as you well know," Madame Pelayo said testily. "The children have taken to you and I must say that you have got them well in hand. It is just that there are pitfalls in Paris for young women, as you must know. When you first came, you were younger than I expected; but I thought that at least you looked . . ." Madame Pelayo stopped suddenly as if she felt that what she was going to say was so uncomplimentary that it would give unnecessary offence.

She hesitated a moment and then turned round, with a swirl of her full, velvet skirt.

"Let us leave it at that, Mrs. Lawson."

She flounced from the room, closing the door behind her with what was suspiciously like a slam. Sheena stared after her and then suddenly her chin went up.

"I won't give up my nice clothes," she said aloud. "I won't go back to looking like I was before."

Even as she said it, she remembered that Fifi had kept her coat and skirt and the Jaegar overcoat which had been a familiar friend for so many years. How wise the little actress had been! Now it was too late to do anything about them; and even if she wished to please Madame Pelayo, she had, in actual fact, nothing to wear but the lovely, exquisitely cut models, of which the Ambassadress so ardently disapproved.

It was impossible for Sheena not to know that she looked pretty. When she took the children out later that afternoon, men turned their eyes to look after her as she walked down the street; and if by any chance she looked at them in passing they smiled at her boldly and with the same admiration in their eyes which she had seen so clearly and so unmistakably in Henri de Cormeille's.

It was only when the children had gone to bed and she had nothing else to think of she began to worry all over again about Uncle Patrick. He had never been able to look after himself; perhaps she had been unwise to come away from him. She thought now how weak and stupid she had been to come here because he had wanted her to, without further explanations, without forcing him to tell her exactly what it all meant.

It must have been the habit of obedience which she had got into all her life which had made her obey him —not only in coming out to Paris, but in not asking him too many questions. Now, because she was away from him, she felt stronger; a personality in her own right; someone who could not just be ordered about without explanation, without a good reason.

Because she was depressed Sheena went to bed

early. But tonight even the comfort of the soft bed could not lull her into sleep as it had done on previous nights. She lay awake, tossing and turning, thinking of Uncle Patrick in trouble, hiding from the Police, being bullied by these strange friends of his who had such power over him.

If only, she thought wildly, she knew more; if only she knew who they were, she could decide for herself if they were really dangerous. It was then, insidiously, incessantly, that there came into her mind the thought of the contract. The Ambassador had said that he had left it on his desk. Was it still there? It was obviously of no moment in itself or else it would have been locked away in the safe.

If only she could see it, she could learn so much. The people whom the Ambassador had seen that morning, who had brought the contract to him, must have some connection in some way with the man who had spoken to her on the telephone. If the contract was about guns, then she would know it was guns that Uncle Patrick's so-called friends were interested in. Or it might be railways or ships or land development. It might be a hundred and one things—and only the contract could give her an idea as to what it was.

Suddenly Sheena sat up in bed. She switched on her bedside lamp and saw that it was after two o'clock. For a moment she hesitated, and then she made up her mind. She got out of bed and going to the wardrobe took from it a house-gown of pale blue satin which Fifi had given her. She slipped it on, tying it with a chiffon sash of two shades of pink.

So preoccupied was she with her own thoughts that Sheena did not look at herself in the mirror, but slipping her feet into a pair of bedroom slippers she walked on tiptoe across the floor and into the Nursery. The room was in darkness but she did not turn on the light. Instead she groped her way to the cupboard where some of the children's toys were kept, and after feeling round the shelves with her hands for a few seconds she discovered what she sought—a torch which Pedro had been given for Christmas.

It was not large and made only a small circle of light to guide Sheena to the door which led out on to the

108

landing. There she stood and listened; the house was very quiet. Madame Pelayo had come home from a party some hours ago. She had heard the car drive up beneath her window. Once the Ambassador and his wife were in, the household usually went to bed.

Everything had been quiet now for hours, and finding that the only sound she could hear was the beating of her own heart, Sheena started down the stairs. The torch guided her feet while she held on to the banister with her right hand. She reached the hall and carefully moved from rug to rug so that her feet would not make a noise on the marble floor.

She reached the door of the Ambassador's study. For a moment she was half afraid it might be locked, but as she turned the handle the door opened and she slipped in, closing it behind her. The room smelt of cigar smoke mixed with the fragrance of carnations. Sheena picked out with her torch a huge bowl of them on the Ambassador's desk.

Slowly she advanced towards them. Her heart was beating almost suffocatingly and her hands were icy cold. By the light of the torch she could see that there were piles of papers on the desk—official-looking documents stacked on the left-hand side of the blotter. Would the contract be amongst them?

She reached the desk and pushed aside the chair which had been drawn closely up to it, so that she could reach the papers more easily. At that moment, she heard a sound. She swung round; there was a click and the lights of the room flashed on, blinding her momentarily, making it impossible for her to see who stood there even while she recognised the voice which snapped:

"Don't move!"

She felt as if she were paralysed where she stood. But her vision cleared and then she saw that Lucien Mansfield was standing just inside the door. He was staring at her in a manner which seemed to her more frightening and even more sinister than the revolver which he held in his right hand.

Seven

It seemed to Sheena that the breath was slowly squeezed from her body; then, as if a shutter came down before her eyes, she felt a sudden darkness encompass her and knew that she was falling.

Down, down she went into the deep well of unconsciousness, but even as it stifled her, she felt it moving away from her again. Still numb, she was yet aware that she was lifted in someone's arms. She felt herself being carried, and though everything was far away and she had almost lost contact with herself, she felt a sense of strength and protection.

All at once she was conscious again. She opened her eyes to find herself being set down gently in a big armchair. There was a fire burning brightly in a grate and she felt the warmth of it on her hands. A voice said authoritatively:

"Drink this."

She wanted to protest. But there was a glass against her lips and almost before she was aware of it she was swallowing, coughing a little in protest as the fiery liquid seemed to scorch her throat.

"No . . . no more," she managed to stammer, in a voice which seemed strange even to her own ears.

"Are you quite sure?" Lucien Mansfield asked.

She could see him now, towering above her, and as

she looked up towards him she remembered everything. With a sickening throb it seemed to her that her heart started beating again.

He had come upon her standing at the Ambassador's desk in what must, in anyone's eyes and most of all in his, have seemed a guilty and indefensible position. What could she say to him? What explanation could she possibly make? With a sense of rising panic she remembered Uncle Patrick. If she were incriminated, so was he. If she were accused of a crime, it would be obvious, after a very few questions, that she was working not for herself but at the instigation of someone else.

What could she say? What could she say? What could she say? The question seemed to repeat itself over and over in her mind with a throbbing intensity which made her want to scream. But she knew that she must play for time; she must think; she must find some explanation. She closed her eyes.

"You must drink a little more brandy," Lucien Mansfield said. "Come along; I can't allow you to refuse me."

She was too weak from her own fears to wish, at the moment, to do anything but obey him. Obediently she sipped again at the glass he held to her lips, then took it from him, saying:

"No more . . . not for the moment . . . please."

"You still look very pale," he said, and surprisingly he went down on one knee and taking her hands in his began to rub them.

She had not thought that he could be so gentle. She had always thought of him as hard and strong, yet his hands, when they touched hers, had a tenderness which made her feel somehow ashamed. And then, before she could prevent him, before she could say anything, he had lifted her feet on to a footstool, had drawn off one of her bedroom slippers and was rubbing her foot in the same manner as he had rubbed her hands.

"Please don't . . ." she protested. But he smiled at her.

"Sit back and relax. You have had a shock and it always makes one feel cold."

Because of the question which was repeating itself over and over in her brain, Sheena was glad enough to

111

obey him. She felt the blood coming back into her feet; she felt the warmth of the fire, and a warm glow, too, inside herself from the brandy she had drunk.

There was no other light on in the room, which she now realised was Lucien Mansfield's own study. But instead of seeming austere and hard, as it had done the time she had been there before, in the firelight there was a cosiness and comfort. However, it did little to alleviate Sheena's fears.

"What shall I say? What shall I say?"

The soft massage of his hands seemed almost to be in time to the question. So was the crackle of the logs on the fire, the movement of the shadows as the flames threw his reflection, huge and somehow monstrous, upon the ceiling.

"What shall I say? What shall I say? What shall I say?"

The words almost became a prayer—and then she knew the answer. She must appear to be very stupid. She must somehow convince him, at all costs, that there had been nothing sinister in her motive in coming downstairs at this time of night.

It was not for herself she lied, but for Uncle Patrick. His very life might be in danger because of some carelessly spoken word.

"I am . . . sorry to be so stupid. . . ."

"Do you often faint?" Lucien Mansfield asked.

He still held one of her tiny feet in his big hands. Because he was smiling she found herself—despite the fluttering in her breast and the feeling that her throat was closing on every word she uttered—smiling back at him.

"I think the last time was in church."

"I always fainted in church when I was at school. It is as good an excuse as any of getting out of a boring sermon."

"This was different," Sheena said. "I was so terrified when I saw what . . . what you carried in your hand."

"I thought you were a burglar."

Sheena opened her eyes a little wider.

"I don't imagine that burglars would want to investigate the library when there are Madame's wonderful

112

jewels upstairs. I was . . . seeking nothing more valuable . . . than a book."

She forced her eyes to meet his as she spoke. It was an effort which cost her every ounce of resolution. Then, as she tried to read the expression in them and felt the penetrating scrutiny that she feared more than anything else, a falling log brought her a reprieve. It was quite natural to turn her face towards the fire and she hoped that the leaping flames would not reveal too closely the colour rising slowly and almost painfully into her cheeks.

"A book?" Lucien Mansfield questioned quietly.

"Yes, something to read," Sheena answered. "I couldn't sleep; and do you realise there are no books in the Nursery except, of course, the children's? I have read nothing since I have been here."

"But, how remiss!" Lucien Mansfield exclaimed. "I can understand what it must be like to have to sit alone for long hours with nothing to occupy your mind."

"Tonight I could bear it no longer," Sheena said. "So I came downstairs, thinking I would take one from the library. Is . . . is that forbidden?"

"Of course not," Lucien Mansfield answered. "But I'm afraid you will find the books in this library very dull. They are most concerned with the history of Mariposa or with international law and politics. I must introduce you to my own bookcases. I think you are more likely to discover what you need there."

He waved his hand a little vaguely towards the darkness at the far end of the room.

"Not tonight," Sheena said quickly.

Having told her lie she suddenly felt an absolute revulsion at having to carry it further.

"No, not tonight," he replied gently.

He put her slippers back on her now warm feet, and instantly Sheena sat up.

"I must go back to bed."

"But, why?" he asked. "You can't sleep and I very seldom go to bed until far later than this."

"Why are you so late?" Sheena asked.

"Because usually I am working," Lucien replied. "You see, in the daytime there are so many calls on my time. The Ambassador wants me; I have to escort Madame Pelayo; I have the secretaries to instruct—in fact there are a hundred and one things which require my attention and which fill the hours when other people are about. It is only at night, when I can get the place to myself and when nobody interrupts me, that I can get down to really serious work."

"But don't you get very tired?" Sheena asked. "When do you sleep?"

"Like many politicians, I have the virtue of being able to take a cat-nap," he answered. "Besides, I do go to bed eventually, and nobody, as you must know, rises very early in this household."

"I . . . ought to go now." She hesitated. . . .

He shook his head, and pulling a cushion from the chair behind him set it down on the hearth-rug and leant his elbow on it.

It was strange, she thought, to be looking down at him. Usually he seemed so tall, so severe, so unapproachable. But now, in the firelight as he lay sprawled at her feet, he seemed quite an ordinary person— someone to whom in other circumstances she would have wanted to talk. Impulsively, and perhaps because the brandy was making her feel braver than she might have been without it, she said:

"Tell me about yourself."

"What do you want to know?" he asked. "I am thirty-two, unmarried and very interested in my job."

"I have never met anyone quite like you before."

"I wonder if that's a compliment," he smiled. "I have a feeling that you haven't met very many people."

"Why do you think that?" Sheena asked curiously.

"Just an idea I have," he replied evasively. "But you have asked me about myself, so I will answer your question. As I told you that first day you arrived, my mother was a Mariposan. From her I have inherited great, vast tracts of undeveloped land. But it is very poor. The people who live on it have a hard time to scratch a living. Yet it is so beautiful! One could hardly bear to change it.

"I should like to show you the pampas, when the grass is filled with every coloured flower and the birds and butterflies which fly above it are so vivid that they seem almost like creatures from another world. Sometimes one will see ostriches moving in the distance or hear the deep-throated growl of a puma on the slopes of the mountains, which, on the frontiers, reach high towards the sky."

"It sounds wonderful!" Sheena exclaimed. "Why don't you live there? How can you bear to come away?"

"I am here because I believe I am working in the best interests of my people and of the country to which I owe half my allegiance. The other half of me is very British!"

Sheena smiled at that.

"When I first saw you I thought you were English," she said. "And then a little later I wondered how I could have thought so."

"My father tried very hard to make me a typical chip of the old block," Lucien smiled. "Harrow and Cambridge made a further effort. It is sad to think that they have all failed in one particular. Although my loyalties and my admiration lie in Britain, my heart has been captured for all time by Mariposa."

"Tell me more about it," Sheena asked. And like a child hearing a fairy story she sat absorbed while he spoke to her of the country he loved.

He told her about the old buildings and fortifications that had been left by the Spanish conquerors; of the gauchos with their silver embossed harnesses and saddles, and of the Indians with the remnants of long-forgotten crafts and their strange tribal customs.

He spoke of fiestas under the summer sky and fandangos danced as only those who have Spanish blood in their veins can dance them; of strange wines made from the local grapes; and of maté, the tea which every South American drinks from a gourd.

"How I would love to go there!" Sheena said at length, when Lucien's voice fell silent.

She had no idea how lovely she looked as she bent forward in the light of the flames. Her lips were parted as if his words had excited her, and her eyes were wide and full of the dreams and fantasies which he had conjured up for her delight.

"Perhaps one day you will," he answered.

"How wonderful that would be! But if the Ambas-

115

sador and Madame Pelayo were returning home, they might not require an English governess."

Even as she spoke she remembered that by the time the Pelayos were ready to go away her task at the Embassy might be finished. Even as she had been sent to Paris at a moment's notice by Uncle Patrick and his strange friends, so she might be recalled—her usefulness finished, or in disgrace because she had failed in a mission she did not understand.

It was then she realised that she didn't want to go away. She wanted to stay in this strange, colourful world, where the unexpected seemed to happen, so that even moments of terror could change into minutes of delight!

"I ought to go upstairs," she said in a low voice—and yet she did not move.

"It would have been a pity to waste the loveliness of that blue dressing-gown of yours only on an empty library," Lucien Mansfield said.

She fancied there was something dry in his voice.

"You don't think that I expected to see you?" Sheena asked innocently.

He smiled at that.

"No, I am quite sure you didn't expect to see me," he said.

She felt her eyes drop; then, moving forward on to the edge of her chair, she said:

"Thank you for being so kind."

"Have I been kind? I think in reality I have been selfish," he answered. "I, too, feel lonely at times!"

"You feel lonely?" Sheena asked. "That, surely, is impossible."

"Not really," he replied. "You see, in the daytime I am always having to think of other people. I'm not complaining—that is my job, as I see it. But tonight you have let me be selfish and I have talked exclusively about myself. Now it is your turn."

"But I ought to go."

"Wouldn't that be unfair?" he asked. "Conversations, you know, should never be one-sided."

"What is there to tell?" Sheena asked. "My life has been very dull, very uneventful."

"And yet you, too, must have found a place in the world that you loved—your home perhaps?"

"Yes! My home where I lived as a child."

Even as she spoke of it she saw the little house standing on the cliffs; the rollers from the Atlantic breaking on the beach below. There could be no harm in telling him of it. After all, she had confessed to living in Ireland when she was young, and what more natural than that one's affections should be centred in childhood's memories, in childhood's pleasures?

Not realising how expressive her face was, she talked. She told him of how her father and mother had been drowned and how she had lived on, for some years at any rate, in the house on the cliffs with old Marie, her mother's French maid.

"There is no colour in the world like the green of Ireland," she said. "And the strange smell of it after the rain; the sweet tang of the sea and the sound of the gulls swirling around the cliffs. Mariposa may be beautiful to you, but there is no place in Heaven or earth as lovely as Ireland is to me."

"You still call it Ireland?" Lucien asked.

"Yes, of course!" Sheena replied. "I hate the name of Eire, and Uncle Patrick always said . . ."

She stopped suddenly. Why, oh why could she not keep her mouth shut? Here she was quoting Patrick O'Donovan again—the uncle she was not supposed to have seen for many years.

"And what did Uncle Patrick say?" Lucien prompted.

"It was years ago when I was a child. He used to come and stay with us occasionally, and I remember him saying: 'Irish I was born, Irish I was bred; in Ireland I have lived, and I am not calling what is my bones and blood by any other name to please them damned politicians.' "

Lucien laughed.

"It sounds just like an Irishman to me," he said. "I think your Uncle Patrick was the original Irishman who, arriving home, said: 'What's the Government? I'm agin it!' "

Sheena laughed. Suddenly all sense of danger had left her. Perhaps it was the manner in which Lucien had taken her reference to Uncle Patrick. Or perhaps it was because it was difficult to feel afraid of him when he was lying at her feet, when he had held her entranced by the stories of Mariposa, when it was so easy to tell him things and to watch him smile at her so that his eyes were no longer frightening.

"I think I should have known anywhere that you were an only child," he said, surprisingly.

"What do you mean by that?"

"I was one, too," he said. "And I think perhaps we have something in common which makes us recognise each other, even in a crowd. A kind of freemasonry amongst those who make companions and playmates out of their surroundings and the elements because they have no other children to play with."

Sheena bent forward.

"Did you invent another child with whom you played and had exciting adventures?" she enquired.

"But, of course!" Lucien answered. "Mine was a boy a little bigger than myself who was tremendously brave and tremendously tough. He was called Rupert—after Rupert of Henzau."

"And mine was a little girl who would do all the things I couldn't do," Sheena said. "She could fly; she could swim under water for literally hours on end; she could sing like an angel and talk with the leprechauns."

"I wonder what has happened to them now?" Lucien asked.

"I think they have gone to the Never-Never Land to wait until we need them again."

"If we ever do."

"But we will! We were lonely as children, perhaps we will be lonely all our lives," Sheena sighed.

"Not if we find someone who is looking for us, even as we are looking for them," Lucien said.

"I don't think I understand," Sheena frowned.

"I think you do," he answered. "We invented those dream children because we felt not only lonely, but incomplete. Half of us was missing, and that is what men and women all the world over are trying to discover—when they have time to think of it—the other half of themselves!"

"I am sure that is an impossible dream," Sheena said.

"Then, you don't believe in love?"

"Of course I believe in it. It is only that I don't think I know very much about it."

She felt, as she spoke, as if some magnetism in him leapt towards her. She felt a strange, almost enchanted feeling that if she looked into his eyes at that moment she would find something that she had been seeking all her life.

And then, even as a strange sensation seemed to tingle at her very fingertips, she felt afraid and knew she must run away. Swiftly she got to her feet.

"Now I really must go. I shall be so tired in the morning that Madi and Pedro will be taught their English lesson upside down."

As if he knew he could no longer hold her, he rose slowly to his feet.

"I have enjoyed our talk," he said. "Will you tell me something quite honestly? Have you enjoyed it too?"

"But, of course I have!" Sheena answered.

"And you would like to talk to me again?"

"But, naturally. Oh, please, you have been so kind. I don't know quite how to thank you."

"There is no need to do that," he answered. "But I was wondering if it wouldn't be nice to meet again very shortly. There is so much I want to hear about Ireland and your dream friend who could talk with the leprechauns."

"I almost believed I could do it myself at one time," Sheena dimpled at him.

"You must tell me about that, too," he said. "Will you dine with me tomorrow night?"

For a moment Sheena felt she could not have heard him aright.

"But . . . but how can I?" she asked, at length. "I . . . I can't go out until next week."

"But, of course you can," he answered. "Wasn't it explained to you when you came that you could go out any evening that you wished after the children were in bed? It was an arrangement we made for Miss Robinson, whose sister was working here in Paris as a secretary with the United Nations. Jeanne will always listen for the children if you ask her to, although I understand that she expects a small *pourboire* now and then. But don't worry about that; I will see to all details of

119

that sort. So long as you say that you will give me the honour of being my guest."

"I would love it," Sheena said. "But . . . what would Madame Pelayo . . ."

"The Ambassador and Madame Pelayo are both dining out tomorrow night and going on to a Ball," Lucien replied. "That is why I shall be free. Will you accept my invitation?"

"If you are quite certain you want me."

"I shouldn't ask you otherwise, and I am quite certain."

"Then thank you very much!"

She didn't know why, but she suddenly felt shyer than she had ever felt before with him. Perhaps it was because they were standing so near to each other and because now that he was on his feet again he towered above her. She thought how very easily he had carried her from the library here. Because she was so small and he was so tall, how simple it would be at any time for him to carry her anywhere! With a sudden sense of urgency, she turned towards the door.

"I must go."

Even as she went she was aware that she was running away from something stronger, something more virile than her own shyness of him. It was as though, in his very silence, he was saying something to her which, if she cared to listen, she could understand, yet was afraid to hear.

"Good night!"

She actually turned the handle of the door before he moved, and then, in two or three strides, he was across the room to stand beside her.

"I will turn on the lights," he said in a low voice.

"No, no," she answered. "Someone might hear. I will use my torch—Pedro's torch."

She tried to smile up at him; but now, because they were away from the fire, she could not see the expression on his face. She was only conscious that he was very near her; that she had only to reach out her hand to touch him. And then, quickly and yet almost silently, she had moved across the hall and was hurrying up the stairs.

Only as she reached the Nursery landing—a little

breathless—did she look back over her shoulder, stand still and listen. There was nothing to be seen in the darkness, nothing to hear but, once again, the beating of her own heart.

She had come back to the place where she had stood an hour ago—or was it longer? She had no idea how much time had passed since she had crept downstairs to look for the contract which she had believed would tell her about Uncle Patrick's friends. Had Lucien believed her story that she had entered the library to look for a book? He must have believed it, she thought, or he would not have been so kind, so very, very kind, to her.

As she stood there on the landing, she felt a sudden sense of regret that she had left him. Why had she come away? Why had she not stayed to go on talking? Almost as though she was afraid of the answer, she hurried into her bedroom.

She had been certain that when she got back to bed she would not sleep. Yet, surprisingly, as soon as her head touched the pillow she fell into a dreamless slumber, and awoke with a start when the house-maid came in with her early morning tea.

When she was fully awake she remembered there was a busy day ahead of them. Madame Pelayo had made an appointment for the children to be photographed at ten o'clock. A car was to take them there and afterwards they had to fit their spring coats at a shop in the *Rue St. Honoré*.

There was a luncheon party at the Embassy, Sheena learned later, which meant that the meal in the Nursery would be half an hour earlier than the usual time at which they went downstairs. For a moment Sheena felt disappointed. She had wanted, although she would hardly admit it to herself, to see Lucien Mansfield again.

Then she remembered that she was dining with him that evening. She felt herself suddenly glow at the thought. It was because she was going out in Paris, she thought. She was going to be taken out to dinner by a man—a thing she had never thought would happen. And yet at the same time she could not help remembering how kind and understanding he had been.

She wondered, now it was daylight, how she had

ever dared to tell him so much about Ireland and about her own secret and childish dreams. She had never thought she would talk to anyone about such things, and yet he had talked to her with a truth and sincerity which she had never expected from any man—and least of all from him.

She was in the Nursery, while the children were having their after-luncheon rest, when the door opened and the *Vicomte* came quickly into the room.

"I can't stay for a moment," he said. "I only slipped up here while my sister went to put her hat on. How are you, my most entrancing little Sheena?"

He had been talking as he came across the room, and now, as he reached her, he took both her hands in his and lifted them to his lips. It was the first time Sheena had seen him alone since he had kissed her. But now, as the colour came flooding into her face, she tried to snatch her hands away.

"You bewitch me," he said. "I find myself thinking of you all the time. I must see you—and alone."

"You know that is impossible," Sheena said.

"Nothing is impossible," he replied. "When is your day off?"

"Not until next Wednesday," she said.

"I will arrange something for then. We will take my car and go right out of Paris into the country. I know a little inn where we can have good food and a quiet, very happy time together—if you will be kind to me."

There was something in the way he said the quite simple words which told Sheena there was a depth of meaning behind them. She took her hands from his and drawing herself up said, with a touch of pride that he had never before heard in her voice:

"If you mean what I think you mean, *Monsieur,* I should be insulted."

"But you couldn't possibly be insulted by knowing that I love you," Henri de Cormeille said. "Oh, Sheena, Sheena! Why must you be so cruel to me? So cold, so unresponsive. Do you think that after I have kissed you it is possible for me either to forget you or to live without you?"

"I think, *Monsieur,* that you had better go quickly,"

122

Sheena said. "Madame does not take long to put on her hat and if she finds you here she will be very angry."

"But I have got to see you," the *Vicomte* insisted, with almost a note of desperation in his voice. "I will try and slip up before dinner, but I have got to go to this party tonight and it may be difficult."

"Do not risk it, *Monsieur*," Sheena cautioned. "And now go quickly."

"I suppose I must," he said reluctantly. "But before I go . . ."

He reached out towards her, but she was too quick for him. She put the table between herself and him and, when he held out his arms, she said:

"Hurry, *Monsieur*! Hurry! Madame will be very annoyed."

"And they say English women do not know how to flirt!" the *Vicomte* exclaimed, throwing his arms wide in a gesture of despair. But he hurried towards the door, blowing Sheena a kiss before he disappeared.

Sheena sat down again and realised, almost in surprise, that she was relieved that he had gone. She did not know why, but she thought there was something almost flamboyantly theatrical in the way he spoke and his extravagant gestures. Even as she decided this, she remembered how, almost against her will, she had been fascinated by him—that time he had taken her driving in the *Bois,* the evening he had come to the Nursery after dinner.

"Perhaps I am growing up," she told herself. But found herself thinking, as she had already thought a hundred times, how much she was looking forward to this evening. To go out in Paris at night would be an adventure in itself; to dine at a restaurant; to drive home in a car or a taxi, when the lights were lit and the moon was rising high in the sky. That would be an experience almost too exciting to contemplate. And perhaps, too, she admitted to herself, some of her excited anticipation was because of the man who was taking her out.

She could hardly remember that only thirty-six hours ago she had been so afraid of Lucien Mansfield that she had almost hated him. Last night he had been so different. Perhaps in the daylight she would have been disillusioned once again. Tonight he might be as he had been in the firelight—approachable and friendly.

The hours seemed to speed by on winged feet.

"You are happy, Lawie, aren't you?" Madi asked her during the afternoon when she was taking them for a walk.

"What makes you think that?" Sheena asked.

"You are smiling to yourself and sometimes you hum a little tune," Madi replied.

She was a perceptive child and very little escaped her.

"Yes, I am happy!" Sheena admitted. "It is because I am in Paris and because you have both been so good today."

The children digested this for a moment or two and then Pedro asked:

"Becawse I'se good does it make you happy, Lawie?"

"Yes, of course," Sheena answered. "Bad people always create unhappiness."

"We like you, Lawie, because you are so nice to us," Madi said simply. "And so we want to be good. Miss Robinson didn't like us at all."

"Oh, I am sure that isn't true," Sheena said hastily.

"Yes, it is true," Madi insisted. "She used to say: 'Oh, be quiet, you little nuisances,' and sometimes she would smack us when we hadn't done anything naughty at all."

"Well, I should forget all about her," Sheena advised. "I am here now and I will try not to smack you for no reason at all."

"But you never smack us," Pedro remarked, his fat, baby face creased in laughter.

"Nor I do," Sheena teased. "I must have forgotten."

"We love you very much, Lawie," Madi told her in all seriousness. "You won't go away and leave us, will you?"

"Not if I can help it," Sheena said.

"Then Uncle Henri mustn't come to the Nursery," Madi said solemnly. "That's what makes Mamma very angry."

Sheena drew in a deep breath. How much these children knew, and what a mistake it was that they should be involved so early in the intrigues and tangles of grown-up love affairs.

"You are right, Madi," she said. "We mustn't have Uncle Henri in the Nursery. You will see him when you are downstairs."

It was almost as if she made a vow to herself, because she was seeing everything through new eyes. What had seemed exciting and adventurous because the *Vicomte* was the first man who had ever made love to her now seemed sordid and rather cheap. She felt ashamed of herself because she had allowed him, if only by not being more firm at the beginning of their acquaintance, to kiss her lips.

That first kiss, in retrospect, seemed shaming. It had not meant what a kiss should mean, Sheena thought. It did not come up to those dreams that she had dreamed alone. By herself, on the empty sands or when she had been lying half asleep in her little, narrow bed, she had imagined—as so many young girls do—that Prince Charming had come into her life and was about to ask her to be his wife. She knew now that Henri de Cormeille had had no intention of marrying her, any more than he had wished to marry poor, foolish, lovesick Miss Robinson. He was just amusing himself, finding her amusing because her youth and innocence appealed to his jaded taste.

"What a fool I have been," Sheena thought suddenly, and felt that she had lowered herself in her own estimation. Then her chin went up in a little gesture which Patrick O'Donovan would have recognised.

"Never, never again!" she promised herself—and the children's footsteps, tapping along on the pavement, echoed the decision of her heart.

Never, never again!

Eight

As Sheena dressed for dinner that evening she felt a sense of rising excitement at the thought of what lay ahead. She had deliberately lingered over putting the children to bed—taking longer than usual to tuck them up, hear their prayers and tell them a good-night story.

Because her whole instinct was to hurry towards the moment when she would be free to go out into the night of Paris, she forced herself to move and speak slowly, to give both Madi and Pedro more than their usual share of affection.

She had long ago decided that although the children received every luxury and all possible care, they lacked the spontaneous, warm emotion which she herself had seen so often in poorer Irish homes and envied with all her heart.

She had watched the children of the fishermen run to greet their fathers when they came home after a long night at sea; she had seen mothers waiting outside School until their children came out at four o'clock in the afternoon; and often she had been in a croft when a child came in with a bleeding knee or hurt arm, and had heard its instinctive cry for its mother and seen the love and sympathy it received.

That was family love; that was the day-to-day affection which meant not only unity, but a security which a child cannot find from anyone except its own parents.

Madi and Pedro loved their mother and there was no doubt that Madame Pelayo was very fond of her children. But she never did anything for them. She was never there if they needed her because they were hurt or unhappy. They saw her at specified times of the day and would no more have thought of calling out for her at night than they would have considered jumping out of the bedroom window.

"I am going out this evening," Sheena told the children last thing. "Jeanne will be sitting in the Nursery, and if you want her you have only got to call."

"We shan't want her," Madi answered. "We don't like Jeanne much, do we, Pedro?"

"I think that's unkind," Sheena said quickly. "Jeanne's very fond of you both. She does her best to be kind."

"She's not unkind to us," Madi said. "It's only that it's much more fun being with you, Lawie."

She put up her little thin arms suddenly and pulled Sheena's face down to hers.

"Shall I tell you a secret?" she asked.

"I love secrets," Sheena answered.

Madi put her small mouth near to Sheena's ear.

"Pedro and I love you more than anyone else in the world," she whispered.

"Except your Mamma," Sheena said quickly.

There was a moment's pause.

"Except Mamma," Madi repeated dutifully, without conviction.

"And now I will tell you a secret," Sheena said.

"Me too! Me too!" Pedro shouted.

"Yes, you too," Sheena answered, and helped him clamber over the bed until he sat beside Madi.

"Now tell us," both the children cried.

Sheena pressed their heads close together, then whispered:

"I love you more than any other children I have ever looked after before."

There were shrieks of joy at this, and when finally she had got them quiet and tucked into bed, Sheena stood at the door with her finger on the switch.

"Good night and God bless you," she said.

"Good night, Lawie," the children answered sleepily.

Then at last she was free to close the door and go to her room.

She only had a little over half an hour left in which to have her bath and change her dress. She had already decided what she was going to wear, having learned from watching Madame Pelayo that only on big and formal occasions do French women dine out in full evening dress. A short, smart cocktail gown was what was needed for this evening, and a suspicion of a hat to go with it.

Sheena felt anxious that she might not wear the dress she had chosen in the right way or that the hat which Fifi must have meant to go with it did not suit her. But her fears were groundless.

The dress was black and yet somehow it enhanced her youth with clever little touches of white chiffon at the neck. The transparency over the shoulders made her unveiled skin even whiter in contrast, and the hat was nothing more nor less than a halo of tiny black and white rose-buds set on the back of her head and somehow contriving to make her look absurdly like a small girl going to a party for the first time.

"And that is exactly what I am doing," Sheena told herself. Never in the whole of her life had she dined alone with a man—with the exception of Uncle Patrick. She had been to what might be called dinner parties during race week in Dublin and when they had been in Cork and Belfast—but what strange parties they had been!

Uncle Patrick would collect some of his friends on the racecourse or afterwards when the races were over, and they had gone to an inn for a drink. And when they had all had as much as was good for them, he would remember that Sheena would be hungry, and they would troop off to the nearest cheap restaurant or public house which served meals, and call for chops or sausages and mash and sit drinking and smoking and cracking jokes with each other—sometimes until the early hours of the morning.

Sheena had never felt at her ease with these strange men whom Patrick O'Donovan liked and who were obviously on easy and affectionate terms with him. They would pay her heavy-handed compliments when she first appeared and then all too quickly they would forget about her, intent on swapping stories about horses and dogs or speculating on a chance they had of making some money if it wasn't for the Police and the fact that Ireland was going to the devil one way and another.

Each party of this sort always seemed to be a replica of the others, and sometimes Sheena felt that she could almost repeat the conversation word for word before it was said. When she grew older, she grew cunning at avoiding the long boredom of such evenings and the aching head which she usually got through the thick smoke and the heat. When she had eaten, she would whisper to Uncle Patrick that she was tired and thought she would be getting back to the hotel—or wherever they were staying.

"Sure, slip away, Mavourneen," he would say. "And I will be following you in a wee bitty. I'll not be long, I promise you that."

Sheena would smile, knowing only too well what his promises were worth. Sometimes she would hear him come up the stairs in the small hours of the morning, singing to himself or lurching unsteadily against the banisters.

More than once she had gone into his room a little while later, to find him lying fully dressed on his bed and in a sound sleep. Then she would slip off his shoes and cover him with a blanket, knowing that in the morning he would be full of apologies and plausible explanations of what had happened to him.

Those had been Uncle Patrick's parties—this was very different! This was her own party; the first she had ever had. Even as she saw her eyes shining back from her reflection in the mirror she told herself to be careful. She was a married woman of twenty-eight; a widow who would have dined with many men before, and especially with her husband.

"I must not appear in the least excited," she thought. She picked up the little velvet wrap which went over her dress, put a handkerchief and a vanity case into a handbag which must have cost a small fortune when it was new, and chose a pair of black gloves which Fifi had given her because they had a small darn in one of the fingers. No-one would have noticed Anastasia's fairy-like stitches, but Fifi had declared that she could never wear them again.

Sheena gave a sigh of ecstasy as she thought of all the wonderful things that had become hers because Fifi was either tired of them or because they had some infinitesimal thing wrong with them—a spot of coffee the size of a shilling on the blue wrapper; a tear in an afternoon dress of fine lace; a small imperceptible flaw in a dress of fine wool. How glad she was of all these blemishes and Fifi's displeasure at them, because they had given her a wardrobe in which she was able to feel not only smart, but almost as if she were a new person in herself.

There was no doubt that clothes meant far more to a woman than the mere fact that they covered her nakedness. Sheena had already discovered that they gave her confidence, courage, faith in her own attractions, and perhaps, she thought suddenly, also a touch of coquetry. In her old, shabby tweed suit she would never have dared to keep the redoubtable Colonel Mansfield waiting. Because of what she saw reflected in the mirror she deliberately forced herself to stay in her bedroom until five minutes past the time when he had told her he would be waiting.

When slowly she came down the stairs, the full skirt of her dress rustling a little from the silk petticoats beneath it, her head held high, the minute halo of black and white rosebuds framing her face, he was standing in the hall. She knew that he was watching her.

For the first time since she had known him she was not afraid of being watched. Tonight she was not afraid of being seen by any man, or with any man. Because of her clothes she could have gone to one of those smart receptions that were so much a part of Madame Pelayo's life, and would not have appeared out of place.

"I am proud of myself," Sheena thought, with a little inward chuckle at her own vanity; and then she had reached the hall and was looking up at him.

"I had begun to think you had forgotten our dinner engagement," he said.

"I was not likely to do that," Sheena answered. "I am looking forward to it very much."

"To the dinner?" he enquired.

"But of course," she answered, and there was a little smile on her lips as she walked ahead of him towards the taxi.

"I am learning," she thought. "Learning to flirt, to be at ease, to talk nonsense with an air of seriousness—and not to be serious unnecessarily."

Lucien got into the taxi beside her.

"I am going to take you to what I think is one of the most charming restaurants in all Paris," he said. "It is called the *Tour d'Argent.*"

"The Tower of Silver," Sheena translated. "What a lovely name!"

"It is rather a charming place," Lucien said. "At least I hope you will think so."

There was no doubt that it was charming—perhaps, indeed, that in itself was an understatement. High up on the sixth floor of an old building on the banks of the Seine, a young man had created a restaurant where the food was superlative and the view unique.

Sheena, sitting at a table at what was called "the window," but which was, in reality, a wall of glass encompassing two sides of the room, saw below her the Seine and opposite—floodlit so that its beauty was revealed in all its glory—*Notre-Dame.* There was something almost breathtaking about the great and ancient Cathedral, in which so much of the history of France had been written and carved, silhouetted now against the dark, star-strewn sky and reflected in the darkness of the moving river at its feet.

"It is lovely! Quite lovely!" Sheena told Lucien.

"I thought you would think so," he answered, his eyes on her face. And then, as the waiter drew her attention to the enormous menu, he asked: "Would you like me to choose for you?"

"Oh, please do," Sheena said, with a sense of relief. She had no idea what the attractive names of the dishes implied and she was not even certain how much or how little it would be correct for her to order.

Lucien chose the dinner slowly with several discussions with the *maître d'hôtel;* and then he took the

131

wine list from another waiter and, interrupting Sheena's contemplation of the river, asked:

"What would you like to drink?"

"I . . . I don't know," she replied. "What do you suggest?"

"I will order you the wine of the country," he said.

He said no more but when the waiter brought a bottle of champagne for his inspection Sheena looked a little apprehensive.

"You like champagne?" he asked.

She hesitated before she replied—not liking to admit that she had only drunk it twice in her life—once at a wedding in Dublin and another time when Uncle Patrick had heard that he had drawn a ticket in a lottery. It had not been a very successful ticket and the champagne in which he had drunk to his own success had cost him nearly as much as he ultimately received. Sheena remembered thinking at both times that champagne as a drink was wildly over-rated and that if this was the beverage people talked so much about she would much rather have had a glass of ginger ale.

She had no sooner tasted some of the golden liquid that was poured into her glass than she knew that the champagne which Uncle Patrick had bought in the local inn and that which she had sipped at the wedding of one of his trainer friends bore no resemblance to what she was drinking now.

"Is it all right?" Lucien asked.

Sheena wanted to tell him that it tasted like nectar, but she remembered that she must appear blasé and used to such expensive things, and so she merely nodded.

"It is very nice," she said. "I heard someone say once that one should always drink the wine of the country one was in, and I think it is a good idea."

"You sound very grown-up," he said.

She flushed because she felt he must have read her thoughts.

"I am grown-up," she protested.

"I don't believe it," he answered. "I think you are the feminine equivalent of Peter Pan. You are therefore ageless! Or else you are an Easter chicken that has just hatched out of the egg."

"It doesn't sound very complimentary," Sheena smiled.

"Do you want me to be complimentary?" Lucien asked.

There was something in the expression on his face which made her say quickly:

"No, I hate compliments. Men only say things that are insincere and exaggerated because they think women want to listen to such nonsense."

"Who told you that?" Lucien asked. "Actually it is not true. But we won't call them compliments then; shall I tell you the truth?"

"Yes, of course," Sheena answered, a little wonderingly.

"Then the truth is that I am almost afraid to talk to you lest, like your Irish leprechauns, you vanish away."

"If you don't want a leprechaun to vanish, you have to catch him quickly and hold him over water; then he can't escape and has to grant you anything you choose."

"Give me your hand," Lucien said.

Without thinking, but instinctively obedient, Sheena put her small hand in his big one. His fingers closed over it—warm and strong—and instantly she remembered how she had been conscious of his strength when he carried her from the Ambassador's library into his own room after she had fainted. And now he said with a little smile:

"I am holding on to you and, to all intents and purposes, you are over water. Do I get my wish?"

"What is your wish?" Sheena asked.

She suddenly found it hard to raise her eyes to his. Her eyelashes fluttered against her cheeks and she was aware that her breath was coming more quickly between her parted lips.

"My wish is only that you should be happy," he said very softly.

"But, I am happy," Sheena answered.

Even as she said the words she remembered Uncle Patrick. Was it disloyal of her, she wondered, to be enjoying herself so much when he might be in trouble? In the power of those terrible men; being blackmailed or threatened; and perhaps, at this very moment, distressed because she had not been as helpful as she might have been. She thought of what had been said at luncheon only yesterday with reference to the contact. She had done her best to find out more. Was it her fault that Lucien Mansfield had come into the room before she had time to inspect the papers on the Ambassador's desk?

"What are you thinking about?" he interrupted and she started because for the moment she had forgotten that she was there, her hand held in his.

"I think I was afraid because I boasted that I was happy," Sheena said.

"You were made for happiness," he answered. "No-one could look as you look and not draw happiness to her."

"Are you paying compliments to me or to my clothes?" Sheena asked.

It was as if deliberately she tried to break the spell which his soft voice and his words were casting over her. She made an effort to take her hand from his, but he would not release her fingers.

"I know exactly what you are thinking," he said. "You are thinking that I did not say this to you the day you arrived. But now I will swear to you, on the Bible if necessary, that I was staggered by your loveliness from the moment I found you at the *Gare du Nord*."

"You certainly didn't show you were staggered," Sheena said. "You looked very severe. I was frightened of you!"

"There were reasons," he said, "why I was not pleased at your appearance—even while I could not help but acknowledge to myself that you were one of the loveliest people I had ever seen."

She knew without his saying more that the reason he had been displeased was because an attractive governess meant trouble with Henri de Cormeille. She did not say so, but for a moment there was a little silence and then the waiter brought another course and Lucien relinquished her hand. When they had started to eat and more wine had been poured into their glasses, he said:

"I wonder why women, particularly English women, think that clothes must mean as much to a man as they do to them?"

"I think it is because nice clothes make us feel different in ourselves," Sheena answered. "When one is shy and nervous and perhaps afraid, the mere fact that one knows one looks one's best is half the battle."

"You talk as though you were always fighting something," Lucien said. "I feel that is true. I have felt it ever since you arrived."

Sheena said nothing and after a moment he asked: "Why are you afraid of me?"

It was almost impossible for Sheena to lie, to tell him that she was not afraid, which she knew would be the wisest thing to do. Instead she answered simply:

"Because you are a very frightening person."

"Only, I think, if someone has something to hide, or a guilty conscience," Lucien remarked.

"Perhaps I have got both," Sheena laughed.

She managed to make the words sound light, but even to herself she knew the danger of such a remark. She looked up as she spoke and thought there was a frown between Lucien's eyes—and then he laughed.

"I don't believe it," he said. "Your eyes are the most honest eyes I have ever seen in any woman's face. I don't believe that you could stoop to do anything that was dishonest or pretend anything that you did not feel."

The unexpectedness of his reply brought the blood rushing into Sheena's cheeks. And now it was impossible to look at him. She played with the stem of her wineglass.

"Isn't that asking too much of any woman?" she said at length in a low voice.

"Not of you," he replied.

"But how can you say that?" Sheena enquired. "You know nothing about me—nothing at all."

"You forget what the Comtesse de Beaufleur said about you before you arrived," Lucien answered. "She spoke in such glowing terms that one would have been a fool indeed to imagine that they could have been said of any but a very special person. And then, when I saw you, I knew that not only were they true but that there was so much more that had been left unsaid."

"There is an old Irish proverb," Sheena replied, "which says, 'Look in the horse's mouth for yourself.' It means, of course, that you shouldn't take anyone else's valuation or recommendation about a horse you are going to buy. I think, Colonel Mansfield, the same applies to people."

"Very well, I will judge for myself," Lucien answered. "And please, for tonight at any rate, can't we forget formality? I have called you Sheena in my mind for a long time. Won't you call me Lucien?"

"I think . . ." Sheena began, but he interrupted her.

"I know what you are going to say," he said. "But tonight let's forget tomorrow and the cares and responsibilities that are awaiting us at the Embassy. We will forget your position and mine, and the jobs we both have to do and the people we do them for. We will forget what the Comtesse de Beaufleur said and we will both look the horse in the mouth for ourselves. Is that a bargain?"

"A bargain," Sheena smiled.

"Very well then; we will begin at the beginning. There is no past, there is no future, there is just the present—tonight! And here we are, Sheena and Lucien of nowhere. We have met under the stars and have come together beside the river."

"It sounds like a fairy story," Sheena said. "It is not difficult to believe that we are living in one."

She turned her face to look out at the swift-flowing water.

"I think your nose is the most adorable thing I have ever dreamed of," Lucien said suddenly.

It was strange, Sheena thought to herself, how different compliments sounded when he said them than when she had listened to them from the young *Vicomte*. She had the feeling with Lucien that they were almost dragged from him; as if he said them because he could not help himself. Whereas with Henri de Cormeille they came so glibly, so easily to his lips that one almost knew it was from constant repetition, from having been educated, as it were, in the art of what to say to a woman.

"If I were an artist I would draw you as you look now," Lucien went on. "But I don't believe that even one of the great masters, whose paintings hang just over there in the *Louvre,* would do you justice. Perhaps Botticelli could have caught that air of innocence about

136

you; perhaps he, and only he, could have put on canvas that elusiveness, that delicacy, which yet, at the same time, is not fragility."

"You are making me feel shy," Sheena murmured.

"You look adorable when you are shy," he said. "I had forgotten that a woman could still blush. It must be your Irish blood, for it's an art that has long been lost —both in England and France."

"You are not to talk about it," Sheena said, putting her hands up to her cheeks in which the colour came and went.

"But I want to talk about it—and you," Lucien insisted. "Sheena, will you tell me something? Because I must know it. It is not that I am prying into your life, it is not that I want to embarrass you by anything I am saying. But there is one thing I must ask."

Sheena was suddenly still.

"What is it?" she enquired apprehensively.

"Have you ever been in love?"

Her eyes were held by his. She had never seen them so grey or so penetrating, she thought. Because of some strange current which seemed to run between them both, holding her spellbound, making her, for the moment, completely in his power, she had to tell the truth.

"No," she whispered. "No, I have never been in love."

She saw the expression of triumph in his face before his voice echoed it.

"I knew it," he said. "I was sure of it. Oh, my sweet! That has made me happier than anything I have ever heard before."

"But, why? . . . Why?" Sheena stammered.

"Because I want you to fall in love with me. I want to teach you about love. Don't you realise by now that I am already in love with you?"

His words seemed to squeeze the very breath from Sheena's body. She could hardly breathe. It was quite impossible to answer. Her eyes were on his face. She could not move; could only look at him.

"I love you, Sheena," he said. "I think I loved you from the first moment I saw you."

"No! No, you mustn't!"

It was a cry of desperation. Almost violently she

turned her face away from his, her hands in her lap clasped together.

"Why not?"

"There are reasons—very good reasons—why you must not."

"It is too late," he said. "I already love you—and now I am going to make you love me."

"No, you mustn't do that. I don't want . . . to love you."

"Are you sure of that?" he asked slowly.

"Quite sure," Sheena said vehemently. "I don't want to be in love with anyone. I can't be."

It was a cry from her very heart, as she thought of Uncle Patrick and the secrets which seemed to shadow her very life—the lies she had told and the trick by which she had gained entrance to the Embassy. How could she fall in love under such circumstances? And how little he knew, when he spoke of love, that he would turn from her in disgust if she once revealed the truth.

She half expected him to be angry at her outburst, but instead he was smiling tenderly.

"You are so young," he said. "Young and afraid. I think in your heart of hearts you already love me a little."

"But I don't," Sheena answered. "I promise you I don't. And you are not to make me. I don't want to be in love, I . . . I want . . . to be free. Free to go away if . . . I have to."

There was no mistaking her agitation. In answer he put both his hands across the table, inviting hers. After a moment's hesitation she did as he asked, letting her fingers rest on the palms of his hands, feeling the strange vibration come from them before he held them tight in his clasp.

"Listen, Sheena, my darling!" he said. "I promise you one thing. I will never do anything that you don't want me to do. I know you are frightened of me—I don't know why you should be, and yet you are. I can't help loving you; it is too late to prevent my doing that. But I won't even speak of it if you would rather not. I am only certain of one thing—the time will come

138

when the fire in my heart will ignite a flame in yours. I love you so much! Do you understand?"

She felt her agitation subside, ebb away from her. There was a feeling of security and strength about him which was irresistible.

"Thank you," she said after a moment.

Then, as he did not release her hands, she looked up into his eyes and once again was held spellbound. It was hard to know how she felt, to know what was happening to her. There was a magnetism about him which undoubtedly seemed to draw her so that her very will to resist was lost in a kind of whirlpool of emotions to which she could not put a name.

"How very sweet you are!" he said. And then her hands were free and she had a moment of regret because he had let her go.

Almost without her being aware of it they had come to the end of their dinner. Lucien paid the bill and almost automatically she rose to her feet.

"Now we must go back?" she asked.

"Not yet," he replied. "There is no hurry."

They went down to the ground floor in a lift. The porter was waiting and enquired whether he should call a taxi.

"Would you like to walk for a little way?" Lucien asked.

"I would love it," Sheena replied.

They stepped out on to the rough, stone road which ran beside the river; then they walked in silence, feeling the soft night air on their faces, overshadowed by the majesty of *Notre-Dame,* both aware that their hearts were saying things their ears could not hear.

There was a gap in the wall which bordered the river and through it Sheena could see a little jetty from which steps led down to the water's edge.

"Come and look closely at the Seine," Lucien suggested.

He held her arm as she picked her way carefully. Here they were out of reach of the lights and the jetty was not fenced in any way; it would have been easy to fall into the dark river lapping against its side.

It seemed to Sheena as if they had stepped from another world into one where there was only them-

139

selves—the traffic, the lights, the laughter, the people walking about the streets were all left behind. There was only silence and Lucien! It was as if they were both waiting for something. She looked out over the river and then, irresistibly, because he was willing it, she turned towards him.

Without really realising how it happened, she found herself in his arms. She felt her head go back against his shoulder, and he was looking down at her face.

"I love you!" he said. "I love you more than I believed it possible to love any woman. You have bewitched me and yet, at the same time, I want to worship you."

There was something in his voice which told her that the words came straight from his very heart and soul. She was still because if she had bewitched him, he, in his turn, had bewitched her. She knew now that she could not escape him, or herself; and then his mouth was on hers, seeking her lips, kissing her with a mixture of passion and tenderness which, for some reason she could not understand, made the tears start into her eyes.

"I love you! Oh, my darling, I love you so much!"

His voice was low and hoarse and now he was kissing her again—not wildly and irresponsibly with an uncontrollable passion as the *Vicomte* had done, but with a controlled desire, both gentle and possessive, which seemed to Sheena to draw her very soul from between her lips.

She felt the fire of passion rising within him, even though he kept it strictly under control. She felt, then, the flickering flame of which he had spoken kindle within herself and begin to burn its way through her whole body. She felt herself tingle and thrill; she felt her lips give him back kiss for kiss.

She knew then that she loved him. Loved him as she had never loved a man before in her life or had ever dreamed that she might do so. Her whole body responded to his and the love he was asking of her. They were in a magical world—a world of water and sky, of darkness and stars. A world where two people could find each other—and nothing could ever be the same again.

His arms seemed to hold her even closer to him, but still she wanted more. The touch of his lips made her tremble and yet it was not from fear. He raised his head and looked down at her.

"Oh, my God, how much I love you!" he said. "And that, my darling is the real Kiss of Paris!"

Nine

Sheena awoke with a feeling of happiness which made her spring out of bed long before she was called and fling open the wooden shutters of her window.

It was very early. The sky over Paris was still grey with the shadows of the night, and yet she felt as if everything was bathed in sunshine. Indeed, her eyes felt dazzled with the brilliance of her own joy, so that when a little while later the sun did break through it seemed somehow dim in comparison with her own emotions.

"I'm in love! I'm in love!"

The very birds singing in the trees outside seemed to chirp the words; and finally she ran to the mirror to see if her face had changed and if, indeed, she looked a very different person because of the alteration in her heart.

She knew now that this was what she had been waiting for all her life; what she had dreamed about sitting by the shore in Ireland; what, unconsciously, relentlessly, she had been seeking as she had travelled with Uncle Patrick to London and had tingled with a sense of adventure when she first reached Paris.

This was the fulfilment of all her desires, all her wishes, all her ambitions—to be in love and to be loved! What woman could ask more of life?

She thought again of Lucien's kisses last night by

the side of the Seine. She felt herself quiver and tremble with the wonder of them. It was strange how love could transform everything that one said and did, and how a kiss seemed to be something snatched from eternity! Something which made one realise how empty and desolate one had been before it happened.

Lucien had come into her life and all her loneliness was past. The long years when she had seemed to belong to nobody; when sometimes she had yearned, with an almost desperate feeling of loneliness, for a sense of belonging, of being part of a family, of having father or mother, sister or brother of her own to cling to! Now that yearning, too, was past. She had Lucien and asked nothing more of Heaven than that he should go on loving her.

Suddenly she asked herself what he could see in her; and then, as the sunshine crept further into the room, she raised her eyes to the sky and murmured a little prayer of gratitude and thanks.

"If I had never come here!" What lover has not murmured the word "if" and been tortured with the thought of how easily the loved one might have been missed? But she had come and Lucien loved her!

The morning seemed to speed by wrapped in dreams of happiness. And yet, looking at the clock every few minutes, Sheena was counting the hours, the minutes, the seconds, until she should see him again at luncheon time. It therefore came almost as a bombshell for her to learn, shortly after midday, that the children were to have their luncheon in the Nursery.

"Guests are expected," Jeanne told her. "And the chef is swearing fit to singe his beard because he wasn't given more notice."

"I don't mind," Madi said, who had been listening to the conversation. "I think it is just as much fun to have our lunch upstairs with Lawie."

Sheena smiled at the child and wished that she could agree whole-heartedly that it was more fun, as she would have done only too willingly a few days ago. Now, her sense of disappointment and a feeling almost of emptiness was, she told herself, out of all proportion to the small incident of not being able to go downstairs for luncheon.

And then, while she was feeling as if the sunshine had been blotted out by a dark cloud, the door opened and Lucien came into the Nursery. She felt her heart leap at the sight of him. But because she was so afraid of betraying to Jeanne and the children the thrill and the wild joy which ran through her because he was there, she turned her head away and deliberately forced herself to tidy away some lesson books that were spread about the table.

"Good morning, Mrs. Lawson!" Lucien said in his deep, serious voice.

"Good morning, Uncle Lucien!" the children cried, rushing towards him.

He picked Madi up and she flung her small arms round his neck, kissing him affectionately in the slightly coquettish manner which proclaimed that in a few years she would be an accomplished little flirt. Pedro clung to his hand, pulling him towards a parade of soldiers which he had arranged round his toy fort.

"Come and see my tholdiers, Uncle Lucien. They're forming fours like you told me you used to do in the Army."

Lucien allowed himself to be led towards the fort while Jeanne withdrew from the room. Then he looked at Sheena and said softly:

"Are you happy this morning?"

It was so much more than a simple question, and because where her love was concerned she was too honest and unsophisticated to pretend, Sheena told the truth.

"More happy than I believed it possible to be."

There was almost a breathlessness about her voice; and now her eyes, very blue between their dark lashes, met his grey ones. He smiled at that and she felt almost as if he held her in his arms again.

"Do you see my tholdiers?" Pedro asked. "Are they doing the wight thing?"

"Quite right," Lucien said inaccurately. "And now I have come to tell you children something very exciting."

"Exciting?" Madi asked.

"Yes," Lucien replied. "This afternoon you are going to have tea with your grandmother."

"Oh, that is exciting," Madi cried. "I love Grand-mamma. She has such lovely things in her house and always has presents for us."

"I like going to Grandmamma, too," Pedro said.

"I know that," Lucien replied. "And you will have to introduce Mrs. Lawson to her, because they have never met."

"Do you think Grandmamma will like Lawie?" Madi asked reflectively, putting her head on one side. "She didn't like Miss Robinson."

"How do you know that?" Lucien asked.

"It was just the way she spoke to her," Madi replied. "And once when Miss Robinson had gone out of the room Grandmamma turned to Mamma and said in English: 'She is an f-double-o-l, that one.' She thought we didn't understand, but I asked Daddy what f-double-o-l spelt and he said it spelt fool. So then I knew what Grandmamma felt about Miss Robinson."

"You are too sharp, that is what's the matter with you," Lucien said, as he put her down. "And I am quite certain that your grandmother will like Mrs. Lawson very much, and so this time she will say she is very n-i-c-e."

"Nice!" Madi shouted immediately. And although he wouldn't have been able to spell it, Pedro shouted: "Nice! Nice!" at the top of his voice, just to pretend he knew.

"Who is their grandmother?" Sheena asked as soon as she could make herself heard above the noise.

"The Duchesse d'Abbeville," Lucien answered. "And you will love her! She is my favourite person—with the exception of one."

There was no need for Sheena to ask who the exception was. She saw the answer in his face and felt the colour begin to rise in hers.

"Where does the *Duchesse* live and how are we going to get there?" she asked quickly.

"She lives outside Paris. It is about an hour's run," Lucien answered. "And the reply to the second part of your question is that I am going to drive you there."

"You!" Sheena ejaculated, and knew that her eyes were shining.

"Oh, you are coming with us," the children cried.

"Lovely! Lovely! It is fun going with you, Uncle Lucien. Can we take our big car?"

"If you mean the Bentley, that is what I intended to take you in," he answered. "But, of course, if you prefer, we could go very slowly in the van."

The children shrieked with laughter at this, which apparently was an old established joke, while Sheena stood watching, feeling that she, too, was as excited as Madi and Pedro, only, fortunately, she had more control over her feelings.

She had not in her wildest dreams imagined that there would be a chance of her spending the afternoon in Lucien's company. But now he explained that Madame Pelayo had received a letter that morning from her mother, saying that she wished to see the children; but as she was unable to take them herself and wanted her own car and the chauffeur to drive her to some appointment already made, she had deputed Lucien to take the children and her apologies to the *Duchesse*.

"I have ordered your luncheon early," Lucien said. "It ought to be up in a few minutes. We want to get away by half past one if possible. The children like to visit the farm when they go to their grandmother's, and being old and a stickler for etiquette she doesn't like what she calls 'these modern ways of dashing in and out.' In her day people were more leisurely."

"I am only too delighted to be leisurely . . . this afternoon," Sheena smiled.

She paused before the last two words and he knew that what she had been about to say was "with you," and then had been too shy.

The children were already bored with the conversation and were squabbling in a corner over the ownership of a coloured marble which Madi had seen in the moat which surrounded the fort. Lucien moved a little closer to Sheena so that he was looking down at her.

"Are you really looking twice as lovely as you looked yesterday?" he asked. "Or is it my imagination?"

"Your imagination," Sheena answered—even while she knew the real answer was that she was prettier because she loved him.

"You look like a spring daffodil," he said. "Everything about you is gold, radiant, and so very—young."

146

She wanted to cry out then because his words made her so happy; at the same time there was a shadow across her joy because she had lied to him. Soon, soon, she promised herself, she would be able to tell him the truth; to sweep away that faint, questioning note in his voice; that air of surprise which was always in his mind when he spoke of her age.

She half debated with herself whether she should tell him now—and then she knew she would not, for two reasons. Firstly, because of the danger a betraying word might bring to Uncle Patrick; secondly, because, although she hardly dared admit it to herself, she was afraid. His love was so new, so precious, that she dared not risk spoiling or besmirching it by word or deed.

"Shall I tell you something?"

His voice broke in the hurried sequence of her thoughts.

"Yes," she replied, her eyes on his.

"When I brought you home last night, I didn't go to bed but sat in front of the fire downstairs. I thought that I was like a man who had been travelling for a very long time who suddenly, and quite unexpectedly, finds that the end of his journey is in sight. I never expected to fall in love again. I thought I was past love."

"Again?" Sheena questioned, and felt as if the word stabbed her.

"Yes, again," he said deliberately. "I wouldn't pretend to you, my darling. I wouldn't lie and tell you you were the first person whom I had ever loved. I have thought myself in love a dozen times, but I can promise you, by all that I hold holy, it has never been like this— never so wonderful, so perfect, so utterly beautiful!"

She felt as if her whole body quivered at his words, and then, because she was both unbearably moved and, at the same time, ashamed because she could not, in turn, tell him the truth, she could only stand looking at him dumbly and her eyes were suddenly full of tears.

"My sweet! My little love!" he said. "What have I said? How can I have hurt you?"

"Because you make me so happy," Sheena answered.

She turned away from him because she could bear no more. The children came running to them then, protesting shrilly against each other and asking for

147

arbitration in their quarrel. So that by the time their differences were settled the footman was bringing the luncheon in through the Nursery door and Lucien had to leave.

"I must go downstairs," he said. "I'm having luncheon in the dining-room, but I shall leave half-way through. Will you all be in the hall at half-past one?"

"We'll be ready, Uncle Lucien," Madi and Pedro cried.

There was no need for Sheena to say anything. When he was gone she helped the children to chicken, new potatoes and young green peas. Any other day she would have enjoyed the luncheon herself. The beautifully cooked food at the Embassy with its delicate flavours and succulent sauces was a never-ending delight. But today she felt she could eat nothing. There were so many emotions at war within her that she felt as if she would choke if she ate so much as a mouthful.

She was wildly, ecstatically happy even while she loathed herself for the deception and lies she must tell Lucien. But actually there was nothing else she could do except keep up the pretence until Uncle Patrick answered the urgent, almost desperate letter she had written to him in London.

She had played with the idea of telephoning, sending first a telegram to say that she must speak to him and asking him where and at what number he could be waiting for her to ring him. Then she knew she could not do that, because she dared not speak to him from the Embassy and if she went outside to telephone, she must do it after the children were asleep and might have to answer questions as to why she was going out alone.

If only, she thought to herself, she could be content to let things take their course. But because her whole heart and soul were fixed on Lucien, she wanted to be perfect in his eyes, and the idea of that mythical husband, symbolised by the gold ring on her third finger, was all the time an irritant and a reproach.

Sheena helped the children to fruit salad and freshly made sponge cake. When they had finished, they said their grace and ran chattering ahead of her into their bedroom.

Sheena was just putting their napkins into the silver rings which had their names inscribed on them when she heard the door open and looked up to see the *Vicomte* standing in the doorway. Before she had time to greet him he had crossed the room and taking the napkin from her hand flung it down on the table.

"Why did you dine with Lucien Mansfield last night when you had refused to come out with me?" he enquired.

There was no mistaking the anger in his voice or in the expression on his face.

"Colonel Mansfield asked me to dine with him," Sheena replied, a little lamely.

"And I asked you to dine with me, and you refused," Henri de Cormeille retorted.

"You know that your sister would not have approved," Sheena answered, feeling strangely on the defensive and, at the same time, apprehensive lest he should guess the secret of her feelings for Lucien.

"My sister!" he sneered. "You have made that a good excuse, haven't you? If you had wanted to dine with me, you know damned well you could have managed it. I'm not a fool, Sheena, and you are not as simple as you appear. But let me warn you of one thing. You are stoking up trouble for yourself if you think you are going to get anywhere with that gentleman!"

"Lawie! Lawie!" Madi's voice shouting from the bedroom interrupted them, and quickly Sheena turned towards the sound.

"I don't know what you mean," she said hastily.

"You will soon find out," Henri de Cormeille replied.

He turned and strode across the room and going out of the Nursery slammed the door. Sheena heard him run down the stairs, doubtless to the luncheon party for which already he had arrived late.

As she hurried to the night nursery Sheena tried to tell herself that it didn't matter that the *Vicomte* was angry with her. At the same time, it was uncomfortable that he should be incensed and she was also upset by what he had said. What had he meant? What would she find out for herself about Lucien?

She had no time to worry over it now. The children

had to be helped into their leggings, coats had to be fetched from the cupboard and Madi's hair brushed and curled.

"You are putting my gloves on the wrong fingers, silly Lawie," Pedro said a moment or so later. And Sheena chid herself for being absent-minded and thinking of her own troubles instead of concentrating on the children.

When they were ready, she sent them into the Nursery while she hurried to her own room. As she opened the wardrobe, she sent up a prayer of thankfulness for the lovely clothes that Fifi had given her.

It was the first time that she had worn the blue tweed overcoat which went over the pearl-grey suit, and she knew as she put it on that it matched her eyes, as Fifi had said it would. She collected from the cupboards the small grey hat, grey bag, gloves and shoes that matched the ensemble.

When she was ready she looked more like a film star stepping aboard the *Queen Elizabeth* bound for Europe, than a governess taking two children to see their grandmother in the country. And yet she knew it was not so much her clothes but the expression on her face which made her look radiant and glamorous this afternoon. And that, she thought with a smile, was something she couldn't help.

She was in love, and because of it she could no more help the light in her eyes than she could prevent the sun from shining outside. If only, she prayed, Madame Pelayo did not see her before they were able to leave the house. Men were never very perceptive and the *Vicomte*, while he was angry because she had dined with Lucien last night, had not yet guessed she was in love. Madame Pelayo would be more difficult to deceive than her brother!

Sheena hustled the children downstairs and to her relief saw that the dining-room door was shut and that Lucien was waiting for them in the hall. It was only a question of minutes before they were outside and had got into his Bentley which was waiting at the door. They sat as they had done that first day when Sheena and the children had gone with the *Vicomte* to the *Bois*.

But what a difference there was today, she thought;

and looking at Lucien's sunburnt hand on the wheel, she longed to put out her fingers and touch it, just to be sure he was there and that this was not merely a dream, a re-echo of something that had happened before.

He drove well, yet steadily, without attempting to emulate the bursts of speed which the *Vicomte* extorted from his car. In everything he did, Sheena thought, there was that same quiet strength which made her want to rely on him, which made her ask only that she should be in a position to lay all her troubles and difficulties upon him and know that he would protect and cherish her.

And yet, would he ever forgive her for lying? The question would not be denied. It was there always at the back of her brain, and even the glory of the day and Madi's chatter could not entirely dispel it.

Lucien said very little, but Sheena thought there was little need for words between them. Once or twice he looked at her and she felt a sudden tingling warmth just as if his lips had sought hers. When they crossed the Seine, golden and blue in the reflection of sky and sun, he looked at her again and she knew he was thinking, as she was, of that moment last night when the flame of his love had awakened an answer in her.

Soon they were far away from Paris and out on the long, straight roads avenued by trees and with the beautiful undulating country stretching away on either side. It was France as Sheena had longed to see it.

They flashed through little villages with their grey stone churches, brightly painted *estaminets* and perhaps a lovely old château standing back from the road, its turrets and roofs and wrought-iron gates betokening the elegance of an age that was long past.

"Not much further now," Lucien said, as they came to a small village nestling in a valley and turned off the main road down what was nothing more than a narrow lane.

"You mustn't be frightened of the *Duchesse*," he went on, speaking to Sheena.

"Frightened of her?" Sheena enquired.

"She is rather a formidable old lady when you meet her for the first time," he replied. "There are only two things she really dislikes and they are hypocrisy and bad manners—both of which she infers are characteristic of the modern generation."

"I'm beginning to be nervous," Sheena said.

"I will look after you!"

There was a meaning behind his words and she smiled at him just as they turned down a long drive bordered with lime trees.

"We are there! We are there!" Madi cried. "Look, Pedro, there is Grandmamma's house."

The château at the end of the avenue was so lovely that Sheena felt herself catch her breath. It seemed large enough to be a little palace, yet it had an almost fairy-tale fragility about it as it stood, surrounded by terraces which led down to an artificial lake. There were fountains, statues and formal gardens laid out with the symmetry which had been so fashionable in eighteenth-century France.

And then, before she had time to take in anything but the beauty of the scene, the car had drawn up at the door and the children were scrambling to get out, impatient to get to their grandmother.

"I'm frightened!" Sheena said softly to Lucien.

"But, why?" he asked. "You have got nothing to hide."

Sheena felt almost as if he had struck her. Did he really believe that, she wondered, or was he saying it deliberately to test or perhaps to taunt her?

There was no time to say more. A footman in an elaborate livery was holding open the door and Sheena had to get out. The butler helped them from their coats in the hall and they followed him slowly up the stairs, while ahead, almost out of sight, they had glimpses of the hurrying children and could hear their high, excited voices.

On the first floor the butler showed them into a long sunlit room and at the far end of it they saw the children in front of an old lady. With her white hair piled high on her head, she looked like one of the pictures by Fragonard, Sheena thought, and she realised then why Madame Pelayo was so beautiful. Madi was curtsying and Pedro making a most courtly bow over her hand covered in rings.

"Welcome, *mes enfants*!" the *Duchesse* smiled. "Have you come alone? Is there no-one with you?"

"Uncle Lucien and Lawie, our new governess, brought us," Madi replied. "But they are so slow, we ran to get to you first, Grandmamma."

"Perhaps that was not very polite," the *Duchesse* said severely. She looked up as she spoke and, seeing Lucien and Sheena in the doorway, added: "And now, Madeleine, will you present your new governess?"

Madi ran to take Sheena by the hand.

"This is Lawie, Grandmamma," she said, pulling her forward. "Her real name is Mrs. Lawson, but we call her Lawie."

"Good afternoon, Mrs. Lawson!"

"How do you do, *Madame*!" Sheena replied, feeling that she would have liked to curtsy as Madi had done.

"I have heard about you from my daughter and my son-in-law," the *Duchesse* said. "I hope you like being here with the children."

"I like it very much, thank you, *Madame*."

Sheena felt the *Duchesse*'s shrewd eyes running over her, taking note of the smartness of the pearl-grey suit, of the elegant way her hair was arranged under the little grey hat, of her gloves and bag and even of her shoes, which spoke only too clearly of a master craftsman.

"And how are you, *mon cher Colonel?*" the *Duchesse* asked, after a second's pause.

She held out her hand to him and Sheena saw that Lucien kissed it as gracefully as a Frenchman might have done, without the least air of self-consciousness.

"There is no need for me to tell you how delighted I am to see you again," Lucien said. "It is all too long since you have commanded my presence."

"Now you are flattering me!" the *Duchesse* exclaimed. "I am too old at seventy-five to have my head turned by pretty speeches."

"But you are not too old to listen to them, or to believe them," Lucien retorted.

She laughed at that.

"You are incorrigible!" she said. "But you are not here to talk about me. Did you choose Mrs. Lawson?"

"I approved her credentials," Lucien replied. "She

was recommended, as you know, by the Comtesse de Beaufleur."

"A stupid woman! Always intriguing about something or other. I make it a practice to ignore her suggestions."

"But this time she was worth listening to," Lucien said firmly. "And we are grateful to her for her introduction of Mrs. Lawson."

"He seems to think you are a success," the *Duchesse* said, looking up at Sheena. "But you are young, terribly young. Not that time won't remedy that!" She chuckled a little. "Youth is the one thing we all get over! Eh, Colonel Mansfield?"

"Only sometimes—as in your case—it doesn't matter in the least," he said.

"Don't talk nonsense!" the *Duchesse* snapped at him. "Any woman who says she doesn't want to be young is a liar." She looked at Sheena again. "My daughter tells me you are twenty-eight. I don't believe a word of it."

"Everyone keeps saying I look too young," Sheena replied. "Perhaps it would be best if I bleached my hair white."

"That is a threat which need perturb no-one very deeply," the *Duchesse* said shrewdly. "No woman with naturally gold hair dyes it. Now come along. I want you to meet a friend of mine."

She rose slowly as she spoke, leaning on an ebony-headed stick and leading the way into another room where big bow windows jutted out over the lake and a middle-aged woman sat working on a frame of *petit point*.

"Oh, here you are, Vera," the *Duchesse* exclaimed. "My grandchildren have arrived."

"So I perceive," came the reply in English, and the woman who was working rose to her feet.

She was tall, good-looking in a straightforward, unpretentious manner. She bent down to kiss Madi and Pedro and gave them each a clockwork car which she told them she had brought specially from London. As they started to push their toys along the parquet floor, she rose to hold out her hand to Lucien.

"How are you, Colonel Mansfield?"

154

"Delighted to see you," he answered. "I didn't expect you to be here this afternoon."

"I arrived last night for my annual visit," she replied.

"And this is Mrs. Lawson," the *Duchesse* said, introducing Sheena. "Lady Carrington—a very old friend of mine."

"How do you do?" Lady Carrington said, holding out her hand. "I heard that the children were to have a new English governess. Are you enjoying yourself in Paris?"

"Yes, thank you," Sheena answered.

To her discomfiture the *Duchesse* took Lucien to another window so that he could inspect some improvements she had made to the garden on the other side of the lake.

Lady Carrington sat down on the sofa and made a gesture of her hand to suggest that Sheena should do the same.

"You must tell me all about yourself, Mrs. Lawson," she said in a pleasant manner, which somehow managed not to be patronising. "Do you come from London?"

"Yes," Sheena replied, wishing desperately that she could make some excuse to avoid what she felt was to be an embarrassing *tête-à-tête*.

The children were perfectly happy just a few feet away on the floor. There was nothing she could do but answer Lady Carrington's next question.

"Do tell me who you were with before."

"I don't think you would know them," Sheena answered.

"I might," Lady Carrington replied.

"They were some people called Wainwright," Sheena said wildly, saying the first name which came into her head.

"And where do they live?"

"In . . . in . . . Hampstead," Sheena said.

"I used to know some Wainwrights who lived in Herefordshire," Lady Carrington remarked. "I expect they must have been relations."

"I am afraid I wouldn't know," Sheena replied.

"Tell me where else you were."

"In . . . in many places," Sheena answered. "You see, I . . . I was married."

It was the first time, she thought as she said it, that

she had ever been grateful for that mythical husband whom Uncle Patrick had invented for her. But her relief was short-lived.

"Yes, of course! The *Duchesse* told me you were a widow. What was your name before you married?"

"Ashburton," Sheena said.

"Not really! How interesting!" Lady Carrington exclaimed. "The Ashburton's are not only old friends, but cousins of my husband. I know them all extremely well."

"Not the same Ashburtons, I am sure," Sheena said.

"They are all related," Lady Carrington said firmly. "This is really quite extraordinary. Now tell me, which branch are you? The Shropshire ones or the Worcestershire ones?"

"I . . . I don't know," Sheena said, looking wildly towards where Lucien stood deep in conversation with the *Duchesse*.

"But you must have been one or the other," Lady Carrington insisted. "What was your father's name?"

"Rupert." Sheena replied, because there was nothing for it but to tell the truth and hope there were at least a dozen Rupert Ashburtons.

Lady Carrington knit her brow.

"Rupert!" she said. "Now let me see. The only Rupert I remember well married a perfectly lovely girl called Katherine O'Donovan and went to live in Ireland."

Sheena forgot caution and everything else and turned almost eagerly to Lady Carrington.

"Katherine O'Donovan was my mother," she said. "Did you know her?"

How often she had longed to meet someone who had known her mother and someone who could add to the fascinating, elusive memories that she had of someone soft-voiced and pretty who had sung bed-time lullabies to her and had carried her out on to the cliffs by the house so that she could hear the waves coming in from the Atlantic.

To her amazement, however, Lady Carrington's expression was one of sheer astonishment as she said:

"That's impossible! Katherine O'Donovan couldn't be your mother."

"Why not?"

"Because the only child that she and Rupert Ashburton had is dead."

"No! That isn't true. I am their only child."

"Is your name Sheena?"

"Yes, that is my name."

"I simply don't understand it," Lady Carrington exclaimed. "When Rupert and Katherine were drowned, I was staying with the Avons They were not only unhappy at the tragedy, but terribly upset because they had not made up their quarrel over the marriage. They were furious with their son because he married Katherine O'Donovan whom he had only known for a short time and ran away with her to Ireland."

"Why should they be furious?" Sheena enquired.

"Because Rupert was only twenty. He was at Oxford and his father said he was to wait until he got his degree —or at least finished his three years at the University. Instead he threw up everything. But I think no-one could really blame him. I know I didn't—Katherine O'Donovan was the most beautiful person I have ever seen."

Lady Carrington paused a moment and then said, almost as though she spoke to herself:

"It might be possible. You are like her. The same golden hair, the same eyes—and there is a lot of Rupert about you, too. But it can't be true."

"What can't?" Sheena enquired.

"That you are here—alive," was the reply. "I saw the letters that Lord and Lady Avon wrote enquiring what was happening to the child Sheena, and suggesting that she should be brought over to England at once."

"And what was the reply?" Sheena enquired.

"Katherine's brother, Patrick O'Donovan—I believe he was much older than she was—wrote back to say the child was dead!"

Ten

Sheena, driving back to Paris, was thankful that the
two children were so tired after their day in the country
that they snuggled against her half asleep, and she was
free to think her own thoughts.

They returned, not in Lucien's Bentley in which they
had come, but in the big Embassy car with its uniformed
chauffeur and dividing glass between the passengers at
the back and the front seat. The sun was sinking in all
the glory and splendour of golden light and red-flecked
clouds, but Sheena saw none of it, intent only on her
own reflections.

She could not help feeling that fate had been kind to
her, for although when she had set out that morning
at Lucien's side she had felt that she could imagine
nothing more wonderful than to spend the day in his
company, she was thankful now that he had been called
away at a moment's notice.

When Lady Carrington made her revelation about
Patrick O'Donovan's perfidy, Sheena had realised with
a feeling of horror that, if Lucien heard what was being
said, all her elaborate fabric of lies must fall to the
ground. She had given herself away in admitting that
she was Rupert Ashburton's daughter, so that Lady
Carrington had only to reveal the date of her father's
marriage to show all too clearly that she was not the

twenty-eight years she had pretended to be, but under twenty-one.

Despairingly Sheena had looked to where the *Duchesse* and Lucien were still in conversation at the far window. They were talking together so animatedly that she was certain that for the moment they had not heard one word of her conversation with Lady Carrington. Making up her mind with a swiftness which gave her no time for consideration or for doubt as to the wisdom of her decision, Sheena turned to Lady Carrington.

"Please listen to me," she said. "Will you, for the moment at any rate, say nothing to anybody of who I am or what you have discovered about me?"

"But my dear Mrs. Lawson, I must let your grandparents know," Lady Carrington protested. "They are old friends of mine and it is not fair for them to remain in ignorance. For any harshness that they showed their son when he ran away and married your very pretty mother they have, I assure you, been mercilessly and cruelly punished. Over and over again they have regretted that they ever let the estrangement remain for so long. When your father's elder brother was killed in this last war, I think they regretted it even more, despite the fact that he left two sons and a daughter.

"They often spoke of your father, and more than once your grandmother has said to me: 'How stupid we were, Vera, not to have made our peace with Rupert and have begged him to come home.' But Lord Avon was very strict with his sons and I think it was his pride which made him want the first sign of reconciliation to come from Rupert He must have forgotten that all the Ashburtons are cursed with a pride which is often their worst enemy!"

"If you only knew," Sheena said in a low voice, "how much I want to hear all about them! I want you to tell me everything about my father—and my mother too. But, please, please, say nothing to the *Duchesse* or to Colonel Mansfield—not for the moment at any rate. I will get in touch with you. I will write in a few days— perhaps sooner. There is something I have got to arrange first, something I have got to do. I can't explain, but please trust me."

Lady Carrington looked bewildered.

"But, of course, my dear child," she said. "I won't do anything you don't want me to do. It is only that I am so thrilled and delighted to have found you. You are very like your mother. I only saw her twice in my life, but I have never forgotten her. She was so beautiful and at the same time so sweet.

"Rupert brought her to see me and told me that they wanted to be married. I begged him to be very tactful when he broke the news to his father, knowing that Lord Avon would be horrified at the idea of either of his sons marrying before they were twenty-one. But Rupert was wildly impetuous and obstinately determined that he was doing the right thing and that anyone who opposed him must be wrong. He wouldn't listen to me."

"Oh, you must tell me all about it," Sheena said. "But not here. I am terrified lest Colonel Mansfield should overhear what you are saying."

"But why should it matter?" Lady Carrington asked, bewildered.

"It does matter, that is all I can say," Sheena answered. "Please don't breathe one single word of this until you hear from me. I will write as soon as I am able to. Perhaps I can even persuade Madame Pelayo to let me come over and see you."

"But, Mrs. Lawson, I don't understand," Lady Carrington said. "Don't you see that Lord and Lady Avon will want you to go to them at once? You won't have to earn your own living; your home will be with your grandparents. I promise you that they will welcome you with open arms."

"It all sounds very wonderful," Sheena replied. "You see, I didn't realise that my father's relations wanted me. I always understood that they refused to have anything to do with me."

"That is the most wicked lie I have ever heard!" Lady Carrington cried positively.

"Yes, I understand that now," Sheena said. "But please, please do not say any more . . . not here."

Even as she spoke the *Duchesse* and Lucien turned from their contemplation of the garden and came towards them.

"Colonel Mansfield approves of my alterations,

160

Vera," the *Duchesse* said in a tone of satisfaction. "I take his advice because my son-in-law, Carlos, tells me that the gardens of his house in Mariposa are the finest in the whole country."

"We are particularly fortunate in our climate," Lucien said with a smile.

"Yes, of course, that makes a difference," the *Duchesse* said. "But I want you to see the changes I have made in the front of the house. The doctor has forbidden me to go out, alas, because I have had a slight chill, but you must inspect them and the children and Mrs. Lawson can go with you. Madi and Pedro will want to see the fountains."

"Can we work them, Grandmamma?" Madi cried. "Remember, last time you let us make them go higher and higher."

"I expect one of the gardeners will be about," the *Duchesse* said with a smile. "Now run along."

They all rose to their feet preparatory to doing her bidding, and at that moment a footman came into the room.

"You are wanted on the telephone, *Monsieur*," he said to Lucien.

"Will you excuse me?" Lucien said to the *Duchesse*. "I am afraid it must be the Ambassador. He said he might have to ring me here."

"Business! Business!" the *Duchesse* exclaimed. "All my son-in-law ever thinks about is business. But I shouldn't complain, it has made him a successful man."

"Very successful," Lucien agreed.

He gave the *Duchesse* a little bow and walked hurriedly from the room.

Sheena bent to pick up the children's toys. She was well aware that Lady Carrington was watching her with a perplexed expression on her face. But she felt there was nothing she could do about it.

Sheena knew that she must see Uncle Patrick first; must somehow or other get an explanation from him, not only about her own life, but about the position in which he had put her. After that Lucien must learn the truth. The thought of having to tell him that she had lied to him almost superseded the new springing joy in her heart at learning that she had a family of relatives,

161

people of her own blood. And yet, even for them she would not hurt Patrick O'Donovan, who, right or wrong, had loved and cherished her all these long years.

"May we go, Grandmamma?" Madi asked.

"In a moment, *ma petite*," the *Duchesse* replied. "You are waiting for Uncle Lucien."

They had only another few seconds to wait before Lucien Mansfield returned. He came quickly into the room.

"I have to make you a thousand apologies," he said, "both on behalf of the Ambassador and for myself. I have to leave at once."

"At once?" the *Duchesse* queried. "What has happened now?"

"His Excellency and I have to fly to Monte Carlo," Lucien replied. "There is someone we have to see there."

The *Duchesse* gave a little chuckle.

"Business, I suppose, is what you will call it," she said. "In my young day when we went to Monte Carlo we called such a trip by its proper name."

"I assure you the reason for this journey is business," Lucien said. "And rather dull business at that. I daresay at the same time we shall enjoy a few moments' relaxation at the tables. Shall I back your favourite numbers for you?"

"Of course," the *Duchesse* replied. "Nine, seventeen and twenty-nine. You will remember?"

"As though I could forget," Lucien replied. "Last time I watched you play you won a small fortune."

He raised her hand to his lips.

"Good-bye, *Madame*! I am sorry this visit has been cut so short."

"*Au revoir, mon cher*," the *Duchesse* said, "and *bon voyage!*"

Lucien shook hands with Lady Carrington and then turned to Sheena. He murmured something conventional as he looked down into her eyes, but the quick, hard pressure of his fingers told her all that he was forced to leave unsaid.

She could find nothing to say to him. She could only cling to his hand for a moment and then watch him go, the children running beside him, holding on to his hand, to see him off in the car. Sheena longed to go too, but because her own feelings were so deeply involved she dare not make the move, until the *Duchesse* said drily:

"I think you had better go with them, Mrs. Lawson, to see they get into no mischief."

"Yes, yes . . . of course," Sheena murmured, and ran down the stairs and along the wide corridor with flying feet.

She caught up with Lucien and the children just as they reached the front door and stepped out into the sunshine. They must have heard the sound of her coming, because Lucien turned with a smile on his face which made her heart turn over in her breast.

"The *Duchesse* sent me to look after the children," Sheena panted as she reached his side.

"I was hoping that I could have a word with you," he said. "It is maddening that I have to go away now: but it is of great importance and I hope to be back by Monday at the very latest."

The children had run ahead and were climbing over the car. Lucien paused and stood looking down at Sheena. The sunshine was on her hair and her face, as she raised her eyes to his, was very sweet and lovely.

"I love you!" he said in a low voice. "You won't forget that, will you?"

"As though I could! But are you sure, quite sure, that you do love me?"

"I will prove it to you the next time we are alone together," he answered.

His eyes rested for a moment on her mouth and she felt almost as if he kissed her.

"Take care of yourself," she whispered.

She had a sudden vision that the aeroplane in which he was travelling might crash or that he might be involved in some accident.

"I was going to say the same to you," he answered, with a little smile.

He took both her hands in his and raised them to his lips. Then he climbed into the car, waved to the children and drove away down the long avenue of lime trees. Sheena watched him go and felt a sudden emptiness as if he had taken her heart with him. But she had no time for reflection; the children were rushing off towards the fountains and she had to follow them to keep them not only from falling in but from getting themselves wet and dirty.

She had no further conversation that afternoon alone with Lady Carrington. The latter made several attempts to get Sheena to herself, but somehow the *Duchesse* quite inadvertently prevented it, and immediately after they had finished their tea the car from the Embassy arrived to take them home. The chauffeur brought a note from Madame Pelayo to the *Duchesse*.

"My daughter says you are not to keep the car waiting, Mrs. Lawson," the *Duchesse* said, reading it with a long pair of diamond-studded lorgnettes raised to her eyes. "She says it was extremely inconvenient having to send the car and that men always make plans at the last moment which are a nuisance to everyone else."

Lady Carrington laughed.

"That sounds very like Yvonne," she remarked.

"I expect, if the truth be known, she is angry at having to find herself another escort for this evening's parties," the *Duchesse* smiled.

"I imagine there is no lack of those willing to offer themselves in such a rôle," Lady Carrington replied. "Last time I saw Yvonne she was surrounded by *beaux*."

"Let us be frank, my dear Vera," the *Duchesse* said, "and admit that a pretty face is what every woman needs to make life easy and simple for her."

"Easy perhaps," Lady Carrington agreed. "But I am not certain about simplicity."

"It is certainly difficult if one isn't pretty," the *Duchesse* said.

She turned towards Sheena.

"I am sure you, Mrs. Lawson, find life both easy and simple."

"Not at the moment, *Madame*," Sheena answered.

She wondered what the *Duchesse* would say if she told the truth; told her how incredibly complicated and difficult her life was and growing worse, as it seemed, hour by hour.

There was no time for further conversation even if she had wished it. The children had to be helped into their overcoats and farewells hurriedly said, and then they were all in the car and driving back towards Paris.

At last Sheena could begin to think about herself and what Lady Carrington's revelations meant. "How could Uncle Patrick have done it?" she asked herself, and knew the answer.

There were two things he had really hated in his life, Rupert Ashburton—who had taken his sister from him—and England. It was easy now for Sheena to understand why he had told that desperate and perhaps, in a way, wicked lie to prevent her grandparents from taking her away to England. It must have been a nuisance for a man of Patrick's age to take over the upbringing of a child of five. He had no money! But it had been Patrick O'Donovan's revenge against the man he hated and against the country he had always loathed.

He had been so much older than his sister, Katherine, that he might easily have been her father. They had, Sheena had understood, clung together because they were all that was left of what had originally been a large family.

One of Patrick's brothers had joined the Irish Guards in the First World War and had been killed in France. Another brother had died from an English bullet in the clash between the Irish rebels and the Black and Tans in 1920. That clash had, of course, increased Patrick's already bitter hatred of England. One sister had married an American and died in childbirth, and another sister, who had been crossed in love, took the veil and entered a Convent and he was only able to see her at very rare intervals.

It was inevitable that Katherine, the youngest by many years, should, as she grow older, have clung to Patrick and he to her. He tried to keep her completely under his domination, but she insisted on going to Dublin University, and it was when she was with a party of students visiting Oxford that she met Rupert Ashburton.

That much Sheena had gathered, getting the story from Uncle Patrick bit by bit, never coherently, never put together as a full story. But now she could fill in so

165

much that had puzzled her, so much she had never understood.

If her father and mother had been secretly married, Uncle Patrick would not have known of it till afterwards. She could imagine his rage, coming from a deep sense of hurt and unhappiness, not only that Katherine should have done something without his permission, but also because he would have felt by the very fact that she had married an Englishman that he had been betrayed.

Little wonder, as Sheena had gathered from Marie, that Patrick O'Donovan was not a very frequent visitor when her father and mother first married. And yet, if Marie's accounts were to be believed, nothing had worried Rupert and Katherine. They had been crazily, wildly in love with each other. They had been like children, Marie had said—playing at keeping house, playing at being husband and wife, playing at being father and mother.

Sometimes there had been quarrels, but they had been worth it because of the joy of reconciliation. And then, still immersed in their happiness, concerned with no one except themselves, they had died.

Sheena could understand, in a way, what Patrick O'Donovan had felt then. The last sister, and the one he loved best, had been taken from him—and there was an Englishman to blame for it! He would not have made excuses for Rupert. It had been Rupert's fault that he and Katherine had gone out in a storm; that the boat was unseaworthy; that they had taken insane risks.

Patrick could not understand that, because they were young and inexperienced, everything, even danger, seemed fun because they were together. To him everything was Rupert's bad and evil influence—Rupert, the Englishman, the usurper, the man who had come between him and his beloved sister, the man whose country stood for everything that Patrick most hated and despised.

It must in some ways have been a sweet revenge to keep the Avons from having their grandchild. It would also have seemed to Patrick a kind of rough justice. They had not forgiven their son in his lifetime for marrying an O'Donovan, in whose veins ran the blood of Irish kings. They should not get the chance of making their peace once he was dead. The child he had fathered belonged to Ireland. She should be an O'Donovan and the cursed name of Ashburton should never be mentioned if Patrick could help it.

Sheena could understand what he must have felt; and yet she knew now that, much as it would hurt him, she must go and see her grandparents, she must get to know her father's relatives and see where he lived and grew up before he came to Ireland.

Not that she had any intention of doing as Lady Carrington suggested, of giving up Uncle Patrick or making her home anywhere but with him—of that she was determined. Her loyalty and her affection were his for as long as he needed them. Whatever wrong he had done in the past, she must stand by him because he had loved her and because, strange and wrong though his ideas might seem to many people, she could understand the workings of his brain and the strong nationalist feelings in his heart which had made him do such things.

"I will meet my grandparents," Sheena told herself. "I want to meet them. I want to know so much about my father. At the same time I will never forget that I belong to Uncle Patrick."

Her chin went up and she looked, at that moment, very proud and very much an O'Donovan. There were pictures of some of Patrick's sisters hanging in the art gallery in Dublin. Uncle Patrick had taken her to see them and she realised then there was an obstinacy and a determination about them which were echoed in Patrick's face. She had pointed it out to him and he had laughed.

"You are right, Mavourneen," he said. "We are all as obstinate as mules and as proud as kings. That's the O'Donovans for you!"

"And as kind as the saints themselves when it suits you," Sheena added softly.

He had laughed at that and he had been pleased, too; and she thought now how kind he had, indeed, been; and whatever the Avons might have to say about the deception and the pretence that she was dead, she would not hear a word against her uncle.

The car drew up at the Embassy.

"Why, we are home!" Madi said sleepily, opening her eyes.

"Yes, we are back," Sheena answered. "Come along upstairs to bed, you are both tired."

Pedro was so sleepy that he made no effort to get out, so Sheena picked him up in her arms and carried him into the house. He was heavy, but when a footman offered to take him she shook her head. There was something very sweet in holding the sleeping child against her breast and feeling his utter dependence on her.

As she climbed slowly up the stairs, she thought of the many times that Uncle Patrick had carried her to bed when she was the same age as Pedro. Often she had cried when he had wanted to leave her; and then he would sit, big and clumsy, by her bed telling her stories of his adventures, some true, some entirely fictitious, until her eyelids would drop wearily on her cheeks and she would fall asleep with his voice still echoing in her ears.

Upstairs Sheena put Pedro down on his bed while she took off her hat and coat. It was only as she was hurrying back to the night Nursery that she saw there was a cablegram for her on the table. Hastily she slit open the envelope.

Arriving tomorrow two o'clock train, the message read. There was no signature, but there was no need for it. Sheena knew only too well who had sent the telegram and she felt a sense of utter and complete relief that Uncle Patrick should be coming to her. Now at last everything would be cleared up; now at last she would know the truth. And because of her new-found knowledge about the Ashburtons she was sure, for the first time, that she would, indeed, get the truth from Patrick O'Donovan.

She would force him to tell her how he was involved with these strange people and by what right they gave him orders and her, too. She would be able to tell him something else as well—that she was in love with Lucien and that she could no longer continue with the farcical deception of pretending to be an experienced married woman.

168

Sheena put Madi and Pedro into bed, tidied up the Nursery and her own bedroom, and then, at length, went into the day nursery to wait for her supper. Pierre, the footman, brought it up on a tray. He was the youngest and most inexperienced of the three footmen employed by the Ambassador, but Sheena liked him because usually he was smiling. He set the tray down on the table, then drew an envelope from his pocket.

A letter, *Madame*," he said. "Colonel Mansfield gave it to me just as he was leaving. 'Give it to Mrs. Lawson, Pierre,' he said, 'when you take up her supper.' "

He grinned as he handed over the letter and there was no doubt that in his young mind he thought that he was bringing Sheena something which would give her happiness. She found herself smiling back.

"Thank you, Pierre," she said.

"It is a pleasure, *Madame*."

He made her a little bow in the correct Embassy manner and then he winked—a boyish, engaging wink which made her laugh when she should have reproved him.

But she didn't want to think about Pierre, she wanted to read the note that Lucien had left for her. She slit open the envelope. There were only three words written on the sheet of paper inside and for a moment she felt an absurd sense of disappointment. And then, when she read the words, she realised that they were the only ones which mattered.

I love you.

Three words in Lucien's handwriting; three words that had the power to make her quiver and tremble and feel ridiculously and overwhelmingly happy. She read them again and again, and then she lifted the letter to her lips.

It was not easy the next morning to arrange to have the afternoon off. Jeanne, in fact, was extremely disagreeable about it.

"It is not convenient, *Madame*," she said.

"Oh, please, Jeanne. I'm so sorry and I hate to ask you to take the children when I have already been out on Wednesday," Sheena said. "But a friend is coming all the way from London especially to see me and I have simply got to meet him at the station."

"A friend, *Madame*?" Jeanne enquired. "Do you mean a young man?"

"No, I don't," Sheena answered, knowing the French predilection for making every assignation one of love. My friend is quite an old man and it is not at all, as you are trying to imagine, an *affaire de coeur*."

"Then it cannot be important," Jeanne said stuffily.

"Oh, but it is," Sheena persisted. "Please, please, Jeanne, be kind. I will never ask it of you again."

"Very well, *Madame*. Just this once," Jeanne agreed.

She still looked so disagreeable that Sheena remembered that Lucien had said she expected a monetary arrangement when giving her services. Uncomfortably, because she was not used to tipping people, especially those who were much older than herself, Sheena drew her last five hundred francs out of her bag and offered it to Jeanne.

"It is all I have got at the moment," she said. "But when I get my salary I will give you some more."

Sheena expected Jeanne to refuse it, but the Frenchwoman was far too practical and business-minded to refuse money or to feel in the least embarrassed at discussing it.

"Thank you, *Madame*," she said, putting the note into the pocket of her apron. "I will come for the children at one o'clock."

An hour later Sheena was waiting at the *Gare du Nord*. The train was late the loudspeakers informed her, and she walked restlessly up and down the platform for nearly a quarter-of-an-hour before finally the great engine came puffing into the station with the usual cries from the porters, the slamming open of doors and the crowd of passengers descending.

For a moment there was no sign of Uncle Patrick; then with a leap of her heart Sheena saw him towering above the other people around him, getting slowly out of a third-class carriage, his hat on the back of his head, his face wreathed in smiles. He gave a great shout of joy as she ran towards him:

"Sheena, my darling girl! It's a sight for sore eyes to be seeing you again. It's hardly recognising you I am."

Sheena kissed him and smelt the raw spirit in his

170

breath and knew, by the light in his eyes and the elation in his voice, that he had been drinking. Not that he was drunk, for Patrick O'Donovan, as he always said himself, could hold more liquor than most men and drink the majority of his contemporaries under the table while remaining sober enough so that a policeman wouldn't turn his head at the sight of him. But he was in the mood that she knew so well—gay, talkative and finding a friend in everyone he met.

"You must meet my friends, Mavourneen," he cried while she was still kissing him. "It's a party we are having."

Sheena turned to shake hands with a fat, middle-aged Frenchman with a curled moustache, his middle-aged wife and their family of two sons in their early twenties and a daughter who was a little younger. With much noise, gesticulation and joviality they collected their luggage and Sheena found herself crushed into a taxi with the lot of them.

As they rattled off at a breakneck speed to some obscure address, she discovered that the Frenchman was a baker who had gone to London with his family to receive a prize he had won in an International baking competition. The diploma was produced for Sheena's inspection and admiration. The gold medal which had accompanied it was brought reverently from the Frenchman's inner pocket and Sheena also dutifully admired it.

They had had quite an eventful journey, she gathered, because Madame had been sick on the cross-channel steamer and Uncle Patrick, when they disembarked, had nearly fallen overboard.

"It was not that I had drunk too much," he told Sheena solemnly. "Sure, we had had a bottle or two between us, but what was that to men like us? It was that I was awful tired, having been up half last night and having started at an uncomfortably early hour this morning."

He had slept for some hours in the train, Sheena gathered, after which his new friends had been kind enough to share their sandwiches and coffee with him.

"And now they have asked me home with them," Patrick O'Donovan said with a roar, "and I said to my friend, Monsieur Bonnet: 'You might be an Irishman with your warm heart and your open arms. It is only in England that they let the stranger and the foreigner starve to death on a cold doorstep for want of a helping hand.' "

"Perhaps it is inconvenient for you to have my uncle," Sheena said, when she could make herself heard above the general clatter of tongues.

She looked at Madame Bonnet, knowing it was the woman who might find an extra mouth in the house a bother and a trouble. But the Frenchwoman smiled and shook her head.

"We are pleased to have him," she said with a glance at her husband, and Sheena guessed that in the excitement of winning the gold medal and gaining a coveted diploma, Monsieur Bonnet had thrown all caution and economy to the winds and was feeling warmly hospitable to all the world.

Her guess was very near to the truth. They had no sooner arrived at the Bonnets' house, which consisted of a number of small, dark rooms sandwiched between the shop and the bakery, than neighbours came hurrying in and relatives telephoned to hear what had happened. All and everyone were invited to partake of the Bonnets' hospitality, and soon the kitchen was filled to overcrowding and Sheena found herself laying the table and helping Madame Bonnet and her daughter, Renée, prepare a meal.

Not that they would let her do much. She polished glasses and set out the plates and tried to make herself heard above the noisy chatter of a dozen voices. It was quite impossible for her to talk to Uncle Patrick. He had had quite enough to drink when he arrived, and now he was drinking French wine out of a tumbler and smacking his lips over it as if it were the very best Irish whiskey.

He and Monsieur Bonnet and three or four elderly Frenchmen were sitting together in the sitting-room, which opened out of the kitchen, and telling each other stories which brought a roar of laughter at the end of each tale.

Sheena wondered if there was going to be a chance of having a word alone with him before she had to go back to the Embassy. At the moment it didn't look like

172

it, but one never knew with Uncle Patrick. Sometimes he would snap out of a mood as quickly as he had got into one. At any moment he might decide that he wanted to talk to her and leave his new friends.

They could always walk up and down the street, Sheena thought, if there was nowhere else they could talk; and yet she felt that all she had to say needed a quiet, uninterrupted place. She half played with the idea of taking him back to the Embassy. When the children were asleep, they could have the Nursery to themselves, and Lucien was away, so that Uncle Patrick need not be afraid that he might have to disclose his identity. Yet perhaps that was mad; she was not sure, not until she had talked it over with Uncle Patrick himself.

Another roar of laughter made the glasses on the table jingle together. Madame Bonnet looked at her daughter.

"Hurry, Renée," she said. "What they need is something to eat. All this drinking on an empty stomach is not good."

Sheena felt there was a lot of good commonsense in her outlook and when finally the food was ready and she saw Uncle Patrick come walking towards the table, she heaved a sigh of relief. He was not unsteady but putting his feet down with a little extra care.

Renée cut up the yard-long loaves of fresh, crisp bread and laid a piece by everyone's plate. There was a golden pat of butter in the middle of the table and to start the meal Madame Bonnet had made a mushroom omelette which smelt as delicious as it tasted.

Uncle Patrick ate all that was put in front of him and was soon tucking into a plate of pigs' trotters cooked as only a Frenchwoman can cook them. More bottles of wine were opened and the laughter grew louder and the stories which the men told broader, until Madame Bonnet pursed her lips and protested that things had gone far enough.

There was cheese and big cups of black coffee to follow and more wine to start the drinking of toasts. It was Uncle Patrick who made a speech in Monsieur Bonnet's honour. As always when he had had a little

173

to drink, his tongue became round and honeyed and the blarney of his words held those who listened to him spellbound.

As he spoke of France he grew quite lyrical and there were, in fact, tears in his eyes as he told of his deep, abiding love for the country and how France and Ireland had always been sisters linked together through the centuries.

"I ask you to drink, my friends, my dear, close friends," Uncle Patrick concluded, "to a great man, a wise man and a clever man. A son of France of whom we can all be proud—Antoine Bonnet—the greatest baker in Europe today."

At this there were cries and cheers and everyone rose to their feet, while Monsieur Bonnet, pink-faced and delighted, sat sweating with pleasure and pride, the golden medal he had won lying on the table in front of him.

"Antoine Bonnet!" everyone cried, and Sheena sipped at her wine, which privately she thought tasted rough and not very nice.

They sat down again and the glasses were filled. Madame Bonnet got to her feet and began to remove some of the dirty plates. Sheena would have helped her, but she motioned her to stay where she was. And now someone else was making a speech, extolling the praises of Monsieur Bonnet's light loaves and making references to Renée, which made her giggle and blush and wriggle about in her chair.

"Renée! I drink to Renée!" Uncle Patrick cried suddenly, interrupting the speaker to hold up his glass and trying, somewhat unsuccessfully, to get to his feet.

It was the first time that Sheena looked at him in real alarm. It was very hot in the kitchen, for the windows were shut and the fire in the range was giving out a great heat. Patrick O'Donovan was crimson in the face, which seemed almost to have swollen with the amount of food and drink he had consumed.

"To Renée!" he repeated. "The loveliest baker's daughter in all . . ."

He made a sudden strange choking sound; his hands came up towards his heart and then were arrested in

174

mid air. Slowly, like a great balloon collapsing, he subsided in his chair and fell across the table, his glass, still clutched between his fingers, emptying itself in a spreading crimson stain over the white cloth.

Eleven

Sheena was too distraught at the moment to notice anyone or anything save Uncle Patrick, but afterwards
she realised how efficiently Monsieur Bonnet had coped
with the emergency.

It was he who sent one person running for a doctor,
another for a priest. It was he who thought of and
superintended the move of Patrick O'Donovan from
the kitchen into the living-room, where they laid him on
a low couch.

Faintly, in the background of Sheena's anxiety, she
heard them chattering and expressions of sympathy from
the women and realised that the men, too, were offering
her awkwardly their consolations.

Yet she was blind, deaf and oblivious to everything
except Uncle Patrick himself. It was as if she felt that
by concentrating on him she could force some of her
own youth and vitality into him. Even when he died an
hour later, without regaining consciousness, she could
hardly believe that there was nothing more she could do.

It was during that terrible hour, while the doctor
shook his head gravely and the priest strove to adminis-
ter the last sacraments, that Sheena realised that Uncle
Patrick was an old man. She had always thought of
him as being ageless, thinking of him, as a child will, as

someone who had always been in her life and who would always be there.

Now, as the doctor closed his eyes and the priest began the beautiful, age-old prayers for the dead, Sheena, with a stab of almost physical agony, realised that Uncle Patrick had left her.

It was almost impossible for her to believe it, impossible to think that she would never again hear him calling her "Mavourneen" or see his smile as she ran to greet him. And yet, for a moment, she was almost numb with the horror of it, so that she could not cry and could, by some will-power which hardly seemed to be her own, thank Monsieur Bonnet quite composedly for all he had done.

Between them the doctor and Monsieur Bonnet arranged where Uncle Patrick should be taken and planned the details of the funeral. To Sheena's astonishment there was a notecase in Uncle Patrick's pocket with a wad of five-pound notes to the value of nearly thirty pounds. He should not have brought them into the country and it was even more surprising that he should own so much money. How and where he had collected them was yet another mystery, she thought with a little sigh—something that now could never be explained to her, that she would never understand. But that did not matter beside the fact that his funeral could be paid for. She gave the money to Monsieur Bonnet and asked him to see to everything.

There was so much to do, so much to think about, so much to feel, even apart from that dull, empty ache in her heart. It was only long after she had returned to the Embassy and had gone up to the empty Nursery that she realised she no longer need keep up the pretence of being Mrs. Lawson. She was free—free to tell the truth, to say why she had come.

It was then that she had an overwhelming yearning for Lucien; to see him, to be able to tell him what had happened, to explain, as best she could, what had occurred before and after she came to Paris.

Just for a moment she felt afraid of what he might think; and then she knew that, because he loved her, he would forgive her for the lies she had told, the subterfuges she had used.

She had taken off her coat when she came in and now she went to her bedroom to put it away. For the first time since she had had her new clothes she took no note of herself in the long mirrors as she passed them. It all seemed unreal—this luxurious room, which she had begun to think of as a background to herself, and Uncle Patrick dead on the couch of a strange Frenchman's living-room.

Yet, despite the unhappiness which was gradually beginning to percolate through the numbness of the first shock, Sheena could not help but warm to the knowledge that whatever happened she loved Lucien and he loved her. She remembered the note in his voice when he had said good-bye, the look in his eyes; and then she covered her face with her hands because she was ashamed to think of love when all her thoughts should be of Uncle Patrick.

Suddenly she heard a knock on her door and opened it to see one of the footmen standing outside.

"What is it?" she asked.

"Madame sent me up to see if you had come in yet," the footman replied. "There is a lady downstairs who wishes to see you."

"To see me?" Sheena queried.

The man nodded.

"Yes. But do not trouble yourself. I have no instructions. I was only told to find out if you had returned."

He grinned at her in the cheeky way the footmen invariably treated the governesses, thinking her neither dining-room nor servants' hall, and making their attentions, therefore, a mixture half respectful, half impertinent.

When he had gone, Sheena furrowed her brow in perplexity. A lady to see her! Who could it possibly be? The only lady she knew in Paris was Fifi Fontés, and she was not likely to be dining with Madame Pelayo.

She was not, however, curious for long. She went into the Nursery to wait and see whether she was to go down to this unknown visitor or whether she would come up to her. She found her thoughts were back with Uncle Patrick and with Lucien. If only the latter were here, he would be able to help her, she thought. Monsieur Bonnet had promised to see to all the formalities about the funeral, but at the same time it would have been very different if she had someone she knew and trusted.

She wished that Uncle Patrick could have been buried in Ireland. He would have felt happier, she thought, in the soil of his own beloved country. But her religious teaching told her that it didn't matter much where one's grave was. It was Uncle Patrick's soul that was so important and she was certain that, whatever sins he had committed, it was with God.

Sheena was aroused from a reverie so deep that she did not at first hear the door open. Then a voice startled her and she jumped to her feet to see a woman advancing across the floor. She was very like all the women who came to the Embassy and were Madame Pelayo's friends. She was extremely well dressed, exquisitely *soignée* as regards her hair, her skin, her red, lacquered nails and her neatly shod feet, and she wore magnificent jewellery—diamonds that cascaded from her ears and a necklace of huge stones which glistened and shimmered almost dazzlingly in the electric light.

At first glance Sheena realised she had never seen this woman before. As she drew near her, she saw that she was older than she had thought at first and was not exactly pretty, although there was a distinct attraction about her face and her dark, deeply set eyes.

"How do you do, Mrs. Lawson?"

The woman held out her hand and then, as Sheena took it, glanced over her shoulder.

"It's all right," she said quickly in a low voice. "We are alone. I was only afraid that someone would come up with me and you wouldn't know who I am."

"But . . . but I don't know who you are," Sheena stammered.

"I am the Comtesse de Beaufleur," the woman answered. "Now do you understand?"

"Oh, yes, of course," Sheena replied. "It was due to your kindness that I got the job."

"Yes, yes," the woman said quickly. "There is no time for all that. What have you learned?"

"I don't know what you mean," Sheena answered, bewildered.

179

The *Comtesse* was speaking perfect English although it was quite obvious that she was French. Now she frowned and tapped impatiently with her foot on the ground.

"Please, don't be stupid," she said. "You must have discovered something since you have been here."

"Discovered," Sheena repeated—then at last she understood. "Oh, you mean about the contract. How stupid of me! I am sorry but I didn't somehow connect you with that."

"I can't think why not," the *Comtesse* retorted irritably, "considering that it was through me that you came here. Well, what has happened?"

"Nothing," Sheena said.

"Do you mean to say that you have heard nothing?"

"I was told to go to the bookshop in the *Rue St. François* and there I spoke to a man on the telephone . . ." Sheena began.

"I know all that," the *Comtesse* said. "What I want to hear is what has happened. Has it arrived? Has there been any information?"

There was something in the quick, almost greedy way in which she spoke which repelled Sheena and made her lose that last vestige of shyness and almost the sense of fear that had come over her when the *Comtesse* first spoke. Now she drew herself up proudly.

"I think I should tell you," she said, "there is no need for this subterfuge any longer."

"What subterfuge?" the *Comtesse* asked. "What are you talking about?"

"My presence here," Sheena replied. "There is no longer any necessity . . ."

Once again the *Comtesse* interrupted her.

"Now listen," she said. "I have got to go back to the *salon*. They will think it is extraordinary that I should wish to stay up here so long talking to you. I made the excuse that I felt responsible for you. You must have some idea what is happening. I hear that you take the children down to luncheon. Has nothing been said when you were there?"

"There is no reason now for me to answer that question," Sheena said. "When Colonel Mansfield returns, I am going to tell . . ."

"You needn't waste your time talking to Lucien Mansfield," the *Comtesse* interrupted. "He is hopeless. We have all tried to get what we can out of him. You might as well try and induce a brick wall to speak. Besides, as you have very likely discovered, he is immune to feminine wiles."

"What do you mean by that?" Sheena asked.

She could not help the question. She sensed all too clearly there was some inner meaning behind the *Comtesse's* words.

"I mean," the *Comtesse* replied, "what you should have discovered weeks ago, if you had any eyes in your head: that Lucien Mansfield has been Yvonne Pelayo's lover for years."

"It isn't true!"

Sheena hardly recognised the hoarse whisper which came from her lips.

"But, of course it's true," the *Comtesse* said. "That's why we can get no information out of this place. We have tried hard enough, I can assure you of that, and getting you into the Nursery was really our last desperate chance." She paused and then looked Sheena up and down with an expression both of spite and disdain. "It certainly doesn't seem to have been a very successful effort," she added.

"It can't be true, what you have just said about Colonel Mansfield and Madame Pelayo," Sheena cried, and her voice seemed to come from a very long way away and belong to a stranger.

"You must be blind or half-witted if you haven't seen it for yourself," the *Comtesse* said scathingly.

"But, Lucien said . . . Lucien . . ."

Sheena's voice died away incoherently. There was no doubt at all of her distress and the expression of horror in her eyes. The *Comtesse* gave a little laugh that was not a pleasant one.

"So that's the way the wind blows," she sneered. "Well, that tells me that we must be very careful. If Lucien's making up to you, there can only be one reason for it—he is suspicious." She gave a little shrug of her shoulders and turned away. "I must get back to the *salon*. But you know what will happen to your uncle if you betray us, so that you had best keep your mouth

181

shut where Lucien and everyone else in this place is concerned."

She went out of the room and shut the door behind her. For a long time Sheena stood staring at the closed door. She could not move, she could not even think. She could only stare after the *Comtesse* and know that somehow her world had crashed around her.

After a long time she found herself in her own bedroom. She sat down on the bed and found herself going over everything that had happened since she came to Paris. In her own mind she was repeating conversations that she had listened to between Lucien and Madame Pelayo. She was seeing them sitting side-by-side at the dining-room table, walking downstairs together, moving across the hall, stepping out into the sunshine. She was hearing their voices, seeing the expression in their eyes—a look, a smile, a sudden flash of understanding.

Could it possibly be true what the *Comtesse* had said? And then, like a child who was lost in a strange, terrifying place, Sheena knew that she was not experienced enough to deny the implication of the *Comtesse's* accusation.

How should she know whether Lucien loved Madame Pelayo or not, when she had been all too eager to believe that he loved her? What did she know of love save the ecstasy within her own heart, the sudden golden glory which had coloured the world when Lucien said he loved her?

All her new self-assurance, the courage and the little touch of vanity which had come to her when Fifi Fontés had transformed her appearance, fell away to leave her utterly defenceless, humiliated and afraid. She knew nothing; she understood less. She was just a fool amongst a lot of clever, intelligent people who must laugh at her for being so guileless, so utterly and completely gullible.

She knew then that something within her had reached breaking point. First, Uncle Patrick had been taken from her, and now Lucien. And he had gone, not leaving behind sweet and happy memories of kindness and understanding as Uncle Patrick had done, but wounding her so that she wished that she might die from the very pain and horror of what she now believed.

All those words he had said to her, the feeling of his arm around her, the touch of his lips on hers, had just been a method of extorting information from her. No! No! her heart cried; that could not be true. And yet her brain told her it was the truth.

She remembered now the expression in Madame Pelayo's eyes when she asked that Lucien should accompany her to the Argentine Embassy. Now, because she herself loved, Sheena knew what that sudden softness had meant. She had been blind at the time, blind through ignorance and stupidity; but now, because of her own love, bitterly she was able to recognise the signs in other people.

She saw Madame Pelayo's thin, elegant hand go out towards Lucien's arm. She had a sudden catch in her breath when she spoke to him. She saw those two beautiful, painted lips open as she had turned her face up to his. No man who could have the most beautiful woman in Paris for the asking would look for one second at a dull, insignificant governess!

Fool that she had been to believe him, even for a moment, when he had kissed her by the side of the Seine and she had looked up at him to see his head silhouetted against the stars!

"I love you!"

She could hear his voice saying it and now, in a sudden agony, it was repeated over and over again.

"I love you! I love you!"

Her own lips were saying it, echoing the sound in her ears, until at last the tears were running down her face, shaking her like a tempest that could not be withstood any longer. She fell forward on to her pillows, crying as if her heart would break. All the time, over and over again, her lips repeated the same words.

"I love you! I love you!"

It was not yet dawn when Sheena rose and began to pack; when the first wild, uncontrollable weeping had passed, she had been left with only one strong decision in an empty and defeated body—that was that she could not stay here any longer, she could not bear to see Lucien again.

She had thought, in her foolishness, that because Uncle Patrick was dead she would be able to tell Lucien the truth about herself. She had thought that he would understand, that he would perhaps take her in his arms and tell her that nothing she had ever said or done could make any difference to his love for her.

How laughable that seemed now! And she knew that, even if his love for her was false and treacherous, hers for him was unchanged and because of it she could not bear to see the contempt in his eyes, to realise that perhaps he found her not only stupid but comical.

All human beings are vulnerable when it comes to ridicule and Sheena, with a sense of terror, knew that she could not face Lucien's laughter. When she was gone, perhaps he and Madame Pelayo would laugh about her, remembering what she had looked like when she had first arrived in Paris, seeing how proud she had been at the change in herself and how easy it had been to make her believe that Lucien Mansfield, the distinguished, wealthy, intelligent Adviser to the Embassy, was in love with her.

Had they already laughed? she asked herself savagely. Had Lucien repeated to Madame Pelayo everything that they had said? Had he told her about that kiss by the river when the whole world had seemed to stand still and her very soul had gone singing in ecstasy towards the stars? A little groan of pain escaped between Sheena's lips as she thought of what might have been said; and then, because she could not bear to torture herself any longer, she rose from her bed to get dressed.

Instinctively she chose a plain black dress. It accentuated the pallor of her face and the dark lines of sleeplessness and tears beneath her eyes. But she had no time to look at herself. Hurriedly she drew out the suitcases from the little *entresol* where they were kept and started to pack the clothes Fifi had given her, putting them in quickly, one on top of the other, for the first time since she had had them finding no thrill or delight in their softness and elegance.

Dawn was only just breaking when finally she was ready. It was then she realised that she had no money at all with the exception of perhaps ten or twenty francs —but this was not going to divert her from her intention.

Quickly she sat down at her desk and wrote a letter to Madame Pelayo. In a few very brief words she told her that she had received news of the death of a near and dear relative. It was with great regret at causing her inconvenience that she was obliged to leave immediately. She added that she would not be returning to take up the position again. Signing her name, Sheena slipped the letter into an envelope, addressing it to Madame Pelayo.

She listened at the night Nursery door. The children were still asleep and she rang the bell and waited until one of the under-housemaids came in answer to the summons. She asked for Jeanne and again she had to wait for some time before Jeanne came.

"You are early this morning, Madame," she said rather disagreeably as she entered Sheena's bedroom. Then she saw the packed suitcases and realised that Sheena was wearing a hat and coat. "You are leaving?" she enquired.

"Yes, Jeanne. I am leaving," Sheena replied. "A relative of mine has died. I have explained it all to Madame Pelayo in this note. Would you be kind enough to look after the children until she is awake and can make what arrangements she wishes?"

"How can you have got the news at this hour in the morning?" Jeanne enquired.

"I knew last night," Sheena answered, "but I was not certain that I should have to go. Now I am quite certain."

"Madame will be very angry at the inconvenience," Jeanne said, speaking as if she was not particularly distressed at the thought of Madame Pelayo's annoyance.

"I am sorry about that," Sheena said. She hesitated and then held out her hand. "I am afraid I have got no money left to give you, Jeanne," she said, "but I would like to thank you very much for all the kindness you have shown me since I came here."

"It is nothing, *Madame*," Jeanne replied. "I am sorry you must go, but somehow I expected it. You are too young to be a governess. You are little more than a child yourself."

185

"I wish I were a child again," Sheena sighed, with a sudden yearning in her voice. How wonderful it would be, she thought, to be looked after, to have nothing to worry one, to know that all problems and anxieties rested on older and wiser shoulders!

"Will you want a taxi, *Madame?*" Jeanne asked.

"Yes, please," Sheena replied.

It was an extravagance she could not afford, but there was no other way in which she could get her suitcases away from the Embassy.

Jeanne called to one of the footmen who had just begun to open up the lower part of the house. He walked down the road in search of a taxi and after a wait of nearly a quarter-of-an-hour returned with one.

"*Au revoir, Madame,*" Jeanne said, "and *bon voyage.*'"

"Good-bye, Jeanne, and thank you," Sheena replied.

She thought, as she drove away, that it was all for the best if Jeanne imagined that she had gone back to England. She did not wish anyone at the Embassy to know where she had gone, just in case Lucien should try to find her. It was not likely, she thought. Still, there was just the chance that he might come after her and she knew that she could not bear it.

She drove in the taxi to the Bonnets' house, where she asked them if they would be kind enough to keep her suitcases for a few hours. Then blushing with the shame of it and feeling that she imposed too far on their good nature, she asked them if they would be kind enough to pay the taxi.

"I will pay you back as soon as I have changed some English money I have with me," she said, lying because there was nothing else she could do.

Madame Bonnet counted out the francs from a well-worn purse she drew from beneath her skirts. The taxi drove away and Sheena piled the suitcases high, one on top of another, in the small vestibule beside the Bonnets' kitchen.

Monsieur Bonnet and his assistants had been in the bakery since the very early hours of the morning. The smell of the warm bread coming across the yard made Sheena feel suddenly hungry and she realised that she had had no breakfast and very little to eat the night before, but she had no intention of asking further favours of the Bonnets, who she knew had done quite enough.

Hurrying away from the house she took a road which led into one of the main boulevards, of which she had taken particular note as she was coming along. There, in a second-hand shop which advertised outside that it was prepared to buy everything and anything, she sold the lizard-skin bag and the black leather one Fifi had given her. She picked out these because they were in better condition than any of the others—in fact they looked almost new—and although the woman behind the counter tried to find fault with them, she finally gave Sheena four thousand francs.

Thankful to have the money and feeling, for the moment at any rate, that she was independent of charity, Sheena hurried back to the Bonnets' house. She paid for the taxi and asked Madame Bonnet if she could buy a cup of coffee and a *brioche* from the shop. Madame Bonnet instantly offered to give her the coffee and the *brioche,* but Sheena insisted on paying.

"You and your husband have done enough for my uncle and me," she said. "I can never thank you enough for your kindness."

Madame Bonnet's rather hard face softened at the words.

"We all have to do the best we can for others," she answered. "But it is not always easy when one is poor."

"We have a proverb in England which says, 'It's the poor that help the poor'," Sheena said.

Madame Bonnet nodded. "That's often true," she answered. "But do not worry, *ma petite.* There is enough money to bury your uncle in a decent manner. He was a fine man. It was sad that he had to die like that. It was the shock that affects us all."

"I think he died happy," Sheena said softly.

"He was certainly very gay and happy on the journey," Madame Bonnet reminisced.

Her face softened again as if at the remembrance of those gay hours when they had laughed and joked and sung. Sheena had the impression that in a life full of hard work such interludes were few and far between.

"And now," Sheena said, "I have got something else

to ask of you. Can you recommend somewhere I can lodge for tonight? I can afford to pay."

"You must come here," Madame Bonnet replied. "I can put you up a bed in Renée's room."

"No, I will not impose on you," Sheena protested. "There must be some lodgings that are clean and reasonable in this neighbourhood. I shall only be staying until after the funeral."

"You could go to a friend of ours next door," Madame Bonnet suggested, and because Sheena was so anxious not to accept their hospitality when they had already done so much, she went round immediately to the house that Madame Bonnet suggested and was promised a room for one or two nights, whichever she preferred.

Then at last Sheena felt free to go to Fifi Fontés. She had already made up her mind that she must get a job in Paris because she had not enough money to take her home but first she must explain to Fifi about the suitcases which she had not yet had the opportunity of returning, and secondly ask her if there was any chance of her obtaining work at the *Casino de Paris*.

An hour later she was seated by Fifi's bed explaining her predicament.

"Of course, I don't mean that I want to go on the stage," she said. "I wouldn't be good at anything like that. But I thought perhaps dressers were wanted, or seamstresses, or even women to clean the floor. I can do both the last things quite well."

"I can't see you doing them somehow," Fifi said.

Sheena gave her a little smile.

"Don't think of me now as you see me in your wonderful clothes," she pleaded, "but as you first saw me. You wouldn't have been a bit surprised to have been told then that I was a cleaner."

"No, I suppose I wouldn't," Fifi replied. "But why have you left the Embassy? I thought you were happy there looking after the Ambassador's children."

"I can't tell you about that," Sheena answered in a low voice, "so please don't ask me. All I want you to do is to promise that if anyone does happen to enquire where I am or if you know what has happened to me, you will say that you have no idea."

Fifi looked at her quizzically. She was almost over-whelmingly attractive sitting up in bed in a pale blue nylon nightgown with a dressing-jacket of velvet and swansdown.

"Who are you running away from?" she asked. "Can it be Henri de Cormeille?"

"No, no, of course not," Sheena answered. Somehow she had forgotten his very existence. "But I don't want him, of all people, to know where I have gone."

"You look unhappy," Fifi persisted. "Are you unhappy?"

Despite her every resolution Sheena felt the tears come welling into her eyes.

"I can't talk about it if you don't mind," she replied. "There are quite a lot of things that have happened. Perhaps in a little while it will be easier to speak of them, but now I must have work."

"In such a hurry?" Fifi enquired.

"In a great hurry," Sheena assured her, thinking of the small amount of francs in her bag which would not last more than two or three days at the outside, however economical she might be.

"Now let me think," Fifi said. "It is hard, you know, to find jobs in Paris at the moment, unless you are very skilled." She gave a sudden exclamation. "I have thought of something. I have a friend who makes all my hats. When I was choosing some yesterday, I heard her say how difficult it is to get girls as matchers. She was cross because the girl who had taken a piece of my new dress to match some feathers to it had brought them back in quite the wrong colour."

"I am sure I could do something like that," Sheena cried.

"I don't suppose it is very well paid," Fifi warned her.

"It would be a job, at any rate," Sheena replied.

Fifi picked up the telephone and a few hours later Sheena found herself engaged in the shop of Madame Gabrielle. It was not a bit the sort of shop Sheena had expected, not realising that French women very seldom dress in the smart-looking establishments which have goods in plate-glass windows to attract the tourists.

Madame Gabrielle's showrooms were on the second

floor in an old, rather dilapidated-looking mansion in a side street and the workrooms soared floor upon floor above it. Madame herself was a middle-aged, rather hard-looking woman with grey hair and strong, capable fingers, with which she accentuated, by the most expressive gestures, everything she said.

"Mademoiselle Fontés is an old and valued customer," she told Sheena. "I will give you a trial because she has asked it, but this is not a place where I can afford to pay Society women who want to play at working."

"I promise you that I am not a Society woman," Sheena said quietly. She realised it was her clothes which had deceived Madame Gabrielle into thinking that she was what she was not. "I am very hard up," she went on. "My uncle has died and I have to keep myself."

"Very well then, be here tomorrow at seven o'clock," Madame Gabrielle said.

"Seven o'clock in the morning?" Sheena asked in surprise. She had not expected that French shops would open so early.

"Precisely, seven o'clock," Madame Gabrielle told her.

Sheena went to a small café for lunch. It was only when she was seated at a small table with a sandwich and a cup of coffee in front of her that a feeling of utter forlornness swept over her. Why was she doing this? she asked herself. Why didn't she take the easy course of getting in touch with Lady Carrington, telling her that she was now ready to meet her father's relatives? Perhaps she might go back to England with her.

Then, as she asked herself the question, she knew the answer only too easily. At the moment she could not bear to come in contact with anyone who knew Lucien. She loved him and she knew that, were he to appear at this moment, she would be unable to prevent herself showing that love or letting him see all too clearly that whatever he had done to her she was still in love with him.

Was it fear of pride or some instinct of self-preservation that was far deeper than both? Sheena did not know which it was. She was sure of one thing: that she must hide herself from Lucien until her heart no longer

190

ached or the blood flew to her cheeks at the mere thought of being near him.

She had imagined that love, when it came to her, might mean many things; but she had never thought that it would be like this—an almost intolerably aching need of someone to the point when she knew that, were she to see him, she would have no control over herself. If he opened his arms, she would go to him, knowing what she knew, knowing that he had only been playing with her, pretending affection when he belonged to someone else.

The mere thought of Madame Pelayo's beauty or her charms and her allurement made Sheena feel almost faint. She shut her eyes for a moment, felt the café swim round her. She could almost imagine that she could see Lucien's face looking down into Madame Pelayo's lovely dark eyes, as once he had looked into hers. She could hear his voice saying: "I love you! I love you!"

Was there any torture, any misery, like being jealous? Was there any agony like loving and knowing that one was not loved in return?

It was only a small, shabby café in which Sheena was sitting, but she felt as if it was the very gates of hell. Since her utter misery of last night she was past tears; there was only a feeling of utter desolation within her, apart from the knife-like stab of pain and memory which came when she thought especially of Lucien.

After a long while Sheena got to her feet and went back to the Bonnets' house. There there were plans to be made over the funeral, there were forms to sign and explanations to be made to both Monsieur and Madame Bonnet. She told them that she had got a job, and when she told them her salary they looked at her in consternation.

"You are going to find it difficult to live on that," Madame Bonnet said.

"Perhaps Mademoiselle has friends in Paris," Monsieur Bonnet suggested.

Sheena intercepted the glance that Madame Bonnet gave him and knew that the older woman was suspecting a very special type of friend.

"I have no friends," Sheena said quickly, "with the exception of you, of course."

They smiled at that and then, with a practicalness which was so characteristic of their race, settled down to plan her life for her. Finally, and rather to her astonishment, Sheena found herself agreeing to lodge with them for a very small sum a week. She was to sleep in the same room as Renée and give the girl English lessons while they dressed in the morning and undressed at night.

"It will be good for Renée," Madame Bonnet said, "and you will be safer here than elsewhere."

Sheena knew what she was thinking and blushed.

"You need not be afraid, *Madame*," she said quietly. "I shall not get into trouble. I have learned my lessons where men are concerned."

"So that is the reason why you have given up your good job?" Madame Bonnet asked, suddenly perceptive.

Sheena had not meant to tell her the truth, but now she found herself unable to avoid it.

"Yes, I suppose that is the reason why I have given it up," she answered.

Madame Bonnet threw up her hands in a wide gesture.

"Ah, men! They are all devils," she cried, "but what would we poor women do without them?"

Sheena tried to laugh, but later she found herself wondering whether Lucien was a devil or had she, perhaps, misjudged him? It was then she drew herself up sharply. How well she knew the weakness which made one want to make excuses for everybody and everything, and most especially for those one loved!

All her life she had made excuses for Uncle Patrick and where had it got her?—into worse trouble than she had possibly imagined. Now, knowing what she knew, being faced with irrefutable proof of a man's duplicity, she was trying to find excuses for him, because, whatever he was like, she still loved him with her whole heart and soul.

Resolutely she forced herself to unpack some of the things that she was most likely to need; and then, taking one empty suitcase in her hand, she took the 'bus and Metro back to Fifi's flat. She had promised to go back that evening and tell her what had transpired about her interview with Madame Gabrielle.

When she arrived, Fifi had just come in from a drive and was looking entrancingly pretty in a suit of leaf green with a cape of blue foxes over her shoulders.

"You were successful?" she asked gaily, as Sheena came into the sitting-room.

"Thanks to you I was successful," Sheena answered.

"Then that is wonderful," Fifi said. "Do you think that you will like the job?"

"I am sure of it," Sheena answered, trying not to think of the low-ceilinged, crowded workrooms, where there was an overwhelming smell of glue and feathers mixed with the kind of dry airlessness that was characteristic of rooms where too many people worked and too few windows were opened.

"If there is something better at the theatre I will suggest you for the job," Fifi said. "But you understand it is difficult for me to bring in a stranger. Most people have been in the profession for years and they resent the employment of outsiders, especially foreigners."

"But of course I understand," Sheena answered, "and I am perfectly happy where I am. You will promise, though, not to tell anybody?"

Fifi suddenly put out her hands and took Sheena's.

"Must you do this?" she asked. "I know you don't want to talk about it yet, but I can't help guessing that you are in love. Have you told him, whoever he may be, why you are running away?"

"No," Sheena answered. "And he must never know."

"You don't think that he loves you?" Fifi asked, her eyes on Sheena's suffering face.

"I know he doesn't," Sheena answered.

"Oh, my dear, then I understand," Fifi said, "and I am desperately sorry for you."

Twelve

"Wake up, Sheena! Wake up! It's six of the hour."

"Six o'clock," Sheena corrected sleepily, but automatically, as she opened her eyes to see Renée standing by her bed already half dressed.

She found it almost increasingly difficult to wake up in the morning, not only because she was tired from the day before but also because she was sleeping very badly. In the day-time there was so much to do that she had little time to think, but once darkness had fallen and Renée's soft, rhythmic breathing from the other bed told Sheena that she had fallen asleep, her thoughts came chasing back into her mind and with them a misery that was inescapable.

She had believed that work would relieve her unhappiness, but she found herself growing more and more unhappy as the days went by. It was as if every hour brought her realisation of what she had lost. Love, which had never touched her life before she had loved Lucien, had, in its short, swift passage, altered her so much that she wondered now if she was really the same person as she had been before she came to Paris.

And it was not only love that had brought her a realisation of her unhappiness without it. It was because it had broadened and altered her whole perception that everything seemed different. Because of love, which

194

she had known such a very short time, she could understand Uncle Patrick as she had never understood him before. It was inevitable that she should have looked on him always as a grown-up and herself as a child and, as children do, had never for one moment realised that he had frustrations, emotions and moments of unhappiness just as she had.

To children grown-ups are always inhuman, seated godlike on an Olympus where they have nothing in common with the petty miseries of everyday life. Now Sheena, looking back, understood so much that she had missed before. Uncle Patrick's incessant desire to show-off was because he himself was conscious that he was a failure. His love for her and the way that he would bewail that he could not give her pretty things was because he knew secretly that he had deprived her of a very different and much richer type of life.

Even so, Sheena could not bring herself to get in touch with Lady Carrington. It was still part of her happiness with Lucien, still so closely connected with him that the very thought of Lady Carrington would make her remember how he looked as he stood with the *Duchesse* at the window, inspecting the gardens. Then she would go with him into the sunshine, seeing his eyes looking down at her, his lips telling her that he loved her. . . .

"You are late, Sheena!"

Renée's voice called her back to the fact that she was still lying in bed.

"I am getting up this minute," she answered, and with a little yawn sat up and pulled back the bedclothes.

"It is a nice day," Renée said, in her slow, broken English. "And me, I am very happy."

"Why particularly?" Sheena asked.

"Because I am seeing Johan. He is meeting me at *midi*."

"Midday," Sheena corrected. "And, Renée, are you wise?"

"Wise to meet Johan?" Renée asked, her eyes shining. *"Oo, la, la!* Who is wise when one is in love?"

"But, Renée, think of André!"

After a week Sheena had found herself immersed in the family affairs of the Bonnets. It was extraordi-

195

nary, she thought, how little she had known about the close family life that such people lived. Now she had the greatest respect and admiration for them. She saw how hard they worked, how unsparing both Monsieur Bonnet and his wife were of themselves in their efforts to earn money to keep their home together, to do their best for their children.

One of their sons worked in the Bakery, the other was serving his apprenticeship in Madrid. They gave them what they could afford, but they were at the moment concentrating, with an almost religious fervour, on collecting a dowry for Renée.

She was already affianced to a worthy, rather dull young man called André, who was, as Renée proudly but frankly explained to Sheena, of a better family than the Bonnets and with far better prospects than she had dared to hope for in a husband. But this did not prevent Renée from falling in love with someone else. Johan was attractive, impecunious and had a natural gaiety which Sheena, herself, thought almost irresistible.

Renée did not pretend for a moment that she was not attracted by him.

"When I am with André," she said, "I am proud. I think how lucky I am that he should want to marry me when I have so little to offer and not such good connections. But when I am with Johan—well, I forget everything except that my heart goes pit-a-pat."

"Supposing André finds out?" Sheena asked.

"I am very careful," Renée replied. "Very, very careful. And *hélas,* one is only young for a very short time. You sound as though you were already middle-aged."

Sheena laughed, but somehow Renée's words left a little sting in her own heart. One was young for a short time! She knew that she, herself, felt immeasurably older than she had ever felt before. Every night, when Renée was asleep, she would cry silently into her pillow, tears running down her face while her whole body ached and yearned for Lucien. Often she wondered what had happened to her pride—the pride of the O'Donovans that she had thought was always there to help and sustain her if ever she felt humbled against love.

"I love him! I love him!" she told herself, and once

Renée heard her murmuring the words and put her arms round her shoulders.

"You are unhappy, Sheena, yes?"

"Yes," Sheena answered, making a valiant effort to smile through her tears.

"I can see you are unhappy," Renée said, "but what can we do? My mother complains because you eat so little, and there are lines under your eyes that weren't there the first day we saw you. Can you not forget this man who is making you so miserable?"

"No, I can't forget him," Sheena said.

She longed to cry out, but the very words themselves were agony. How could she forget that moment of almost divine ecstasy when the world had been utterly transformed and she had given her heart, her soul, her living into Lucien's keeping? On his part it had just been a scheme to find out what he wanted to know, but for her it had been a revelation, a miracle which had changed everything and herself.

"I love him!"

She found herself repeating the words as she walked to work; as she scrambled on the crowded 'buses to stand in the open place at the back because it was cheaper than the seats; as she climbed up flight upon flight of dark, back-breaking stairs to the wholesale departments of the great silk stores, or hurried homewards in the evening, exhausted, with swollen ankles and the feeling that it was impossible for her to do a single thing more except, of course, to go on loving Lucien.

How cruel, how relentless love was! And yet once it was there it was impossible to escape from it.

Sheena had got permission from Madame Gabrielle to go to Uncle Patrick's funeral. It had been a dull morning with a touch of rain in the clouds, and there had only been Monsieur Bonnet and herself at the service and afterwards to stand beside the deep, wide grave in the overcrowded cemetery.

Sheena found herself weeping bitterly as finally the coffin was lowered into the grave. Monsieur Bonnet was kindness itself, and as they left the churchyard she turned to him and taking his hand in hers said:

"I don't think I can ever thank you for all you have

done for us. I had no idea that anyone could be so wonderful to strangers as you and your wife have been."

Monsieur Bonnet's good-humored face took on an expression of embarrassment.

"*C'est rien,*" he said a little gruffly. "I liked your uncle. He was one of those people with whom one has a warmth and a friendliness from the first moment he appeared. One does not always feel like that about the British," he added, with a little smile which somehow made Sheena want to smile back at him despite the tears that were still running down her cheeks.

As they rode back into Paris in the Metro, Sheena said:

"Are you quite sure that you don't mind my continuing to lodge with you? I like being with Renée, but I wouldn't like to feel that I was a burden on you."

"A burden, when you are paying?" Monsieur Bonnet asked. "But, of course we like to have you, and already Renée's English has improved out of all recognition. One day, when she is the wife of André, she might find it useful. He will go far, that young man."

"You mean as a lawyer?" Sheena asked.

"Perhaps as a politician," Monsieur Bonnet answered. "Not that I have much use for them, but . . ." he shrugged his shoulders, "they get the applause and the glory."

It was, Sheena thought, a typical way of looking at public life; but when she told Renée what her father had said, Renée had made a grimace.

"They are ambitious *pour moi,*" she said. "Me, I shall be content to have a good home, a kind husband and plenty of children."

"Content if you marry André?" Sheena asked.

"But, of course," Renée replied. "It is a great mistake to confuse marriage and love."

It was no use, Sheena thought; she could not understand Renée's point of view and Renée would never understand hers. Renée, the practical, thought that it was time Sheena looked for another man. Her heart might be broken but there were other men in the world, weren't there? And sooner or later, with her looks and her beautiful clothes, she would find one.

But as far as Sheena was concerned it wouldn't have

198

mattered if the world had been peopled with nothing but women. Now she did not even notice the glances that followed her as she walked down the street or hear the compliments that were often paid her as she fought her way on to a 'bus or when she went with the Bonnets for an evening stroll round the boulevards.

It was when she arrived at Madame Gabrielle's, hot and panting because, despite Renée's instructions to hurry, she had very nearly been late at her work, that she realised, almost with a sense of shock, that she had been working there for over a week. She would not have thought of it had not a message come through to say that Mademoiselle Fontés was expecting her hat, which had been promised for over a week, and she was not prepared to wait any longer.

On the day Sheena had gone, on Fifi's introduction, to see Madame Gabrielle, Fifi's parting words had been: "And tell her I am not going to wait a week for my blue hat. I want it tomorrow."

Now, as Sheena heard the girl taking down the message over the telephone, she looked at the calendar hanging above it on the wall and saw that it was, indeed, seven days since she had come here. She had moved from one type of existence into another, and the hours and minutes had little relation to her feelings and emotions.

Seven days since she had left the Embassy; eight since she had last seen Lucien. She felt her heart quiver at the thought so that she almost missed hearing the telephonist say:

"I understand. Mademoiselle Fontés wishes Madame Lawson to bring the hat to her."

"She asked for me?" Sheena enquired as the girl replaced the receiver.

"Yes, but I must go and ask Madame first if you may go."

The girl disappeared and Sheena stood waiting, looking at the little piece of ribbon in her hand to which she had been matching some silk flowers. How much she had learned in this last week—of colour and shades of tones which blended and didn't blend, and the different hues which materials took on by night and by day!

She wondered how many miles she must have walked,

199

and somehow it seemed longer because her thoughts had always been unhappy and she had not felt, as she had when she first came to Paris, that she wanted to dance along the sunlit streets.

The telephonist returned.

"Madame says you can take the hat at once, but you are not to linger. She says it oughtn't to take you more than an hour if you hurry."

"Very well," Sheena said.

She was used to Madame's peremptory commands when it came to any of them wasting time.

"Time is money! Time is money!" Madame Gabrielle would repeat it over and over again, coming swiftly round the corner to rebuke a girl who had stopped work to powder her nose or another who might be arranging her hair in the mirror or sitting down for a second to rest her aching feet.

"Hurry! Hurry! Hurry!" she would say to Sheena.

Sheena thought sometimes that those words were an accompaniment to everything she did, even in her hours of freedom.

"Hurry! Hurry!"

The words sang themselves now as she ran downstairs with the elegant, round hat-box on her arm and jumped aboard the first 'bus which would carry her towards the *Champ Elysées*. It actually took her only a little over quarter-of-an-hour to reach Fifi's apartment, and as she hurried up the stairs she was conscious of feeling excited at the thought of seeing the pretty star again.

Fifi was sitting in front of her dressing-table and as Anastasia showed Sheena into the room she jumped up and held out her hands.

"I was expecting to hear from you," she said reproachfully. "How is everything going? You like the job?"

"I am very grateful to you for getting it for me," Sheena said. "I was hoping so much that I would get a chance to see you and to tell you all about it."

"But you should have come here. I was longing to see you," Fifi insisted.

Sheena said nothing. She did not wish to reply that she had no intention of pushing herself or being a

200

nuisance to the young French woman who had already show her such extraordinary kindness.

"Tell me all about it," Fifi insisted. "Do they work you hard?"

"Very hard," Sheena smiled. "But it is interesting and one does get away from the shop. I am beginning to know Paris quite well."

"And where are you lodging? I was so annoyed with myself for not asking you that before you left," Fifi said.

Sheena told her about the Bonnets and how kind they had been.

"The French are kind," Fifi agreed, when she had finished. "I know people think we are grasping and mercenary, but underneath we want to help people. It is only that many are so poor that they have to count every sou."

"I can understand that now," Sheena said, "although I have never understood it before. But don't let's talk about me; tell me about yourself."

"I have got a new song," Fifi said, "and a charming new partner to sing it with. One night you must come and see me. They have been very difficult about letting me have free seats up to now because the place has been so full, but in a little while it will be easier. I will give you a ticket and three for your friends, the Bonnets."

"Thank you so much," Sheena said. "That would be kind of you."

"Unless, of course, you would rather have only two and take a young man," Fifi said, with a question in her eyes.

"I have no young man," Sheena answered.

"Are you sure of that? I cannot understand it," Fifi sighed. "You look so pretty—much prettier in those clothes than I did. I should have thought everyone would have been mad about you."

"I must go now," Sheena said.

She felt she could not bear to stay and talk about men when there was only one man for whom her heart cried.

"But, no! Not until you have had some coffee. Anastasia's bringing it. Besides, there is no hurry. Don't be afraid of Madame Gabrielle. She is much more afraid of losing my custom than you could ever be of her."

"I expect that is true," Sheena agreed, "but she is a very frightening woman."

Anastasia brought the coffee and biscuits and as Fifi poured out she said casually:

"Someone has been making enquiries about you."

Sheena sat up suddenly and her cup rattled against the saucer.

"Who?" she asked.

"I don't know his name," Fifi replied. "But it was a man with a very charming voice. He asked me if I had seen you. Of course I said no, but he was very insistent and kept me talking for a long time."

"You are quite sure you didn't tell him anything?" Sheena asked.

"Quite, quite sure. But he sounded very attractive. Are you wise to run away from him?"

"Very wise," Sheena said. "And you promise me, promise me truly, that you didn't . . ."

"I haven't said a word," Fifi interrupted her. "I am not so stupid as that. If you don't want to see him, you don't want to see him. I was just wondering if you were doing what was the best thing for yourself."

Sheena gave a little sigh.

"It is always very difficult to know what is best," she said. "I only know that there is nothing else I can do."

She was thinking, as she spoke, of how, if she saw Lucien, she would still want to run into his arms, knowing what she knew, knowing that he must now have no further use for her—she still wanted him.

"Women are very stupid creatures," she cried aloud, with a little jerky laugh, and putting down her empty coffee cup got to her feet. "Thank you for everything. You have been so wonderful to me."

"Don't be ridiculous. I have done nothing," Fifi replied. "I am still looking out for a better job for you. I am sure Madame Gabrielle's an old harridan, but at least it will fill in time until we can find something better. I shan't forget you, don't be afraid of that. You brought my luck back to me and I'm sure you are lucky to me always."

"I hope I am," Sheena said. And then, as Fifi kissed

202

her, she said: "Do you think that you will ever find happiness, real happiness, again?"

Fifi waxed suddenly still, her eyes wide, and then in a very different voice from what she usually spoke she said quietly:

"I think, *ma chérie,* that there are many sorts of happiness and many sorts of love. I have had one sort, which can never be taken from me, but I have to go on living. Because I am young and successful I want to live fully, and so I shall go on looking, not for a second best, but for something which will be quite different and therefore, perhaps, very nearly as wonderful in its own way."

"You are so sensible," Sheena sighed. "So much more sensible than I am." She kissed Fifi again and went towards the door. "I must hurry back," she said, "or I shall get the sack and then I shall be here asking for your help once more."

"Au revoir," Fifi replied. "And don't be so long before you come again."

"I will try not to be," Sheena promised, but knew, even as she said it, that she would not go to Fifi without an invitation—not unless she was absolutely desperate.

She remembered Uncle Patrick once saying to her: "One must never wear out one's friends!"

It was such a good thing to remember, she thought, not to encroach on other people's lives, not to ask too much of them without being able to give anything in return. She did not want to wear out her friendship with Fifi, any more than she wished to wear out the kindness and affection the Bonnets always showed her.

The sunshine outside was really quite hot and for a moment she felt herself luxuriate in it, and instead of hurrying towards her 'bus, as she should have done, she started to stroll along the *Champs Elysées.* The cars were speeding up the broad roadway, brightly coloured awnings made a splash of colour outside the shops, the trees were now in full flower, and for the first time since she left the Embassy Sheena felt the beauty of Paris warm the cold, frozen misery of her unhappiness.

She almost felt as if the ice within her began to melt a little. She raised her face towards the sunshine, her eyes half shut, walking mechanically but with a little

203

spring in the movement. It was almost like being startled by a douche of cold water to hear a voice say:

"Is this where you have been hiding?"

She started, half turned, and saw Henri de Cormeille walking towards her. For a moment she was overcome with panic, she wanted to run, she wanted to hide, she wanted to do anything, however wild or crazy, to avoid him. And then her better judgment, or perhaps it was her sense of humour, came to her aid. She could not run away as if she were a girl in the films or a heroine of some strip cartoon, and so a little unsteadily she stood her ground until he reached her side.

"Sheena!" he ejaculated. "Where have you been?"

"Do I have to answer that question?" she enquired.

"You certainly have," he replied. "Come, I want to talk to you."

"I can't stay," she answered. "I have got an appointment."

He put out his hand and grasped her wrist.

"You are going to give me an explanation," he said, "so come quietly, as they say in the Police Force."

She found herself half smiling at his determination even while she knew that she was so nervous that she was trembling. As if he sensed what she was feeling he drew her across the broad pavement to where there were seats amongst the flower-filled beds under the shade of the blossoming chestnut trees. Sheena seated herself and the *Vicomte*, slipping his arm along the back of the seat, turned sideways, his other hand still holding hers.

"Where have you been?" he asked.

"That's a secret," Sheena replied.

"Why did you go like that?"

"I gave your sister an explanation," she replied.

"Do you suppose any of us believed that for a moment?" he enquired. "Who is keeping you?"

Sheena started.

"I don't know what you mean by that."

"I think you do," he answered. "There is a man behind this. I am not such a fool as not to realise that. Who is he? Do I know him?"

"You are making a terrible mistake," Sheena answered.

"Don't lie to me," Henri de Cormeille said sharply.

"Someone has been cleverer than I was. You have a lover, someone we never guessed that you even knew, and now you are with him. Is he making you happy?" There was something almost savage in his question.

"Listen!" Sheena said. "I promise you that I left the Embassy for the reason I gave your sister. A relative of mine died—my uncle as it happens."

"Then why haven't you returned to us?" Henri de Cormeille enquired. "Has he left you rich, so rich that you can afford not to work?"

Sheena did not answer and looking into her face at her downcast eyes he said more gently:

"You don't look well. You are thinner. Sheena, can't you see that you are driving me mad?"

There was so much passion in his voice that she raised her eyes at that.

"I am . . . sorry," she faltered.

She felt his hand grip her shoulder and he drew her closer to him.

"What were you waiting for?" he asked. "Come and live with me, as I asked you to do before. I will give you an apartment, I will give you clothes, money, anything you want. I love you, Sheena. I wanted you from the very first moment I saw you. We will tell no-one. No-one need ever know. It will be our secret—yours and mine—and we will be together. I will make you happy, I swear it."

His lips were near to hers, but Sheena turned away, pushing him away from her with her free hand even while he tightened his hold upon her.

"Please don't say such things to me," she begged. "I can't live with you; I can't do anything that you want. As I told you before, I don't love you."

"Does that matter so very much?" Henri de Cormeille asked. "I am not asking you to do anything which must last for eternity. We can have a great deal of fun together. I can teach you how to enjoy life! How not to look serious, so very solemn, about the things that should make you joyful and glad. Come with me, Sheena. Come with me now.

"No! No! No! It is impossible," Sheena cried.

She tried to get to her feet, but he prevented her.

"Please let me go. I have got to go back to work," she begged. "If you keep me here I shall lose my job."

"Where are you working?" he asked. "I will take you there."

"No! No!" she protested. "That will not help matters at all."

"Are you trying to say that I am not to see you?"

Sheena nodded.

"Yes, I am trying to say just that. We can mean nothing to each other. You live one sort of life, I live another."

"But the whole thing is fantastic," he said. "You come to the Embassy, recommended as a governess. You are good with the children, we are all delighted with you, and then suddenly you disappear. You tell me that you are not living with any man. Do you really expect me to believe that you have walked out to find another sort of job? What is it? What is the mystery?"

"I know it all sounds ridiculous," Sheena answered, "but I can't give you any explanation. I just want to be left alone."

"And supposing I refuse to leave you?" Henri de Cormeille enquired. "You say you are going back to work. Very well, I shall follow you. I shall find out what you are doing. I will come in and see your boss. I will tell him, if you like, that I am offering you a far more congenial situation."

"It is not a he, it is a her," Sheena corrected, half laughing, half exasperated by the *Vicomte's* persistence.

"A woman?" Henri de Cormeille enquired. "Then that makes it easier still. A woman will understand whatever she can give you I can give you something better."

"I don't want what you are trying to give me," Sheena said. "Oh, please understand. I am not shocked or upset because you are asking me to be your mistress. I know you meant it as a kind of compliment. But I can't accept because I love someone else."

The *Vicomte* sat up suddenly.

"So you are living with a man."

"No, I am not living with this man. I am not even seeing him," Sheena answered. "But I love him and that is the truth. So now you understand why I can't go with you. I . . . I shall . . . have to leave you now and go back to my job."

The *Vicomte* looked at her and then suddenly he reached out his hand to put his fingers under her chin and tip up her face towards his.

"Do you love him so very much?" he asked, and now his voice was kind, in a way understanding.

"Yes, very much," Sheena replied. "More than I could ever love anyone else ever again."

He looked at her for a long moment and then, with quite a surprising tenderness in his voice, he said softly:
"Ma pauvre petite!"

Just at that moment a shadow fell across them and they realised that someone was standing there. It was Sheena who turned her face first and then gave a little cry which seemed to come from the very depths of her being.

Lucien was towering above them. Lucien, with his face dark and almost contorted with an expression she had never seen before.

"Hello, Lucien . . ." Henri de Cormeille began, but before the words had left his lips Lucien had spoken first.

"I saw your car," he said. "So it is you who has been hiding her all the time."

"I don't know what you mean by that," Henri de Cormeille snapped.

"I think you do," Lucien retorted. "I thought of many explanations, but not this. You dirty little swine! Now you'll get what I've been wanting to give you for some time."

He stepped towards the *Vicomte* as he spoke and Sheena gave a little scream. Lucien pulled Henri de Cormeille to his feet and then swung back his right arm and hit him hard on the chin. The Frenchman staggered against the bench and the support it gave him saved him from falling.

Then, with an oath which was literally spat from his lips, he sprang at Lucien. The latter was bigger, but the *Vicomte* was more wiry. In a moment they were fighting fiercely, struggling and scrapping, their hats falling from their heads, their feet slipping as they strove to get a grasp one on the other.

It was then that Sheena managed to throw aside the paralysis which had held her spellbound. With a little incoherent murmur, like an animal whimpering, she turned and ran away from them both.

She ran blindly, without looking where she was going, down the *Champs Elysées*, pushing past people and children, running on, on, on and on—with the one idea in her mind—to escape.

Thirteen

Sheena ran until her breath was coming sobbingly between her lips and there was a pain in her side. She had no idea where she was going or really what she was running from. She had only a sense of urgency to be free, not only from Lucien but from the horror of seeing him and Henri fighting—the blows they struck at each other sounding as dull and ominous as the beats of her own heart.

On, on, she went swerving in and out of the groups of people sauntering in the sunshine. She did not know that a grey car was speeding down the *Champs Elysées* or that the man at the wheel was leaning out searching the crowds for her. She did not see the car pass her, moving far more quickly than she could manage, or know that the driver had stopped the engine and descended.

Only when he loomed up in front of her, when he was actually so near that she could not prevent herself from bumping against him, did she see who it was. Breathless as she was, Sheena managed a little scream as Lucien took the full force of the collision, then held her closely in his arms.

"Why are you running away?" he asked.

It would have been impossible for her to answer him even if she had wished to. She could only gasp for breath, her eyes closed for a moment as her head rested against his shoulder. He looked down at her, so frail in appearance and yet so tenacious of purpose. Her fair hair was curling riotously against her cheeks, which were bright with colour. Only her eyes were veiled, the long, dark lashes quivering with each breath she drew so painfully.

Suddenly Lucien made up his mind to some course of action and his lips tightened as, bending down, he lifted Sheena in his arms. It was then that her eyes opened and she struggled against him.

"Let me go! Let me go!" she gasped.

"Not until you have given me some explanation," he answered grimly.

She fought against him, but to no avail. He carried her across the pavement to where his car was waiting, set her down in the front seat and got in beside her.

"I refuse to come with you," she cried desperately, but she was too late.

He started the car and drove away, turning out of the *Place de la Concorde* down a less frequented road which ran parallel with the Seine. Sheena saw the water glimmering silver in the afternoon sunshine, but for once its beauty evoked no response within her. She could only feel angry and frightened, combined with some other emotion to which she was too afraid to give a name.

They drove for some minutes and all the time in silence till Sheena found it easier to get her breath and gradually the pain in her side subsided. Finally Lucien drew the car to a standstill in a quiet street in which there was little traffic. On one side of them lay the river, on the other a row of centuries-old grey houses in front of which bloomed a row of chestnut trees scattering their pink and white blossom like snowflakes on the ground.

"You have no right to bring me here."

Sheena spoke quickly, rushing into speech because of the fear of what Lucien might say if he spoke first. Slowly he turned his body round to look at her, one arm over the wheel, the other on the back of the seat.

She had forgotten how handsome he was, she thought, or how penetrating his eyes could be. Then she saw that his face was bleeding from a long cut on one cheek. Henri's signet ring might have done that, she thought, and she had a sudden impulse to put out her hand and wipe the blood from it.

Then, with a sickening leap of her heart, she realised that Lucien had not answered her but was looking at her, looking at her in a way which seemed to Sheena to strip away all the pretences, the lies and subterfuges of the past weeks, and see the pitiful, shameful truth which lay in her heart.

"I am not going to stay here," she said frantically. "I'm going to get out."

She put out her hand towards the door, realising even as she did so that it was a futile gesture. Lucien merely reached out and took her hand in his. She felt herself tremble at the strength of his fingers; felt, too, another emotion, warm and sweet, run through her veins, and knew, with a sense almost of horror, that she had weakened at the touch of him.

"You have got to tell me where you have been."

His voice was deep, a little hoarse.

"Not where you imagine," she retorted. "I met the *Vicomte* only a few minutes before you found us together. I had not seen him since I left the Embassy."

"I might have known that," Lucien said. "I have only to look at you to realise that you are all you appear to be."

She felt herself stiffen at that. She was certainly not all she appeared to be, but at least she had not sunk to becoming the *Vicomte's* mistress.

"I am not responsible to you or to anyone else for my actions," Sheena told him in a low voice. "May I go?"

"No!"

The monosyllable was sharp and authoritative. Lucien released her hand and now Sheena made a little gesture almost of despair.

"Very well then. What do you want to know?"

"Why you ran away."

There was a moment's silence while Sheena fought vainly for words. What could she say? What was there to say to him?

"I thought the explanation I gave to Madame Pelayo was quite clear," she prevaricated at last.

"What you say to Madame Pelayo and what you say

211

to me are two very different things," Lucien answered. "I was sure when I went away with the Ambassador that you loved me."

Sheena turned her face away from his. How was she going to bear this? she thought. How much longer could she go on pretending, schooling herself to appear indifferent when he was sitting beside her?

"I love him," she thought wildly. "I love him so much that I am ready to go down on my knees and ask him to take me back, under any conditions, under any circumstances. I don't care if he lives with a thousand other women as long as he wants me too."

She felt her defences crumble; she felt the treacherous yearning of her body quiver and tremble because he was so near. And then the pride of the O'Donovans came to her rescue. With a sudden lift of her chin, which in its very bravery was somehow infinitely pathetic, she said:

"I suppose we all make mistakes in our lives, and you must remember that I am not very experienced."

There was a long silence. Then in a voice which she had never heard before he said:

"Sheena, what are you trying to tell me?"

"Haven't I made that clear?" she asked. "I want only to be left alone."

"I don't believe it," he said slowly. "You love me. I know you love me. And if you don't I will make you."

She felt his arms go round her shoulders and then, as she made one despairing effort to escape him, he tipped her head back against his shoulder and she felt his lips on hers.

He kissed her passionately, fiercely, almost brutally for what seemed to her almost an eternity of time. She fought him wordlessly, with tight lips, her body stiff and unbending in his arms. Then suddenly, as a flame of delight shot through her, she could resist him no longer. She felt herself collapse, close and warm against him. Without her conscious volition her arm crept around his neck and then her mouth, soft and warm and open, was beneath his and they were joined in a kiss which seemed to transport her once again into a paradise of wonder and glory.

Only, as it seemed to her, when she reached the very

zenith of unutterable joy, did he take his lips from hers and look down at her face, flushed and quivering against his shoulder.

"And now tell me that you don't love me," he said, with that light of triumph in his eyes that she had seen there before—the triumph of a man who has attained what he most desires.

"But . . . you don't . . . understand."

Her voice was hardly above a whisper but he heard what she said.

"I only know that you love me."

"But, I . . . I . . . do you . . . want me?" Sheena asked.

She stared at him, still too bemused by the joy his kisses had brought her, to think clearly or coherently.

"How could you leave me like that?" he asked. "Don't you realise that I have been crazy, distraught with worry? I thought you must have gone to England. The Police were looking for you there."

"The Police!"

The very words were like a splash of cold water in Sheena's face. She sat up, freeing herself from his encircling arms.

"Yes, the Police," he repeated. "I am sorry, darling, but I had to find out what had happened to you."

"But, why are they looking for me? What for?" Sheena asked, her voice apprehensive.

"They are looking for you because I want you," he answered. "Because, Sheena, I can't live without you; because, having found you, I can't let you escape me now."

She stared at him, hardly believing what she had heard.

"But . . . but . . . Madame Pelayo . . ." she stammered at last.

"So that was it!" She saw no guilt in his expression. "Who told you?" he asked.

"The Comtesse de Beaufleur," she replied. "She said . . . that you . . . had been her . . . lover for years."

"An exaggeration. The *Comtesse* is noted as one of the biggest liars and trouble-makers in all Paris. But you weren't to know that. My sweet, did it really worry you? Why, why didn't you ask me about it instead of running away?"

"It isn't true?" Sheena asked.

He picked up her hands and kissed them one after another.

"Listen, my darling! There is usually a grain of truth in every rumour, which makes it all the more difficult to contradict, all the harder to combat. Yes, it was true —but ten years ago, during the war."

"And you don't love her any more?"

Lucien smiled.

"Love! It is such a very big word, isn't it?" he said. "It covers so many different forms of emotion. Yvonne and I never loved each other, but we were very infatuated for a short while. It was when I entered Paris with the American troops. The Army of Liberation! We were all of us heroes and the French women were, like us, carried away by the spirit of victory, the joy and excitement of knowing that peace had come at last.

"For a few months Yvonne and I were very happy together. She had suffered greatly during the war, for her first husband, a Frenchman, had been taken to a concentration camp, where he died."

"She was married before!" Sheena exclaimed. "I had no idea of that."

"She never speaks of it," Luicen said. "It was a sad and miserable time for her and when she decided to marry again all those who were fond of her were delighted. The part I played in her life was perhaps important only in that it drew her out of a despond of misery. It made her realise that the world could still hold other joys and happiness besides those which she had lost."

"I had no . . . idea," Sheena stammered.

"Why should you have?" Lucien asked. "But if you had asked me instead of running away and making me so anxious, so worried, I would have told you. The whole Embassy has been upset."

"I am sorry."

"And so you should be," he smiled. "Perhaps I will have to punish you for what you have done, but I will do it, my darling, with kisses—the kisses I have missed this past terrible week, when I have been unable to find you."

His face drew nearer to her and he would have kissed her again, but resolutely Sheena pushed him away.

"No," she said. "I have got something to tell you."

"Can't it wait?" he asked, his voice a little hoarse.

She looked up to see the rising passion in the darkness of his eyes.

"No! No!" she answered. "You have got to listen." She drew herself up, twisting her fingers together in her lap. "Don't touch me," she said. "It would be hard for me to say what I have to say if you are touching me."

Suddenly her voice broke on a little sob.

"Perhaps . . . when you have heard . . . you will no longer . . . want to."

Lucien did not speak, he only sat staring at her. Sheena drew a deep breath.

"You have got to know why I came to Paris," she said. "You have got to hear that I have deceived you, that I have lied and pretended many things that weren't . . . true." For a moment her voice was choked in her throat and then she added: "But it is true that I have loved you. I love you with all my heart and soul. I love you so much that all these last weeks I have wanted to die because I thought I should never see you again."

"Isn't that all that matters then?" Lucien asked.

His arms went out, as though he would have drawn her to him.

"No! I have got to tell you," Sheena insisted.

She began the story of how she had lived in Ireland with Uncle Patrick; of how, for some mysterious reason which she did not understand, they had gone to England and stayed in that dark, sinister house in the Fulham Road. She told him how Uncle Patrick had brought her the news that she was to go to Paris to be governess to the children of the Ambassador to Mariposa and to pretend to be married.

"I am not married. I never have been," Sheena said in a very low voice.

Lucien said nothing and after a moment she continued with her story. She told how the letter had come to her commanding her to go to the bookshop in the

Rue St. François. She described the voice on the telephone and how it had threatened her and how, terrified and afraid for Uncle Patrick's sake, she had written and begged him to come over and see her.

"He came," she said. "Perhaps if I had not sent for him he would have been alive today. Because he came, he died. He must always have had a bad heart, the doctor told me, but the excitement of the journey and too much food and drink was too great a strain on it. He died . . . and I still feel it was . . . my fault."

She was crying now, the tears running down her cheeks. She made no attempt to check them, forcing herself to sit motionless while she told her story, conscious all the time that Lucien's eyes were on her, that he was watching her.

"I wanted to tell you the truth," she finished. "I swear that I wanted to tell you, but how could I betray Uncle Patrick? How could I do anything which might endanger his safety, or even his life? I had to go on lying, even after I loved you. Please, please, understand."

Her voice broke and now, because she could bear it no longer, her hands went up to her face, hiding her eyes and the shame which she felt must be written there.

And then, as it seemed to her that she went down into the depths of the darkest hell—a hell of self-accusation and of guilt—Lucien's arms went round her.

"My poor little darling," he said. "Why didn't you tell me? It all could have been explained so easily in a few words, and yet you went on suffering. I ought to have forced you into the open. I ought to have accused you that night when I found you looking, so obviously guilty and yet so utterly adorable, by the Ambassador's desk."

"You guessed?" Sheena gasped.

"But, of course," he smiled. "I knew from the very first day you arrived at the Embassy that you had been sent to spy out the land."

"How did you know?" Sheena asked.

"Because, my sweet, you looked so very unlike a governess. When I saw you at the station, I felt there must be some mistake; and then, when you were so mysterious about your relations, your husband and where you had come from, there was nothing I could do but make enquiries."

"And what did you discover?" Sheena asked.

"That your Uncle Patrick was very much alive and that it wasn't years since you had last seen him," Lucien answered.

The colour rose in Sheena's cheeks.

"I am such a hopeless liar."

"Do you think I am not glad of that?" Lucien asked. "You will never be able to deceive me, my darling, however hard you try."

"Why didn't you say something to me? Why didn't you face me with it?" Sheena asked.

"To tell you the truth I was rather amused to see what you would do," Lucien said. "You see, I realised how absurdly inexperienced you were. They had sent other people to get information, all of whom had been past masters of intrigue and espionage, and they had all failed. I suppose really you were their last resort."

"But, who are they? What does it all mean?" Sheena asked. "And why should Uncle Patrick have been involved in it all?" She hesitated and then she added: "You do believe that I don't know that?"

In answer Lucien took her chin between his fingers and tilted her head up towards his.

"I always know when you are telling the truth," he said. "I can see it in your eyes, darling, and it is sacrilege to make your lips tell lies."

He kissed her then, but lightly, and almost before Sheena could thrill to the touch of his mouth he had released her again.

"I think it is time you were given an explanation," he said. "And really, it is such a simple one that half the horrors you have anticipated have been quite unnecessary. The facts are these:

"Mariposa is a very undeveloped and backward country, but it does contain large deposits of valuable minerals. We have known for years that there are copper and gold and a certain amount of tin there, in fact the Incas discovered it first. It was only recently we had a suspicion that the country possessed an even more valuable commodity—uranium.

"Now we had always been told by the experts that

the other minerals were hardly worth the trouble of getting them out. It meant building railways, roads; finding transport of every sort and shape. It meant importing labour as well as machinery and everything else which goes with a mining operation on a large scale. But uranium was different. That, as you know, is in very short supply the whole world over. The point was, had we got enough of it?"

Lucien paused for breath.

"Is that what Uncle Patrick was trying to find out?" Sheena asked.

Lucien nodded.

"Exactly," he said. "Not only your Uncle Patrick, but a large group of rather unscrupulous and incredibly persistent financiers. I don't know how they met your uncle, but I have a suspicion that some of them, at one time, were connected with a little gun-running in Southern Ireland and there is no doubt at all that your uncle played his part in the same organization."

Sheena stared at him wide-eyed.

"Do you mean that he was bringing guns into the country with which to fight the English in Northern Ireland?" she asked.

"Exactly!" Lucien said. "Your uncle was mixed up in various activities; most of them were extremely patriotic. You can't blame a man for wanting to fight for his own country or for what he believes is the best for it."

"Uncle Patrick loved Ireland," Sheena said.

"That I can well believe," Lucien replied. "But these friends of his love nothing but money. They are an unscrupulous lot who have a certain amount of power, and they could, if they had found out what we were about to do, have turned the information to their own advantage."

"And the Comtesse de Beaufleur is one of them?"

"Her boy-friend is," Lucien explained. "Her husband is a poor old man whom nobody worries with very much, but she has a *cher ami* with whom she goes everywhere. He is undoubtedly one of the moving lights behind this organization, or whatever they call themselves. He knew, as did a number of other people, that we had sent out the finest engineer in France to make a report on the mines where it was thought the biggest deposits of uranium were likely to be found.

"They found out, by some method of their own, that if the report was favourable, the Mariposan Government intended to offer the whole development of the scheme to the Anglo-French Engineering Company. That was the contract they wanted to hear about."

"But, how could they benefit?" Sheena asked.

"It is too long for me to go into the details," Lucien said. "But briefly, there are Companies already floated which control the shares of some of the mines of Mariposa. These are gold, copper and tin mines, but to get at the uranium it would mean coming to some arrangement with the shareholders or giving them some participation in the new uranium mines. That's where your Uncle Patrick's friends intended to be very clever. The shares have slumped practically to nothing. They would have bought them up at a very low price and then held us to ransom when it came to an amalgamation or a concession."

"I understand," Sheena said. "And so, if I had been able to tell them there was a contract, they would have rushed to buy up the old and comparatively valueless shares."

"That's right! The Bourse and the Stock Exchange would have been flooded with orders within a few minutes of hearing from you that a contract had been arranged."

"But I did hear it," Sheena said. "And I did nothing."

"You heard it? You heard that a contract had come?" Lucien asked in surprise. Then he began to laugh. "I know what you are talking about. I thought at the time that it might bewilder and surprise you. That day at luncheon when the Ambassador said the people he had been seeing that morning had been trying to make him sign. So that was the contract you were looking for when you came down that night! Fool that I was, I never connected the two; it has only suddenly come to me now."

"And that wasn't the right contract?" Sheena asked.

"No, darling," he said. "The men the Ambassador had been seeing that morning were a firm of landscape gardeners whom he wished to employ to lay out the gardens of the Embassy. They were in such a bad state that the Ambassador was determined to make them look more worthy of the prestige of Mariposa.

"Personally I thought it a waste of money and told him so, but he wouldn't listen to me and I only with difficulty managed to make him promise to get an estimate from several firms and not to take the first one he was offered. That's why he was explaining that he had not signed the contract despite the fact that the firm in question were very anxious to have his signature."

"Oh, I see," Sheena said. "So if I had had time to look on his desk that's all I would have found."

"You wouldn't even have found that," Lucien said. "You see, my sweet, the Ambassador has a very good Financial Adviser who doesn't allow him to leave valuable documents of any sort lying about the place."

Sheena bent her head.

"How stupid you must think me!" she whispered.

He put his arms round her and drew her close.

"Shall I really tell you what I think about you?" he asked. He did not wait for her answer but went on: "I think you are the sweetest, most foolish and the most wonderful girl I have ever met in my life. The only thing that puzzled me for some time was if you had really been married. If you only knew how much I hated that unknown husband of yours! And then gradually I came to the conclusion that he never existed. No one, my little love, could be so innocent and so utterly unspoilt as you if they had been married, or even in love with anyone else."

He waited a moment and then his arms around her tightened.

"It is true, isn't it?" he said. "You have never loved anyone else?"

Bravely she raised her face to look up at him.

"I have never loved anyone before," she said, "and I never shall love anyone but you."

Her words were almost lost against the hungry impetuosity of his lips; and then, as he began to kiss her, she put her fingers against his mouth.

"One thing more I haven't told you," she said. "When I went with you to see the *Duchesse*, Lady Carrington was there, you will remember. Through her I discovered that my father's family believe that I am dead. Uncle Patrick told them that I had died because he did not wish me to go to England."

"I know that, too," Lucien answered. "When you disappeared, I went over to see the *Duchesse* to ask her if by any chance you had said anything while you were there which might have led her to think you were upset. It was then Lady Carrington told me about your family."

"I feel I don't want to see them," Sheena said.

"They will be longing to see you, darling," Lucien replied, "and I feel it would be cruel to keep you away from them for ever. We will go and visit them on our honeymoon."

"Our honeymoon?" Sheena questioned.

"Yes, our honeymoon!" Lucien repeated. "You don't think I am going to let you escape me again, do you? I have learnt my lesson. What I have I hold, and I am not going to let you out of my sight until you are my wife."

"Are you quite, quite sure that you want me?" Sheena enquired.

"Must I answer that ridiculous question?" Lucien asked. "Look at me, darling."

She tried, but she was suddenly shy. It was not only her new-found happiness flooding over her, but the feeling of being possessed, of belonging, of knowing that in his arms there was a security that she had never known before, which made her suddenly shy of him. As if he understood, he laughed softly and drew her even closer.

"Do you really imagine anyone would take you for a sophisticated married woman?" he asked. "But the day after tomorrow you will be one. It will be my ring you will wear on your finger then—a ring that will stay there until you die, for I shall never let you go."

Sheena gave a little incoherent murmur and turned her face against his shoulder.

"There are so many things for us to do together," Lucien went on. "Somehow, my sweet, I don't think you will ever be bored. I have got to go back to Mariposa within the next month. Before we go we will have a honeymoon in Italy and a week, perhaps, in England. We could even go to Ireland if you wished it."

"Could we really?" Sheena eyes were suddenly radiant.

"Would you like that?"

"I would love it more than anything in the world. I would like to go to my home, the only home I have ever known. I suppose now Uncle Patrick is dead it belongs to me, but I have never thought about that. What I have dreamed about sometimes is being there with you—standing on the cliffs looking out towards the Atlantic; lying on the sands in the shelter of the bay and listening to the waves breaking against the rocks. There are caves where I played when I was a child, imagining that I was a smuggler or a pirate or any of the other colourful characters which I read about in my fairy stories."

"And was your dream companion with you there?"

"Yes, of course. She was the only person I had to play with; the only person who understood."

"And do you think I will be able to take her place?"

Lucien was not laughing, his face was serious. There was something in the expression in his eyes which told Sheena more truly than any words could have done how lonely he had been and how he, too, had longed for a companion.

"There will never be any more need for dreams," she said softly. "Not so long as we are together. We will be, won't we?"

His arms were around her again and now his lips were seeking hers.

"You and I—together," he whispered against her lips. "Yes, my darling, my sweet, we will always be together."

ON SALE WHEREVER PAPERBACKS ARE SOLD
— or use this coupon to order directly from the publisher.

BARBARA CARTLAND

V2734	Open Wings $1.25 £ (#37)
V3242	Out Of Reach $1.25 £ (#60)
V3243	The Price Is Love $1.25 £ (#61)
V3373	The Private Life Of Elizabeth Empress Of Austria $1.25 £ (Biographical Romance)
V2650	Reluctant Bride $1.25 £ (#34)
V3518	Royal Pledge $1.25 £ (#18)
V3428	The Runaway Heart (#69) $1.25 £
V3331	The Scandalous Life Of King Carol $1.25 £
V3565	The Secret Heart $1.25 £ (#7)
V2429	Stars In My Heart $1.25 £ (#21)
V2887	Stolen Halo $1.25 £ (#44)
V2689	Sweet Adventure $1.25 £ (#17)
V3189	Sweet Enchantress $1.25 £ (#58)
V2920	Sweet Punishment $1.25 £ (#45)
V3388	Theft Of The Heart $1.25 £ (#67)
V3272	The Thief Of Love $1.25 £ (#63)
V2577	The Unknown Heart $1.25 £ (#29)
V2146	The Unpredictable Bride $1.25 £ (#6)
V2996	Wings on My Heart $1.25 £ (#47)
V2504	Wings of Love $1.25 £ (#25)
V3293	Woman, The Enigma $1.25 £ (Nonfiction)

Send to: PYRAMID PUBLICATIONS,
Dept. M.O., 9 Garden Street, Moonachie, N.J. 07074

NAME

ADDRESS

CITY

STATE   ZIP

I enclose $_____, which includes the total price of all books ordered plus 50¢ per book postage and handling for the first book and 25¢ for each additional. If my total order is $10.00 or more, I understand that Pyramid will pay all postage and handling.
No COD's or stamps. Please allow three to four weeks for delivery.
Prices subject to change.

P-17